A DEVIL AT THE HIGHLAND COURT

CELESTE BARCLAY

All rights reserved.

No part of this publication may be sold, copied, distributed, reproduced or transmitted in any form or by any means, mechanical or digital, including photocopying and recording or by any information storage and retrieval system without the prior written permission of both the publisher, Oliver Heber Books and the author, Celeste Barclay, except in the case of brief quotations embodied in critical articles and reviews.

PUBLISHER'S NOTE: This is a work of fiction. Names, characters, places, and incidents either are the product of the author's imagination or are used fictitiously. Any resemblance to actual persons, living or dead, business establishments, events, or locales is entirely coincidental.

Copyright © by Celeste Barclay.

0 9 8 7 6 5 4 3 2 1

Published by Oliver Heber Books

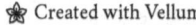 Created with Vellum

A heartfelt thank you to everyone who traveled along this two year journey as we met and fell in love with *The Highland Ladies*.

I hope these couples have given you as much joy and escapism as they have me.

Happy reading, y'all,
Celeste

THE HIGHLAND LADIES

A Spinster at the Highland Court
A Spy at the Highland Court
A Wallflower at the Highland Court
A Rogue at the Highland Court
A Rake at the Highland Court
An Enemy at the Highland Court
A Saint at the Highland Court
A Beauty at the Highland Court
A Sinner at the Highland Court
A Hellion at the Highland Court
An Angel at the Highland Court
A Harlot at the Highland Court
A Friend at the Highland Court
An Outsider at the Highland Court
A Devil at the Highland Court

SUBSCRIBE TO CELESTE'S NEWSLETTER

Subscribe to Celeste's bimonthly newsletter to receive exclusive insider perks.

Have you read *The Highland Ladies Guide*? This FREE series companion with insider information is available to all new subscribers to Celeste's monthly newsletter. Subscribe on her website.
Subscribe Now

PREFACE

The Highland Ladies series is a spin-off of my first series, *The Clan Sinclair*, and follows the lives of ladies-in-waiting at King Robert the Bruce's court. If you are a fan of Highlander romances, then you're surely familiar with the time that spans the Wars of Scottish Independence, along with the rise and reign of Robert the Bruce (late 13th and early 14th centuries).

While I was intentionally vague about the time and reigning couple in *The Clan Sinclair*, there is little way to avoid the history of Robert the Bruce when this series takes place predominantly at Stirling Castle after he was crowned king. I have taken creative license in several areas, especially the creation of the protagonists, but the events and clan dynamics are true to history.

Throughout this series, I have made the rule of King Edward I longer than it actually was. Longshanks died only a year after Robert the Bruce became king. His son, Edward II, hardly lived up to his father's reputation, so I chose to ambiguously extend Longshanks' reign. I took quite a lot more liberties with the true historical timeline in this book. While the events I describe between Clan Dunbar and the Earl of Salisbury

PREFACE

are true, I condensed them and included situations that occurred during the reigns of Edward II and Edward III as though they happened during the lifetime of Edward I.

William Montagu, the Earl of Salisbury, was a renowned knight during reigns of both Edward II and Edward III. He played a prominent role in the Wars of Scottish Independence, and the events I detail between the Dunbars and him are real. He joined the royal household of Edward II as a ward when his father died. It was as children he formed a close relationship with Edward III, despite legend saying Edward III raped his wife, Catherine. It's believed the story was concocted as French propaganda. Catherine and he had six children together, and his heir was also named William, just as I wrote in this story. He died from injuries in a jousting tournament, and the younger William became the second Earl of Salisbury.

Lady Agnes Dunbar was known as "Black Agnes," and she defended her home against Salisbury's nineteen-month siege in 1337–1338. Edward III was on the throne at the time, and Scotland and England were embroiled in the Second War of Scottish Independence. Her strategies that I recount in this story are true to history; even the quote I use is accredited to her. I'm particularly fond of Black Agnes's resilience and spunk. She sent a loaf of bread and a flask of wine to the Earl of Salisbury merely to taunt him while he suffered the winter outside during his siege. As I mention in the story, he began the siege with nearly 20,000 men, and it did cost the Crown nearly £6,000. He was able to engage in the futile battle because he was still considered Edward III's closest confidant.

It was William Montagu, 2nd Baron Montagu, the Earl's father, who had a strained relationship with Thomas of Lancaster and Leicester during the reign of

Edward II. I once more shortened the timeline for the sake of enriching this story, with facts that prove truth is stranger than fiction. Thomas of Lancaster and Leicester was related to the Plantagenets and was a cousin of Edward I. Through his marriage to Alice de Lacy, he held the title of the Earl of Salisbury in 1311. This predates William Montagu, who became the Earl of Salisbury in 1337. Interestingly, this is a title that has been recreated several times throughout British history. William Montagu was known as the 1st Earl of Salisbury, despite his nemesis having already held the title. However, Lancaster fell from grace when he was one of the baronial leaders in the rebellion against Edward II. Upon Thomas's execution, the title shifted once more. Between Lancaster's exploits in the Lowlands, his contentious relationships within the English courts, and his death, I knew I had plenty to work with.

John de Warenne married Joan of Bar, a granddaughter of Longshanks, and their marriage was as much a disaster as I describe. She was a child bride who he abandoned before she was even fourteen. He attempted to petition for divorce, but it was never granted—even after he was excommunicated. He had six children with Matilda de Nerford, but they eventually parted ways when their relationship soured over his failed marriage to Joan of Bar. Predictably, de Warenne moved on and formed an attachment to another woman. It's recorded that he sired nine children altogether; none were with his wife. Much like William Montagu, de Warenne was also a ward of the Crown, and it is likely they grew up together. De Warenne was drawn into a feud with Thomas of Lancaster and Leicester when one of the former's knights abducted and assaulted the latter's wife. De Warenne did nothing, so Lancaster sought retribution. Ultimately, de Warenne came out the winner when he

PREFACE

helped seal the other man's fate as a traitor, leading to his beheading.

The MacLeods of Assynt and the Mackenzies were rivals throughout history. This created a rather complex web when I decided to make Michail MacLeod the hero of this story. I'd already linked the Mackenzies and MacLeods of Assynt in *His Bonnie Highland Temptation*. I used the death of Rose MacLeod, Siùsan's mother, as a catalyst to another round of feuding that spilled over into this book. Since Siùsan Mackenzie married Callum Sinclair, and her half-brothers went to foster with the Sinclairs during that installment of *The Clan Sinclair*, I knew I could bring back the Sinclairs and the Hartleys (Blythe's sister, Isabella Dunbar, married Dedric Hartley in *A Spy at the Highland Court*) in preparation for my next series, *The Clan Sinclair Legacy*.

A Devil at the Highland Court is the final book in a series that has taken me two years to write and publish. I've loved every couple I crafted in *The Highland Ladies*. Each holds a special place in my heart, so no, I don't have a favorite. I worked with great purpose to incorporate emotional and thought-provoking themes into each story. My goal was to create stories that have messages that are as relevant and relatable to modern readers while maintaining the spirit and appeal of historical romance. I hope you've enjoyed this journey with me.

Until next time, I bid you adieu.

Happy reading,

Celeste

CHAPTER 1

Michail MacLeod reined in his horse, the world spinning around him as he clung to the reins. He listened to the cheers from his men, who urged him on to win his race against his younger brother, Adan. While the crowd clapped and laughed, Michail kept swallowing to keep down the barrel of whisky he'd consumed well into the early hours of the morning. His bleary eyes looked past the bailey's main gate as he tried to recall the course along which he'd pushed his steed to gallop. He could barely recall where the brothers' competition began. They'd charged over hill and dale because Michail accepted a dare that he couldn't remain mounted all the way from the outermost fields to the keep's gates.

He knew Adan and his other younger brother, Edward, prayed he would see the risk and come to his senses. But it had only baited him. He rubbed his hand over his throat, then the back of his neck, amazed that he hadn't broken it. Closing his eyes to stop his spinning surroundings, he inhaled before more sliding than dismounting *Cunnart*. He'd name his horse Risk because he knew he took one when he insisted on nursing the sickly colt. Now the name fit even more because Michail took one risk after another on horseback to feed his daredevil nature. He always drew the line at doing anything that would most certainly endanger his horse, but he knew he toed the line too often.

"Michail," Adan hissed as he came to stand behind his older brother's left shoulder. Ostensibly, he stood alongside the MacLeods' of Assynt tánaiste, but in reality, he propped up Michail. "Father is coming."

"Fwine," Michail slurred. He tried to wipe the haze from his eyes, but two hulking Highlanders marched toward him, and neither of his father's shapes looked amused.

"Get yerself sober before yer mother returns from the village," Laird Torrian MacLeod snapped. "If ye give yer mother one more moment of worry, I will take the strap to ye." Torrian crossed his arms, squinted his eyes, and swept a look of disgust over his oldest son. But in the back of his mind and within his heart, the ever-present ache burned more sharply. He understood his son better than most, understood his grief, but he could never condone the constant danger Michail sought.

"Aye, Father." Michail made to walk toward the keep's steps, but he pitched forward the moment he lifted his left foot. Adan caught the neckline of Michail's leine while Torrian pressed upward on his shoulders. Michail flinched before covering his mouth. He stumbled to the stable's side wall, tripping, then landing on his belly, pressing the vomit from him. It spewed against the wall, some dribbling onto his right hand.

"That's it," Torrian growled. "Adan, Ward, take yer sotted brother into the barracks. Dinna let him leave until he's sober." Torrian crouched beside Michail and whispered, "I love ye, son. But if ye dinna mend yer ways, I canna keep ye as ma heir. I canna endanger the clan if I canna trust ye."

Michail rolled onto his back, shading his eyes from the sun. He sniffed, first inhaling the scent of his own vomit, then the alcohol on his own breath. He couldn't disagree with his father. He wouldn't disagree. He almost wished that very thing would happen.

"I'm nae giving up on ye just yet, so ye can rid yerself of the idea that ye can force ma hand," Torrian whispered. "I'm sending ye back to the Sinclairs."

"What?" Michail sat up too quickly, forcing him to turn his head before he cast up his accounts for a second time, barely avoiding it landing on his father's lap.

"Aye. I need ye to take the barley and rye we sold to Liam, and I think it would do ye some good to see yer cousin. Mayhap she can talk some sense into ye. Nay one else seems to."

"When?"

"Ye have a sennight until ye leave. Ye willna get drunk again before that, and ye had best nae embarrass us by getting drunk there. Dinna let Tavish and Callum goad ye."

"Aye, Father. Ye ken even I draw the line at doing aught to disgrace the clan."

"See that ye dinna." Torrian grasped Michail's hand and pulled his son to his feet as he rose. "Michail, I grieve ma da's death just as much as ye. But I dinna have the luxury of drowning maself in whisky, ale, and mead. This isnae how yer grandfather would wish ye to behave. I canna tell ye simply to forget yer grief, but ye must find a different way to cope. Ye've always had a wild streak, but ye're hurting yer mother. And ye ken she will never say aught to ye because she understands, too. But I am. Yer hurt is hurting everyone around ye. It terrifies yer brothers that they're going to bring yer dead body back to us. It terrifies yer mother that she's going to be sewing yer funeral shroud. And I'm terrified I'm going to lose the mon I still trust the most. We're all holding on by a thread, lad. Dinna drive us all away, or ye will find a new form of grief."

Torrian nodded to Ward and Adan, who stepped forward, each taking one of Michail's arms as they steadied him and guided him into the barracks. Michail hung his head, ashamed of his actions, consumed by grief, and wanting nothing more than to be left alone.

"We were fools for thinking we could give ye a dare so wild even ye would turn it down. We ken better," Ward murmured as they moved into one of the small rooms that currently stood vacant. He and Adan stripped Michail of his leine and plaid, leaving him naked. "But we truly thought ye'd finally see yer limits."

"And I was already too drunk to ken there are such things as limits," Michail muttered. "If ye werenae ma brothers, I would think ye wished for me to break ma bluidy neck."

"It's nay secret ye were grandfather's favorite—" Adan jumped back as Michail spun toward him.

"Nay, I wasna. Grandda loved each of us as much as the other. Dinna ever doubt that. I'm the auldest, so he had much to help teach me as ma father's heir. We may have spent more time together the last few years he was alive, but I wasna his favorite. But he was mine. Ma earliest memories are of him. I remember the day each of ye was born because it was Grandda who held me and told me stories because Mama's cries scared me." Michail blinked away the tears that pricked his eyelids, and he swallowed the lump threatening to steal his words. "I remember he was the one who taught me that nay one is more important than family, and there will never be a mon I can trust more than ma own brothers. It's his sword I carry. So there isnae a day that goes by that I dinna think of him, remember him, miss him. That doesnae mean he didna love ye both as much as me. Dinna say that."

Laird Thormud MacLeod died three years earlier, but Michail's grief hadn't subsided with time. It was raw and angry every day. He saw his grandfather in everything he did and everywhere he went. He tried to wash away those memories with enough alcohol to sink a ship, but that only made his grandfather's voice louder in his head. He only continued to imbibe because it lessened the physical pain of his loss, the constricting feeling that took hold of his heart and lungs. He knew only a hangover and emptiness would greet him when he sobered, but for the time the alcohol kept him inebriated, the pain was bearable.

While Ward fetched a bucket of water and Adan searched for a lump of soap and drying linens, Michail stood naked and alone. It was rather symbolic of his life these days. His recklessness might amuse the clan's guardsmen, but it had pushed away many of his childhood friends. It was only his immediate family who tolerated him, only they who understood the depths of his ever-present sorrow. He would confide in only Adan and Ward, and he recognized his grief in his parents' eyes. His self-isolation only fed his loneliness and his recklessness.

Da may be right. If I can ignore Callum and Tavish's jests, then I might actually listen to Siùsan. She may nae have kenned Grandda her whole life like I did, but she was as close to him as I was. She's the only one who likely understands. I canna keep doing this. I ken others think I'm wallowing and weak, but I just dinna ken how to move past ma grief. I have duties to this clan and to ma family. Ma grief is ma own to keep, but ma actions dinna just affect me. If I keep drinking as much as I do, I'm soon going to be at the point where I need to keep drinking as much as I do. I'm likely to do maself a mischief and get Cunnart hurt in the meantime. He might be as wild as I am, but he trusts me. If I canna even keep ma horse's trust and keep the beast safe, what the bluidy hell will the rest of the clan do?

"Michail?" Ward murmured as he and Adan returned to the small chamber. Michail hadn't moved, hadn't even noticed their return. Even when three sheets to the wind, Michail was always aware of his surroundings and potential threats.

"Aye. I was just lost in ma thoughts. Bring the bucket and soap over. Please." Michail accepted what his brothers brought for his ablutions and quickly scrubbed himself, starting with dunking his head in the frigid water. He kept his head submerged until the pinprick sensation from the icy water threatened to make him gasp. It had a powerfully sobering effect, and by the time he finished and pulled on the fresh clothes Ward found, he felt almost normal.

"Better?"

"Aye." Michail clapped Adan on the shoulder as he nodded in response. "Da is sending me to Siùsan and her family in a sennight. I promised him I wouldnae drink between now and ma journey. I really dinna want to." He frowned and shook his head. "I'd rather stay at the keep at night. We all ken I must stop. I ken I must before I canna. Dinna think ye must stay behind to be ma nursemaid. There's nay reason to end yer fun when ye ken how to have it responsibly."

"How long will ye be away?" Ward gathered the sopping-wet linens and glanced at his brother.

"Three sennights at least, but likely a moon with the time to travel across the Highlands to Dunbeath. Who kens what the weather will do?"

"Do ye wish—" Ward glanced at Adan, uncertain he should finish his questions.

"I would wish for yer company, but I dinna need ye

to ensure I dinna louse it up." Michail's reassuring smile appeared more like a grimace. With matching rueful nods, Adan and Ward walked from the barracks with Michail. Once inside the keep, the three brothers approached the dais in the Great Hall, but Torrian poked his head out of his solar and called Michail to join him.

It surprised Michail to find his parents and the entire clan council seated around the massive oblong table in the center of the chamber. His mother, Catriona, often joined council meetings, offering information about the family lives of the clan and pertinent information about supplies and food stores. But it was a Friday, and the council met on Wednesdays. Michail always attended if he was in residence.

"Father, Mother," Michail greeted his parents with a smile before sweeping his gaze over the gathered men. He nodded and took his customary seat at the foot of the table, across from his father. Catriona MacLeod sat beside her husband.

"Michail," Torrian began. "Ye ken I'm sending ye to the Sinclairs, but it isnae just for trade. I couldnae risk anyone overhearing ma real reason." Without thinking, he reached out and took Catriona's hand, lacing her fingers with his as their hands rested on his thigh. "The Gunns have turned their eye back to us. Despite yer mother being a Gunn for the first half of her life, they've decided we make a far better target than continuing to take on the Sinclairs and Sutherlands. Never mind, marriage and blood now connect us to both clans."

Torrian didn't need to explain the complicated history their clan shared with the Gunns. Catriona was the younger cousin to two now dead lairds, Tomas and Farlane, and a dead middle brother, James. Her other cousin, Elizabeth, had a disastrous marriage to the father of her niece, Siùsan. Her Gunn cousins had caused Siùsan's mother's death. Rose MacLeod was her husband's dead sister. As if that family tree weren't twisted enough, Siùsan's younger half-brothers had fostered with the Sinclairs. Siùsan's husband, Callum, the Sinclairs' tánaiste, agreed to bring them back to Dunbeath when Siùsan finally severed ties with her abusive stepmother, Elizabeth, and her neglectful father, Ulrich.

Michail wanted to rub his temples as he ran through his familial ties and realized he might not be as sober as he assumed. He couldn't understand why the Gunns would be interested in them. While the current laird, Edgar, hadn't been alive when Catriona lived at Clyth Castle, she was still a Gunn by blood. It made Edgar his cousin once removed. It further mystified him why they would be interested in the MacLeods of Assynt when they knew it would just bring the Sinclairs back into the fray. And wherever the Sinclairs went, so did the Mackays and Sutherlands. Laird Tristan Mackay married Mairghread Sinclair, the youngest of the Sinclair siblings and only sister. Her four older brothers—Callum, Alex, Tavish, and Magnus—and their father, Liam, were fiercely protective of the knife-wielding woman. Liam was married to Laird Hamish Sutherland's sister, Kyla, before she died. There were times like this when Michail wished someone would map out the clan connections on a sheaf of parchment.

"Aye. It gives me an aching head, too." Torrian's voice permeated Michail's thoughts. "I dinna ken why they'd want to. They're nearly surrounded by the Sinclairs, Sutherlands, and Mackays, and there is little room for them to run before they reach us. Kieran already kens aboot the trouble, and he's offered to send men. But I dinna want to accept. He's having his own troubles on Lewis. I'm sending ye to Dunbeath because

Tristan will be there. He hasnae had to use them before, but he has skills that his father taught him."

The MacLeods of Assynt were a smaller branch of the larger MacLeods of Lewis. As part of the chieftain's family, Michail, his brothers, and his father had a distant relation to Laird Kieran MacLeod of Lewis, who was married to Maude, Hamish Sutherland's daughter. It added yet another connection to the Sutherlands and Sinclairs.

"Skills?" Michail's brow furrowed. They all had skills. There wasn't a man in the chamber who hadn't been wielding a sword since he was five. They'd all started with wooden swords, then moved onto steel before they were adolescents. Every man on the council was nearly old enough to be Michail's father, so they had at least twice the experience as he. They weren't short on seasoned warriors.

"Tristan's father was a mercenary in France for many years alongside Innes Kennedy. They both were younger sons who never thought to inherit, but they became lairds around the same time. The tactics Tristan learned arenae meant for a battle. They're meant for a sole mon or a small group with a specific target. The auld laird learned from the French *routiers* and returned home an accomplished spearman and slinger. There are plenty of us here who are superior marksmen with a bow and wield pikes like we were born with them in our hand, but we dinna have the same knowledge with slingers."

"Slingers?" Michail scoffed. "Ye taught me how to use one to hunt before ye even gave me a wooden sword."

"Aye, and that was fine for bringing down small foul or catching rabbits and squirrels. Ye havenae used one to fell a mon. The French use a *fustabile* with a long staff to improve speed and power. It's like a siege engine ye can carry. It works from the same sort of idea on how to launch the rock. Tristan can also teach ye more ways to kill a mon up close than with a dirk or snapping his neck."

"Why would I need to ken how to kill in closer range?" Michail squinted, knowing there was something his father hadn't yet told him.

"Because of the reason I'm sending ye and why we're meeting. While ye were—out—we captured half a score of Gunn spies. They were nearly to the keep's walls before we recognized them as strangers. They'd blended in with the villagers at the market. It was yer mother who recognized them. They were young men, but apparently they bear close resemblances to people yer mother remembered." Torrian squeezed Catriona's hand, encouraging her to tell what she'd seen.

"Edgar was Tomas's son by Tomas's leman. Tomas married the woman, but nae until after Edgar was born. Nay one recognized Edgar as legitimate until all the successors before him died. In less than a score of years, they lost Tomas, then Farlane and his sons Arlane and Beathan. James was dead. There were nay other men with our family's bloodline within the clan. Edgar is kenned to make poor choices, like getting mixed up with the MacDougalls' attempt to ruin the Campbell-Ross alliance. He never should have interfered when Brodie and Laurel married. But from what we ken, Edgar is a shrewd mon with nay morals. He takes after his father."

Catriona was a soft-spoken woman by nature, often shy when people focused attention upon her. It also meant people underestimated her willpower and tenacity. She'd acted as Lady MacLeod since the day she married Torrian, since his mother, Aoife, had suffered poor health and died not long after Ward was born. She could command an army when Torrian rode out, and her word was law. While she might describe her second cousin as shrewd, there was no one in the northern Highlands who didn't know that word best described Catriona.

"Two men I saw today are aulder than Edgar. I was already living here when Edgar was born, but I ken I saw Edgar's aulder brothers. They had a different father from him, but they all looked like their mother. Three other men are the sons or grandsons of men I remember from the clan council. I remember them as weans, or they look like their sires. The rest I didna ken. There were enough though that I'm certain they were Gunns."

"Were they trying to enter the keep or scout?" Michail asked as he leaned forward, his hands clasped and now resting on the tabletop. *I should have been here. I should have been on that wall walk even if it wasna ma shift. I should have seen them rather than Mama.*

"Ye wouldnae have kenned who they were, Michail," Catriona spoke quietly. "The only person here who could, was me. It was their bad fortune that they approached as I returned. Had they waited until dusk, they might nae be enjoying our dungeon's accommodations."

"We think they intended to enter with villagers for the evening meal. What they planned from there, we dinna ken. None have been forthcoming despite our encouragement," Torrian explained. Michail understood the kind Torrian meant, since he'd doled out his own incentives to prisoners in the past. "We suspect ye and yer brothers were the targets, either for murder or abduction. It was just as well the three of ye were away from the keep."

Michail watched Catriona flinch, but she said nothing, nor did she meet his gaze. He was certain she'd heard about the state he was in when he returned to the keep, and he didn't doubt that in the short time he and his brothers were in the barracks, she'd heard about his breakneck race. Adan had ridden hard, but at a far more responsible pace. She'd abandoned asking him not to drink to excess or to act with such disregard to his safety. Her silence now made Michail feel far guiltier than anything she said.

"Yer mother, the council, and I have decided ye will go to Dunbeath with the sacks of grain and remain there for a fortnight to train. Ye'll have half a score of men traveling with ye. I'd send Adan and Ward, but I am nae comfortable sending all three of ma sons in the Gunns' direction. Ye can barely make it to Dunbeath and still stay off their land. I have the most confidence in yer ability to foil any of Edgar's moves."

"Thank ye, Father."

Father and son locked gazes for a long moment, both knowing Michail's appreciation went far beyond Torrian's compliment. Michail swore to himself he would never again risk breaking his father's trust and faith in him. That wasn't the man he wanted to be, even if sometimes he wished he could walk into the hills and never return.

CHAPTER 2

"Michail!" Siùsan Sinclair hurried down Dunbeath's steps and across the bailey with three children hurrying after her. She flew into her cousin's embrace as Michail handed off Cunnart's reins to a stable boy. They squeezed before leaning apart, Michail dropping a cousinly kiss on her cheek.

"Wife, what aboot me? Have ye nay greeting for me?" Callum Sinclair opened his arms to his wife and received a cocked eyebrow in exchange. But it was only a moment later her mountainous husband engulfed Siùsan. People throughout Scotland knew the Sinclair brothers to be four of the largest and best warriors in the country. "I missed ye."

"Ye didna even take yer horse, ye daft mon. Ye walked outside the gates. I havenae been out of yer sight more than five minutes."

"And I missed ye the entire time," Callum offered an unrepentant grin as his hand slid low on his wife's back. She swatted at him and turned to their children, Thormud, Rose, and Shona.

"It's good to see ye," Thormud said as his chest expanded, and he stuck out his arm for Michail to shake. At three-and-ten, Thormud was nearly as tall as his father, but he looked like a sapling next to the mighty oak. Michail remembered being the same age and wanting to command the same respect. He thrust out his arm and gripped Thormud's forearm. Named for Siùsan and Michail's mutual grandfather, the adolescent resembled Callum more than Siùsan. But beside him stood his twin, Rose Kyla. Named for Siùsan's and Callum's mothers, she shared the same light-red hair both Siùsan and Michail inherited from the elder Thormud.

Michail offered his embrace to Rose, then bent to include ten-year-old Shona in the warm greeting. Shona shared the same chestnut-brown hair that all five of the Sinclair siblings possessed, but her features resembled her mother's. The two girls wrapped their arms around their second cousin and giggled as he pretended to squeeze. When Michail stood, he watched three more couples approach. He recognized them all. To the left were Alex and Brighde. In the middle were Magnus and Deirdre, and to the right were Tavish and Ceit. As Michail greeted the couples, Thormud, Rose, and Shona dashed off to find their herd of cousins.

"Michail, it's good to have ye at Dunbeath," Laird Liam Sinclair boomed from the top of the keep's steps. He approached his family, pulling Michail into a rib-crushing, back-pounding embrace rather than accepting the proffered forearm. Michail laughed, trying to hide how he gasped for air.

It was clear from where the four Sinclair brothers got their height, breadth, and good looks. They were all the spitting image of Liam. Though he was approaching the middle of his sixth decade, there were still only hints of gray sprinkled through Liam's dark locks. His leine strained across his arms and chest as he moved, his muscular frame showing he hadn't gone to fat with age. He and Tavish shared a barrel-chested build, which made the aging laird even more intimidating. While he didn't ride into battle as often as he once did, no one underestimated Liam and lived to tell the tale.

"Come inside. Ye and yer men must be starving," Siùsan mused.

"Starving? The sun's barely been up three hours," Callum teased.

"Ye may nae be hungry because ye've done naught this morn, but ma cousin and his men have been riding since sunup."

"They werenae the only ones," Callum reminded his wife with a wink. Even after fourteen years of marriage, Callum still embarrassed Siùsan, making her blush. But she offered him the same cocked eyebrow and now an unrepentant smile. The couple, along with the three others, were still as in love and in lust with their mates as when they each wed. Liam turned away from the younger generation, but only to hide his smile. He and his wife, Kyla, had been the same until she drew her last breath far too many years ago.

The Sinclairs and Michail moved inside, each taking a seat at the dais. Siùsan organized food and drinks for everyone before taking her place beside Callum. Michail looked around but couldn't find who he sought.

"Mair and Tristan will be back," Magnus shrugged, "at some point. They went for a ride too."

Siùsan spluttered, causing Callum to pat her back as her wine went down the wrong pipe. Mairghread and Tristan, married the longest of the all the couples, were just as enamored with one another as they had been when they met. With four children of their own—three lads and a lass—their arrival filled the keep to capacity, making it difficult for any of the couples to share a moment alone. Michail nodded as an image—or rather, more of a memory—of white-blonde hair flashed through his mind.

The jovial nature of the family's conversation shifted when Liam leaned forward to look at Michail. "We can start yer training in the morn. The lads will be out there with ye. Tristan taught them nae long after he and Mairghread wed, but ye can all do with some practice."

At first, Michail thought Liam referred to his older grandsons, but he soon realized "lads" referred to the four men who were all older than he was. He looked around the Great Hall, but he didn't see the other couple for whom he searched.

"Will Ric join us?" Michail asked.

"Aye. He kens ye took to the javelin and spear when ye were younger. He's the only one here who trains with them." Liam pointed toward the doors as a couple entered. Michail's belly clenched as he watched a stunning woman with the white-blonde hair from his memory approach, a warrior at her arm. Isabella Hartley was the older version of the woman who haunted Michail's dreams. The three Dunbar sisters— Isabella, Emelie, and Blythe—shared the same features and unique hair color. The only other woman he knew with such pale hair was Brighde. Isabella married Dedric Hartley while she was a lady-in-waiting at King Robert the Bruce's court. They'd left the border soon after they married and joined the Sinclairs. Ric was among the Sinclairs' senior warriors. Scottish by birth and by choice but forced to grow up at the English royal court of Edward I, he brought knowledge north of the border that no Highlander could match.

"Michail," Isabella smiled warmly as Michail bowed over her hand. "Have you been to court recently? Any news of Blythe?" She pressed her lips together, embarrassed to bombard their guest.

"It's been a few moons since I was there, but last I saw, yer sister was hale." Michail could offer little more, since Blythe had barely spoken to him the last time he was at court. He knew the only one to blame was himself. He'd made one error after another, some more unforgiveable than others. But that didn't mean she wasn't constantly on his mind. If he wasn't focused upon swinging his sword or staying on his horse, then he was thinking about his grandfather or Blythe. He often thought about what his grandfather would say to him about Blythe. Reflecting on it now, he nearly winced.

"Greetings," Ric grinned, his English accent jarring against the Highland burr that filled the Great Hall. Stolen from his home near the border when he was seven, Dedric Hartley hadn't made his home once more in Scotland until his tenure as a knight drew near its end. Forced into serving King Edward "Longshanks," the very man who organized both his father's and his mother's deaths, Ric was only too happy to live in the Highlands after acting as a spy for both the English and the Scottish kings. Neither he nor Isabella had returned to Robert the Bruce's court in Stirling in more than a decade.

"Good morn," Michail returned. "Cunnart is eager to remind MacLellan who's braver and quicker." He waggled his eyebrows, matching Ric's grin. It still amused Michail that Ric named his steed after his mother's clan, partly to remind him of his family and partly to spite Longshanks. The horses might enjoy the sport, but it was Ric and Michail who reveled in a jousting competition. Ric's hearty chuckle rumbled from his chest, but he only shook his head. They would meet on the field in the morning.

"How long will you be visiting?" Isabella asked, her Lowland accent as much a contrast to the Highland burr as her husband's English accent. Michail saw the hopefulness in her gaze and knew she wondered if he would travel to court again soon. She would certainly ask him to pass a missive to Blythe. He'd traveled to court many times over the recent years, ostensibly to report to the king about ongoing trouble with the Mackenzies, but he used any excuse to escape from his grandfather's ghost.

"A fortnight, ma lady. Then I'm returning to Ardvreck." Michail's home sat on a rocky promontory that jutted into Loch Assynt. Isabella nodded with a tight smile. He knew his answer disappointed her. He wondered if he could use carrying a missive to Blythe as an excuse to return to court rather than Ardvreck.

"Michail, ye should ken Magnus Óg and Seamus are arriving before the midday meal," Siùsan interrupted his thoughts. He looked at his cousin and recognized her nervousness. It had been a couple of years since he'd seen his cousin's younger half-brothers, with whom he shared a blood relation through his mother. He'd liked the men when they were lads fostering with the Sinclairs. They'd been caught between parents who could barely stand one another, so it had been a blessing when Callum and Siùsan returned to Dunbeath with them. But Siùsan's ties to both the MacLeods of Assynt and the Mackenzies had done little to ease the animosity the clans shared. There'd been ongoing hostility between the two clans for three generations. There'd been a brief time when it eased, when Ulrich Mackenzie handfasted with Rose MacLeod, but it was short-lived because Rose died, falling from her horse while traveling to Ardvreck.

Rose had been pregnant with Siùsan at the time and went into labor, delivering Siùsan just before she died. Ulrich's father forced him to marry Elizabeth Gunn, a cousin of Michail's mother, and he spent more than two decades resenting and blaming Siùsan for Rose's death. He despised Siùsan with such ferocity that he'd told the MacLeods she'd been stillborn and hid Siùsan from Michail and his family. When Thormud discovered the lies and Siùsan's years-long mistreatment, it stoked the feud to its worst point. Michail was unsure how Magnus Óg, called the "lesser" or "younger" because Magnus Sinclair was older, and Seamus would receive him.

"Dinna fash," Michail assured Siùsan. Neither Magnus Óg nor Seamus liked their father. They had no choice but to follow his edicts, especially since Seamus was the Mackenzie heir and tánaiste, and Magnus was Seamus's second-in-command of the clan's warriors.

When Siùsan's eyes watered, Callum tucked her against his chest and shook his head. Thormud, Torrian, and even Michail had never convinced Siùsan she wasn't the reason for the feud continuing. Thormud, then Torrian, insisted it was Ulrich's choices, not Siùsan herself, that kept the animosity from ending. It was out of respect to Siùsan being trapped in the middle that the MacLeods ceased raiding the Mackenzies, only defending themselves. The Mackenzies' continued reiving of MacLeod cattle forced Michail to ride out on hot trots to retrieve them, leading to deaths on both sides.

Mairghread and Tristan walked through the keep's main doors, saving Michail from pursuing the awkward topic. Holding hands, the couple chatted with one another until they reached the dais. Michail rose to shake forearms with Tristan and to offer Mairghread a loose embrace. The youngest Sinclair sibling resembled her father and brothers, but where the men shared whisky-hued eyes, Mairghread had inherited her mother's blue-gray eyes. Coming to only the middle of her husband's chest, and those of her father and brothers, Mairghread appeared as petite as the women who married into the Sinclair clan. But it was well known that Mairghread was a physical force to reckon with, wielding knives with ease. She'd won the knife-throwing competitions—the women's and the men's—at the Highland Gatherings for more than a decade, much to Callum's chagrin, as he was the best of all the men.

Tristan's black hair was windswept and tousled as he pushed it from his face. His emerald eyes sparkled, and lines crinkled beside them as he laughed. He pulled a chair back for Mairghread, then slipped into the one beside her. He whispered something in his wife's ears that made her giggle, then press her lips together. Michail forced himself not to roll his eyes. Mairghread and Tristan were no less conspicuous than any of the other married couples. As he caught sight of Brighde and Isabella talking together, their uncanny matching platinum-blonde heads close together, Michail once again felt his chest constrict.

"I think I should refresh maself before any more of yer guests arrive," Michail said to any and everyone. He just wanted to escape.

"Come with me," Siùsan said as she rose. "The chamber on the third floor ye used the last time ye visited is ready for ye. I'll send the tub and hot water up as well. Nearly a sennight of travel is never enjoyable when ye spend every night on the ground."

Michail followed Siùsan abovestairs, the cousins remaining quiet until they reached Michail's guest chamber. He turned to Siùsan as they stepped inside. "I really dinna want ye to worry. Everything will be well with Seamus and Magnus Óg. They arenae yer father."

Siùsan nodded, her eyes drifting from Michail's until she looked at the rushes strewn on the floor. She shook her head before her gaze met Michail's once more. "It might be well with them, but I ken nae all is well with ye."

Michail waited for Siùsan to continue, to share what he was certain his parents told her in whatever missive they sent to arrange this journey. He waited for her to offer her commiserations and condolences. He waited for her chastisement, since he assumed his parents mentioned his overindulgence and recklessness. But she remained silent. It was as bad as when his mother was silent. He wanted to shift like a naughty wean brought forward for punishment.

Siùsan watched Michail, waiting for him to share anything he wished to say. She understood pushing him to expose his feelings would only create a barrier. She still grieved their grandfather's loss. She'd only met him a decade before his death, but they'd become close in the few years she'd known him as an adult. Once she established a relationship with Michail and his family, Callum accompanied Siùsan on thrice-yearly trips to Ardvreck. While he'd been alive, Thormud had traveled to Dunbeath at least four times a year.

When Thormud died, Callum had been the silent strength Siùsan needed. He'd already grieved the loss of his mother when he was a young adolescent. He understood Siùsan couldn't, and didn't want to, speak aloud her emotions whenever she grew overwhelmed. Instead, he kept her company, held her, distracted her, but never pressed her to talk or to rush through her grief. She recognized Michail needed the same as she had—did.

"It's been three years and how many journeys here, and it still feels odd to enter the gates without Grandda ahead of me." Michail moved to the window embrasure and looked out toward the main gates. Siùsan came to stand beside him. She slipped her hand into his and squeezed, but she still said nothing. "I ken in the beginning ye were close because ye reminded Grandda of Aunt Rose, and ye wished to learn all ye could aboot our family. But ye were so fond of one another because ye were so much alike. How do ye manage?"

"I dinna always. I still cry, but I only allow Callum to see it. Someone will say something, or I'll have a memory from one of our visits together, and the grief steals ma breath. Whenever I smell birch, it reminds me of his soap. And peat. The scent of it in winter reminds me of the early visits when we sat together to learn all we could aboot one another." Siùsan fell silent as they both gazed out of the window. This time, Michail squeezed her hand in support. They were quiet for five minutes before Michail continued.

"Everywhere I look, I see him. His voice echoes in ma head, his sayings and jests. But he's also the voice of ma conscience. I ken I shouldnae keep drinking and taking dares as I do. I hear him telling me I'm being selfish, and that I'm nae making him proud. I've been drinking to excess to drown all of ma grief away."

"It's harder for ye because ye're at Ardvreck, where ye're surrounded by things and people connected to Grandda. I understand that. But are ye really being the mon he and yer father worked so hard to raise?"

"I ken I'm nae. But by the time night falls, I'm beaten down by the constant reminders that he's nae there. Losing maself in a few flasks of whisky numbs the grief. I'm too busy during the day to suffer the sadness and loneliness. But at night..." Michail shrugged. "The alcohol makes it easier."

"But does it? And the bets? The races? The diving into the loch in the middle of winter? The challenging Callum and Tavish with the cabers and tree climbing? Ye ken how Ceit and I feel aboot that."

"I do. It's why I dinna offer the dares anymore."

"But ye let Callum and Tavish coax ye into these

competitions. At least, they have the sense to ken when to stop. Ye dinna." Siùsan turned toward him. "What happened with Blythe? I thought…"

"I canna say more than I ruined it. I had the chance, and I let it slip away. Mayhap if we hadnae lost Grandda when we did, then I might have married her. But I couldnae see night from day, and I said things I never should have. Things I'd take back, but I dinna think she'll ever let me."

"That's nae how Isa makes it sound."

"What?" Michail's heart raced as he looked at Siùsan.

"From what Isa's told me aboot the missives she and Blythe exchange, Blythe regrets whatever pushed ye two apart."

Michail froze. Not only did his heart pound, but his ears rang. He knew what Blythe regretted because she'd told him as much. More than once. But he doubted Siùsan knew the true reason. From Isabella's warm welcome, Michail realized she didn't know either.

"Michail, why nae see if ye can make things right with Blythe? It's obvious ye care for her. I'm nae saying use her as a distraction or marry her to forget aboot missing Grandda. But I think ye would find life easier, better, with a partner."

Michail couldn't confess that he'd done just that—used her as a distraction to forget aboot his grandfather—and that's what ruined his future with Blythe. It was what his conscience gnawed on him about every day. He knew his life would be better for having Blythe by his side, but he'd squandered the chance.

Their conversation ended when servants arrived with the tub and buckets of water. Siùsan waited until the last servant left before stepping toward the door. She turned back to Michail. "I ken ye dinna enter the races and dare to have fun. I dinna think ye've had fun in three years. Let yerself enjoy yer time with the brothers, Tristan, and Ric. Ye arenae selfish for taking part in the joy that surrounds ye. It's what gets me through each day. It did when I was moving on from severing ties with ma father. And it's what helped me cope with losing Grandda. Just ken this: the pain we feel isnae aught we'd want to put our family through, but that is just what ye're likely to do."

Michail watched Siùsan leave. He knew she was right. He didn't know why hearing it from her carried more weight than from his parents and brothers. He supposed it might be because their grief seemed so similar. She'd commiserated with him over the past three years, even offered advice he knew he should have taken, but for reasons he hadn't yet understood, what she said that day finally made him want to change. He stared at the door for a long time before stripping bare and soaking in the tub.

CHAPTER 3

The midday meal arrived sooner than Michail realized. After bathing, he joined the men in the lists. As they stood together at a trough to rinse their faces and necks, the Mackenzie entourage rode through the gates. While he didn't mind spying Seamus and Magnus Óg leading the group, he kept his head down and grumbled as he recognized more than one Mackenzie warrior from hot trots he'd led to recapture the MacLeods' stolen cows and sheep. He followed Callum and the others as they greeted the Mackenzies.

"MacLeod," Seamus said as he came to stand before Michail after greeting the Sinclairs, Tristan, and Ric. The men stood eye-to-eye, Michail only two years older than Seamus and five years older than Magnus Óg. When Seamus and Óg arrived at Dunbeath to begin their fosterage at five-and-ten and two-and-ten, Michail had felt much older than them, having already been riding on patrol for a couple years. But now, as one future laird looked at the other, it was clear they were equals. Both were tall, broad shouldered, and with a brooding edge. Óg elbowed his brother out of the way as the greeting slipped toward a standoff.

"MacLeod," the younger Mackenzie brother repeated the greeting, but his tone was much lighter. The brothers resembled one another as much as the Sinclair siblings did, except they were both fair-haired, with hazel eyes. Óg's gaze locked with Michail's green eyes, and Óg's left eyebrow twitched while the right corner of his mouth drew up.

"I'm starving," Magnus Sinclair announced.

"Ye're always starving, Mòr," Callum complained.

"I'm still a growing lad," Magnus Mòr, nicknamed so for being the bigger or the older of the two men with the same given name, grinned.

"Keep that to yer wife," Tavish scoffed. "We dinna need to ken that."

"Ye mean any more than we needed to ken yer wife walking by was the real reason for yer plaid sticking out this morn and nae the wind like ye claimed." Alex nudged his younger brother, who pretended to kick him in the shins.

Michail chuckled, the Sinclairs reminding him of his relationship with his own brothers, except none of them had wives to tease one another about. Michail entered the keep alongside Ric, who he'd practiced jousting against. They knocked one another from their horses twice before they abandoned their competition and called it a stalemate. Both warriors sported aching backs and sore backsides, but they'd enjoyed themselves.

"You did well today," Ric spoke quietly. "Have you considered entering any tourneys in the Lowlands?"

"Ye mean sneak across the border and knock some Sassenachs on their arses? Nae seriously enough to want to go to England. *Ever.* Ye ken the tourneys are a wee south of the Lowlands."

"You could trounce your opponents. You're good enough."

"Thank ye, and mayhap I am, but I still dinna want

to go to England. They'd ken me for a Highlander the moment I opened ma mouth, never mind how I look."

"I sent my spurs back, but I kept my armor. If ever you change your mind, I will lend it to you."

"I dinna have a squire to help with that prickly lot."

Ric's mouth turned down in a quick frown as he shrugged. "I can do that. I was a squire before I was a knight."

"Teach me or go with me? I dinna imagine Isa would agree to ye going back to England."

"No. She wouldn't fancy that if I left her behind here. But if we make another trip to Druchtag Motte, then she might be a little more agreeable. We could stop at court along the way."

Michail halted. "Neither ye nor Isa has been back to Stirling since ye left Barsalloch Point and gave it back to Isa's father. Ye swore ye would never return. Neither of ye even visited Emelie or Blythe there. Why now?" Michail feared something happened to Blythe, but he was more apt to think Ric was maneuvering him.

"I'm not trying to force you to see Blythe. I don't know what happened. If she doesn't cry foul against you, then it's not my business. But there have been more problems with the Earl of Salisbury lately. Laird Dunbar fought Salisbury and came out the victor, but it didn't resolve aught. I know Salisbury, and I know how the man thinks. I also know how the English fight."

"Ye would take Isa and Blythe to where there's likely going to be another battle?"

"Salisbury won't cross far enough into Scotland to reach us while we travel. You've not been to Druchtag Motte, but the keep will protect them for no other reason that Lady Dunbar will be there to defend it. My mother-by-marriage may be called "Black Agnes" because of her dark hair, but the countess deserves the moniker nearly as much as the Black Douglas does his. You've surely heard the tale."

"Aye. How she defeated Salisbury once before? Something aboot her servants dusting the battlements."

"That's right. Salisbury laid siege to the keep for nine-and-ten moons while Isa and Blythe's father was on campaign. He used his catapults to hurl boulders at the keep. In between rounds, Agnes sent her maids dressed in their very best out with white linens to wipe off the marks the boulders made when they struck the walls. Completely goaded by my mother-by-marriage, Salisbury tried his siege engine next. But he never considered what the Dunbars did with all the boulders he lobbed at them. Agnes ordered them collected, then ordered them dropped on Salisbury's men. They shattered the siege engine and sent the men scurrying with their tails between their legs."

"But didna the siege continue? I dinna remember hearing aboot the English retreating before winter."

"They didn't. More fool were they. Salisbury assumed he would starve them into submission and nearly did. But Alexander Ramsay of Dalhousie sneaked in by boat through a hidden arch that I didn't even know existed. Not until Isa told me this story once we'd been here for a year. He brought in food and supplies. Agnes, unwilling to pass up the chance to taunt Salisbury, sent him a loaf of fresh bread and a chalice of wine the next morning."

"Is that when Salisbury summoned the Earl of Moray?"

"Yes. The earl is Agnes's brother. Salisbury thought the earl could make her back down. Instead, she pointed out that if Salisbury carried out his threat to kill the earl if she didn't concede, then she would inherit her brother's land and title, since he has no children. She would be a countess twice over."

"And that sent the mon back to England in disgrace," Isabella finished as the men took seats at the dais, where the family had already gathered. "My mother is a kind and generous soul, but she's loyal to her last breath and fiercely protective of our family and clan. My sisters and I still lived there, so I remember it clearly. Emelie and Blythe don't recall as much as I do because they're several years younger than me."

Michail remained quiet, not knowing if Ric had discussed his idea with his wife. He watched the couple as he considered whether he could ever enter a jousting tournament and win. He would fight alongside Ric if they asked, if not for Blythe's sake, then for Ric and Isabella's, but he wasn't interested in crossing the border.

"We know you're expected home, but if you can journey south with us, then we'd appreciate your company. A tourney would give me an excuse to return to England and learn what I can about Salisbury."

"I'll have to see what ma father thinks aboot that," Michail hedged. "I canna give ye an answer without asking him."

"Fair enough." Ric nodded before turning his attention to something Liam said. Michail fought to push aside how desirable the idea was to see Blythe again. If he accompanied Ric and Isabella, then he would have time away from court with Blythe. He wondered if he could at least earn her forgiveness if he helped her family.

"I hear the only thing ye've been lifting lately are pints of ale," Seamus muttered across the table to Michail. The latter took a bite of quail to keep from responding with something that would likely wind the men up in a fight, with words or fists. When he didn't answer, Seamus pressed on. "Drink up. Ye look a might parched."

Michail clenched his jaw, not pleased that the

Mackenzies had obviously heard about his excessive drinking. He rued every drop he'd drunk in the past three years if word had spread. If the Mackenzies, and likely the Gunns, believed the clan had a weak tánaiste, they would think it was only a matter of time before they defeated the MacLeods of Assynt. Michail would one day switch from being tánaiste to laird. Both clans had already proven they were patient and could hold grudges.

"Nae so thirsty that I canna lift ma sword and ma mug. I believe I lifted ma sword high enough to take yer cousin's hand from his wrist the last time he paid us a visit." Michail took a long, slow draw from the mug of ale before him. Seamus's eyes narrowed, but he said nothing. The raid Michail referred to had been an unsanctioned one, not one Ulrich Mackenzie ordered. His nephew had acted on his own accord, so Ulrich had wisely kept quiet when Michail sent the ringleader back with his hand in his saddlebag.

It was one of the few times Ulrich accepted being in the wrong. Michail glanced at Óg, who studiously ignored them both, talking to Mòr instead. The elder Magnus had taken responsibility of the Mackenzie brothers' training when they arrived at Dunbeath. The two Magnuses had grown close, making Magnus Mòr no longer feel like the youngest brother in the family.

"Tristan, what would ye have us practice first?" Michail shifted his attention to the Mackay laird and immediately regretted it. He didn't know how long the Mackenzie brothers intended to stay, and he didn't wish for them to discover the MacLeods would soon have another tactic in their arsenal.

"Practice?" Seamus pounced.

No one spoke. No one looked around. Suddenly, the food fascinated everyone. Michail wondered if he could test the waters and see whether the Mackenzies would actively side with the Gunns or merely be spectators.

"The Gunns have a mind to cause us trouble." Michail watched as matching venomous glares turned toward him. He was no surer of the brothers' position than he was before.

"What have they done now?" Óg demanded.

"Sent some men to take a gander at ma home—from the inside." Michail watched as Seamus set his eating knife down and leaned back. Óg continued to glower.

"Ye ken they're our mother's people," Seamus pointed out. Michail glanced toward Siùsan, who shifted anxiously.

"I'm aware."

"Ye ken our relationship with that part of our family is—strained." Seamus's lips tightened as he chose his words.

"I'm aware," Michail repeated.

"Did ye ken our mother returned to Clyth Castle?" Seamus raised his chin.

"I hadnae heard. I suppose she thought to visit her nephew."

"She thinks to live there," Óg interjected.

Michail drew a whistling breath. It suddenly became very clear why the Gunns now set their sights on the MacLeods. Elizabeth Gunn would resent Rose MacLeod until she drew her last breath. She'd entered her marriage, eager to replace Rose in Ulrich's heart, in his home, and his bed. She was utterly unrepentant for the part she and her brothers played in spooking Rose's horse and causing her death. But Ulrich had barely done his duty by Elizabeth, siring Seamus and Magnus Óg. Once he had, he became even more embittered and belligerent toward Elizabeth.

The woman had never forgiven Siùsan for being Rose's daughter. While Ulrich might have neglected her, Elizabeth viewed Siùsan as a constant reminder that Ulrich still loved Rose. When her middle brother, James, took an interest in Siùsan at far too young an age, she did nothing to dissuade him. James helped the Mackenzie warrior Siùsan grew up with abduct her when Ulrich rejected both their suits and betrothed her to Callum Sinclair. Both James and Robert Mackenzie died for their choices.

"How easily yer mother forgets she's ma mother's cousin," Michail noted.

"Which makes us kin. How easily yer father forgets that," Seamus retorted.

"He hasnae forgotten for a minute, *Cousin*." Michail laid down his eating knife, leaning back in his chair, his posture matching Seamus's. "Neither have I." Michail glanced toward Siùsan, who fidgeted with one hand and clutched Callum's arm with the other. Seamus and Óg followed his gaze. Neither man said any more during the meal, but the conversation had hardly ended. It merely moved to the lists when the meal finished.

Seamus and Michail stood toe-to-toe, their postures menacing. Both sets of hands were fisted as a set of green eyes glared into a set of hazel. Seamus's blond hair whipped around his face, while Michail's red hair with hints of strawberry-blond lifted from his neck. The Sinclairs, Tristan, and Ric watched, each prepared to end the brewing fight if it grew too violent, but none willing to intervene yet. It was Magnus Óg who did.

"MacLeod, ye ken we dinna agree with most of what our father does, and our mother was barely better to us than she was Siùsan. Neither of us has missed her since the day she rode out without looking back. We're loyal to our clan, which makes us loyal to our father. But that doesnae mean we see things as he does."

Michail didn't shift his gaze from Seamus, but a

sliver of tension eased from between his shoulders. Still on guard, he nodded, not convinced Óg didn't speak merely as a distraction. But he relaxed further when Seamus unfurled his hands.

"Ye would never ken we're related to the Gunns for all we've had to do with them since Farlane and Arlane's death at the Highland Gathering the Grants hosted. Our mother cared when James died because it happened in her home. Tomas died for his foolishness, as did Farlane. Arlane died for his cruelty and self-centeredness." Seamus explained.

"I ken aboot all that. Ye're fortunate to be Siùsan's brothers because, to the Sinclairs, ye're Mackenzies, nae Gunns." Michail offered a mocking smile. The Gunns further angered the Sinclairs when Tomas aided Randolph de Soules and Laird Albert Kerr with their claim that de Soules was legitimately betrothed to Brighde Kerr, the laird's daughter. She married Alexander, but not without a battle that claimed all three men's lives. In less than five years, the Gunns lost James and Tomas at the Sinclairs' hands. Farlane and Arlane died when the Gordon twins defended Eoin's wife, Cairstine.

"Beathan wasna any better than his brother, Arlane," Óg mused. "We were here when that nightmare happened." The complicated clan politics escalated further when Farlane's younger son, Beathan, wouldn't accept a failed betrothal with Arabella Johnstone and tried to keep her from her now-husband, Lachlan Sutherland. Lachlan was Laird Liam Sinclair's nephew-by-marriage and the Sinclair siblings' cousin. Marriage joined the Sinclairs and Sutherlands, binding the two powerful clans into one of the strongest alliances in all of Scotland.

"Why are ye telling me history I already ken,

Mackenzie?" Michail wondered. "I ken how complicated our family tree is."

"So ye can understand how the branches dinna always meet and the roots tangle until one strangles another." Seamus looked at his brother before turning his attention back to Michail. "One day, ye and I will lead our clans. We liked each other well enough when we were younger. The only reason we dinna now is because of choices made generations before we were born and continued by men who will pass the mantle to us one day."

"Are ye saying ye dinna want to continue the feud?" Michail kept his voice low.

"That's what we're saying," Seamus answered, including his brother in his statement.

"Yer mother may have returned to Clyth, but the Mackenzies and Gunns maintain their alliance. It's only time before we're battling both sides of yer family."

"We dinna control Edgar and his men," Óg spoke up. "But we will have a say over our men, just as ye will yers."

"That helps nae at all. Ma father and yers are both in fine health. Neither is bound for the Lord's Kingdom soon. That still leaves ma clan battling both ye and the Gunns, and ye're allies."

"True enough. But Edgar is a fool to look in yer direction." Seamus shook head dismissively. "Even if we came to his aid, the Sinclairs will come to yers. Siùsan may be how the Mackenzies' alliance began with the Sinclairs, but the Sinclairs' feud with the Gunns goes back as far as ours does with ye. And where the Sinclairs go, the Sutherlands and Mackays ride alongside. Where the Sutherlands go, the MacLeods of Lewis go too, which is yer extended kin to boot. We arenae looking to have the entire northern Highlands and half the Hebrides descend upon us."

"Seamus is right," Callum said as he stepped forward. "We'll defend the Mackenzies against any foe who isnae the MacLeods of Assynt. But we will never ignore the Gunns threatening one of our allies. Our history with the Gunns goes back much further than just Tomas and his brothers. Elizabeth wasna Tomas's only sister."

Michail, Seamus, and Óg turned toward Callum, surprise and confusion clear in their expressions.

"Aye, they had a younger sister named Ceana," Callum explained. "Ma father had a younger brother, Dugan. Ma uncle fell in love with Ceana, just as she did with him. The feud was already going, but they would meet where our lands border. Ma grandfather was still laird then, and he approved of their match. They believed they would soon marry. However, when Tomas discovered their relationship—rather, when yer mother told him—nae only did he lock Ceana away after nearly beating her to death, he led a raid and killed Uncle Dugan. I was a bairn so I only ken what I've heard. Someone helped Ceana escape Clyth, and she came here. Mama and Da offered her a home, but her grief made her see Dugan everywhere. She eventually asked to retire to an abbey. Ma parents escorted her to Inchcailleoch Priory, where she gave birth to ma stillborn cousin. She named him Dugan. So ye can all see, the Gunns have stolen a great deal from us and done us more harm than anyone else. Da doesnae seek vengeance, but neither does he turn a blind eye to yer mother's people. Ma mother and Siùsan's were best friends growing up, so ma father arranged ma marriage, in part to honor Mama, but also because he wouldnae allow a Gunn to keep harming Rose's daughter. I didna ken that until after I married Siùsan."

"That is why we will defend the MacLeods of Assynt," Alex said as he stepped forward. "It doesnae change our feelings toward ye." Alex nodded to Seamus and Magnus Óg. "It's all our misfortune that ye're related to the Gunns."

"We ken," Óg grunted. "We dinna blame any of ye for who ye stand beside. Seamus spoke the truth. Neither ma brother nor I wish to continue this. We would stand beside the Sinclairs before the Gunns. We *will* stand beside them."

"That means we willna stand against the Sinclairs' allies," Seamus declared. Michail wasn't so quick to believe Seamus and Óg, not because he thought the men were lying, but because he understood they wouldn't easily change their clan's belief that the feud was justified. Nonetheless, Michail thrust out his arm, both as a peace offering and to ensure everyone witnessed Seamus give his word. Seamus looked down at it for a moment before clasping Michail's forearm. They each squeezed, both a silent competition and threat in what was supposed to seal a future truce. When Michail grasped Óg's arm, the challenge wasn't there. Óg held Michail's forearm in a powerful grip, but there was no test. The younger man's smile told Michail he understood Michail would hold Óg to the same pledge should he ever become laird.

"Ye're still all clishmaclavering?" Ceit said as she slid her arm around Tavish's waist. The other women came to join the men. Michail offered a reassuring smile to Siùsan, who leaned against Callum, her eyes darting between her cousin and her brothers. Ceit poked Tavish in the belly, her finger hitting a solid wall. "Ye canna eat as ye do if ye dinna work it off."

"Shall I show ye how I swing ma sword, ma little bee?" Tavish teased.

"I've seen ye do that plenty of times before. It's nae as impressive as it once was," Ceit retorted. Callum, Alex, and Magnus guffawed while Ric and Tristan choked on their laughter. The wives winked at Ceit, and Seamus, Óg, and Michail shifted uncomfortably. It was always endearing at first, seeing the longtime married couples still jest with one another and share affection. But eventually it became uncomfortable for the bachelors.

Taking pity on the unmarried men, Tristan kissed Mairghread's forehead, then said, "Come. I'll introduce ye to the slinger."

Michail still wasn't certain it was a good idea for the Mackenzie brothers to join his lessons. He didn't doubt their refusal to support the Gunns, but he worried he would be on the receiving end of one of their rocks once they all departed Dunbeath.

CHAPTER 4

The next sennight passed with the same ease Michail and the Mackenzie brothers shared while the younger men fostered with the Sinclairs. Michail held his reservations, but his trust grew as he became better acquainted with the men they'd matured to be. It was clear from mannerisms they failed to hide that they both disliked their father and held little respect for him as a man or as a parent. They were kind and helpful to their sister, and the Sinclairs' younger generation thought they were wonderful because they led excursions to go swimming and fishing.

"Michail, will ye join us?" Óg called as the oldest of the third generation of Sinclairs gathered at the postern gate. Thormud and Rose stood beside their cousins Saoirse, who was Alex and Brighde's oldest daughter, and Maisie, Magnus and Deirdre's oldest child. Along with them stood Kirk Hartley, Isabella and Ric's oldest son.

"Aye. Let me—"

"Riders approach. MacLeods," a deepening adolescent voice called from the wall walk. Michail spun around, glancing at Wee Liam—named for his grandfather, and not so wee anymore—then toward the gate as his clansmen charged into the bailey. Adan led the entourage, and Michail's stomach dropped. He raced to meet his brother, grabbing the horse's reins before it stopped.

"What's happened?" Michail demanded, but Adan was looking past them. He pointed to Seamus and Óg.

"They happened," Adan spat. "Mackenzies raided three of our villages. Taking our cattle wasna enough. They burned crofts, violated lasses barely auld enough to be called women, and killed dozens of men."

Michail stilled. He looked at Adan. The pure hatred that poured from his brother shattered any truce in the making. Adan lunged forward when Seamus and Óg hurried toward the MacLeod brothers.

"What happened?" Seamus demanded. "Who led the raid?"

"I dinna ken, and I dinna care. He wore yer plaid," Adan snarled as he once more lunged. Michail fought to restrain his brother, pushing against his chest.

"Cease. Nae here," Michail whispered, then called out, "Laird!"

"Aye. I'm here," Liam responded as he jumped down the last four steps from the keep. "To ma solar. All of ye." The aging laird swept his gaze around the gathering crowd, and his sons fell in step with the MacLeods and Mackenzies, keeping them apart.

Siùsan ordered food and drinks served to the newly arrived men before she hurried to join her family in Liam's solar. She stood between her brothers and her cousins, knowing that despite the animosity, she was likely the only person who could keep them apart. She was confident not a one would ever harm her, either on purpose or by accident.

"Explain," Liam ordered. Adan opened his mouth, but the laird was looking at Seamus and Óg.

"We dinna ken." Seamus shook his head but paused and looked at Óg. "That's why he sent us here."

"Aye."

"What do ye mean?" Siùsan asked.

"Óg and I had a huge row with Father a fortnight before we arrived here. We did it in his solar, but we're certain half the clan heard all of us."

"What were ye arguing aboot?" Siùsan wondered.

"Them." Óg jutted his chin toward the MacLeods. "Father thinks we should raid farther east from Ardvreck, hoping we'd be less likely to be caught. He even thinks ye might blame the Gunns. I think he wishes that to spite Mother. We refused."

"Ye refused," Adan scoffed.

"Aye. We refused. We may have crossed swords more than once, Adan. But I dinna lie." Óg crossed his brawny arms and narrowed his eyes.

"Enough," Liam boomed once more. "Ulrich claimed ye both wished to see Siùsan."

"We did. That's why we thought Father sent us," Seamus explained. "Obviously, he wanted us gone, so we wouldnae stand in his way again."

"Again?" Michail asked. The Mackenzie brothers exchanged a look. Óg shrugged, so Seamus answered.

"Two days after Marcus returned with his hand amputated, Father wanted to send a war band across yer eastern lands. He wanted to do what Adan just described. That's what we argued aboot. Óg and I refused to lead the men. He threatened to disown us. I couldnae help it, and it didna help the matter, but I laughed. Laughed hard and in his face. It's nay secret the men follow ma orders better than they do our father's. Even if he'd forced us to lead the war band, we wouldnae have done more than filch some sheep."

"Father waited for us to leave," Óg took up the explanation. "Because he kenned Marcus would lead the men again. This time, Father would sanction it, and Marcus would feel justified in revenge. He didna want us there, so he manipulated all of us. We came here in good faith."

"And now ye shall leave in disgrace," Adan taunted. Michail shoved his shoulder into Adan's upper chest, where it met his shoulder. He slipped between his brother and the Mackenzies.

Speaking over his shoulder to Adan, Michail whispered. "We will learn naught if ye dinna stop. Dinna make me send ye away." Adan took a step back, but the tension flowing from him radiated against Michail's back.

"Nay. We leave to resolve the matter of the lairdship finally," Seamus responded.

"What?" Siùsan stepped toward her brothers.

"The clan council has been talking aboot it for a while, but Father doesnae ken. Or if he does, he doesnae believe they would ever do it. They want him to step aside for me." Seamus appeared almost embarrassed, but Óg looked hopeful.

"Father has only gotten worse with age. He favors Marcus because our cousin believes he'll prove to the council that he should become laird once Father dies. He believes he can convince the council to disinherit me. He's nearly convinced Father." Seamus looked at Liam, then Callum. "After what happened to Siùsan because of our Uncle James, the clan lost respect for Father. Nay one agreed with how he neglected Siùsan, but he had seemed a capable and just laird. After Siùsan's abduction, he seemed like a broken mon for a long time. From what we ken, once we left to foster here, Mother took advantage of Father's moroseness and spewed vile things aboot Siùsan and the Sinclairs. Father hadnae really changed. He eagerly believed all that

Mother said aboot Siùsan. He believed a woman he can barely stomach looking at."

"She was smart enough never to say aught against Rose. She did it once when we were vera young, and Father nearly strangled her to death," Óg explained. "But she spoke against the MacLeods, blaming Siùsan for outrageous things that were utter nonsense. Father believed it all. Or at least, he believed it enough to argue it justified raiding ye. Yer grandfather only reacted to our father's aggression. He was well within his rights. Seamus and I were here, and we were too young to understand then what we do now."

"Do ye really think they'd make ye laird?" Callum asked as he stood behind Siùsan, wrapping his arms around her waist. She leaned against the solid frame that had been providing her comfort and security for nearly a decade and a half.

"After this? Aye. I dinna doubt it," Seamus nodded.

"How can ye be so certain?" Michail demanded.

"Because the Sinclairs and Mackays are aboot to arrive at our doorstep to support the MacLeods." Seamus locked eyes with Michail, even though he'd just commanded Liam and Tristan to send men to fight.

"Ye would have us support yer mutiny," Tristan spoke up.

"I would have the Sinclairs remind ma father they defend their family. Ma father doesnae recognize Siùsan as a Mackenzie; he believes she's a MacLeod. Where the Sinclairs go, the Mackays ride beside. If there's time, ye might rally the Sutherlands too," Seamus grinned as he finished his rationalization.

Michail looked back at Adan before looking at Tristan, then settling his focus on Liam. "We will accept yer support if ye wish to offer it. But we willna ask ye to be in the middle. Either way, Adan and I leave in the morn. I need to speak to ma brother." Michail nodded to Liam before nodding toward the door, indicating Adan should lead the way from the solar. Neither brother spoke until they reached the chamber they would now share.

"Michail, Da wants ye to go to court to deliver a missive to the Bruce." Adan reached into his sporran and pulled two folded sheets of parchment from it. Only one was sealed. "They say the same thing. Da wants ye to ken exactly what he wrote to the king, but he had to seal the one ye're to hand over."

"Do ye ken what they say?"

"Aye. Ward and I were in the solar with him and the council when he wrote them. He's threatening to declare war on the Mackenzies and invoke every alliance we have. He says he'll call upon our allies' allies. Ulrich has gone too far this time."

Michail nodded as he read the missive in their father's script. Adan hadn't exaggerated. Torrian demanded—with flowery prose—that the Bruce intervene or accept a clan war across the Highlands. He reminded King Robert of how hard the man had worked to unify the clans, and that Ulrich would be to blame when it all came crashing down. Without saying it outright, Torrian issued the Bruce an ultimatum. Michail swallowed. He dreaded being in the Privy Council chamber when the king came to the end of the missive. But he also knew the Bruce would side with the MacLeods, if for no other reason than the Sinclairs and Sutherlands would get involved. Lairds Liam Sinclair and Hamish Sutherland had fought beside Robert the Bruce since the king first began his quest for the crown and then throughout his battles with the English.

It was a well-kept secret that all the Sinclair and Sutherland siblings were King Robert and Queen Elizabeth de Burgh's godchildren. If the Sutherlands heeded the call from the Sinclairs and so did the Mac-

Leods of Lewis, Michail's distant relatives and Hamish's family-by-marriage, it would also prompt the Camerons to join the fray. The allies would almost surround the Mackenzies. The MacLeods of Lewis and Assynt, the Sinclairs, the Sutherlands, the Mackays, and the Camerons would descend upon the Mackenzies before they could rally any ally. It would decimate their clan.

"Do ye believe Seamus?" Adan interrupted Michail's thoughts.

"Aye. He might deceive ye and me, but he wouldnae tell such a bold lie in front of Siùsan and the others. Never."

"I thought the same."

"The past sennight gave me a chance to get to ken them as men, nae the lads I remembered. They respect their father because they must, but they are loyal to their clan. I canna fault them for it. But both have made it clear they willna support the Gunns, and they wish the feud to end once Seamus and I are lairds. Ye saw their faces. They didna ken, Adan."

"I realized that once I could see straight. It doesnae sooth ma rage, but I believe them too."

"Do ye ride to Stirling with me?" Michail asked.

"Nay. Ward and I must go to the villages and survey the damage. He already set out for them. I'm to join him rather than go home. I could smell the smoke, Michail, even when I couldnae see aught. The fires must have been massive. I suspect they caught some of the woods ablaze."

"Killing our game and trees. It'll make hunting harder, and it'll keep us from selling our timber. They kenned what they were doing." Michail shook his head. "If we remain here instead of going to the Great Hall, it willna look good. People will think we're sulking or plotting. I'm in nay mood for a crowd, but we must."

"I ken. I dinna wish to be here, but since I am, I want to visit with Siùsan and her kin."

A soft rapping on the door made the brothers look toward the portal. When Michail bid the person enter, Siùsan opened the door. She and Adan exchanged embraces, finally greeting one another while the servants set up a bath for Adan. Once the brothers were clean and wore fresh leines, they made their way belowstairs.

The evening meal was subdued for all who sat upon the dais. Michail learned Liam was sending Callum and Tavish along with Seamus and Magnus Óg when they returned home. They would delay their departure for three or four days to give Magnus Mòr time to call upon the Sutherlands. Tristan would ride with the Sinclair and Mackenzie warriors. The three score warriors who accompanied Mairghread and Tristan would follow their laird, and Liam would send five score warriors with his sons. They expected Hamish would send at least three score, but it would surprise no one if the Sutherlands equaled the Sinclairs.

Despite the developing plans they all prayed would resolve the feud, Michail and Adan remained suspicious. Seamus and Óg had slipped away to talk privately before the meal. Michail noticed that while talking to Adan had calmed them both, Seamus and Óg seemed angrier than they had when they first learned of their father's deceit. Their anger simmered, directed at no one on the dais. Michail and Adan confirmed they still planned to leave in the morning, Michail riding straight to Stirling. He was eager for the Sinclairs and their allies to set off, not happy that they would wait four days, but he trusted Liam and Tristan would keep their word.

Michail fell into an exhausted sleep, barely noticing that Adan lay next to him. His mind filled the hours of restless slumber with nightmares about deaths among his clan and dreams of seeing Blythe again. He awoke as tired as he had been when he retired for the night. But he couldn't ignore that he looked forward to seeing Blythe, even if the coldness between them forced him to keep his distance.

CHAPTER 5

Michail leaned forward and patted Cunnart's neck as he approached Stirling. He and his men rode hard for ten days, stopping during the day only long enough to rest the horses. They slept during the darkest hours of the night, so they were on the road well after dusk and well before dawn. He was filthy and exhausted.

Michail and the MacLeod guards were unprepared for the sound of charging hooves from behind. They drew their swords and pulled their horses to a halt before spinning them around, prepared to defend themselves from attack. They were all unprepared for the three women surrounded by their guards—or rather the two women with hoods pulled over their hair surrounded by their guards and one very blonde woman leading the pack. The leader was nearly a furlong ahead of the others and riding at a speed only Michail dared when he was most inebriated. A cloak billowed around the rider as she stood in her stirrups, but kept her body crouched over her steed's withers. She veered at the very last moment to skirt the MacLeods, who sat motionless, stunned at the daredevil. The horse and rider passed in a cloud of dust moments before the rest of their party caught up and passed through the castle's gates.

Michail and his men followed once they'd sheathed their swords and swiped their sleeves over their faces to wipe away the dust. Michail recognized the leader, but he could only guess who the other women were. The men all wore Lowland breeks, even though he suspected most were Highlanders. He entered the bailey, set on going directly to the stables.

"Look who's here. MacLeods."

Michail turned toward the feminine voice that announced his arrival. He wanted to groan and turn Cunnart around when he recognized his cousin's voice. Before him stood Sileas Gunn, Blythe Dunbar, and Evina Murray. Michail had no choice but to acknowledge them since they blocked his path. He dismounted and led Cunnart toward the women. His men fanned out and continued to the stables.

"Ma ladies," Michail greeted them. He offered a genuine smile to Sileas. She was Laird Edgar Gunn's cousin, too. Despite being unquestionably legitimate and Farlane's youngest child, she hadn't inherited the lairdship because she was a woman. Some clans acknowledged a woman's right to lead and inherit the title, but the Gunns were not one of them.

"Hello, Michail." Sileas's smile was just as warm. "How is your mother?"

Michail grinned at Sileas's refined speech. They'd known each other since they were weans, even though Catriona was no longer close to her family. They'd seen each other annually at the Highland Gathering. He remembered when she'd once sounded like a Highlander.

"She's well." Michail offered nothing more, making Sileas frown. "Have ye had word from Edgar recently?"

Sileas shook her head. "Naught more than he's signed my betrothal papers. What happened?"

"Ma felicitations, Cousin. Mayhap that is why our cousin sent men to ma home. Mayhap it was to share the good news." Michail watched Sileas's shoulders slump as she closed her eyes.

"Ye ken—"

"I do, Sileas." Michail proffered a kiss on her cheek before turning to the other two women. "Lady Blythe, Lady Evina, I trust ye are well."

"Quite well," Blythe answered, infusing smugness into her tone. She met Michail's gaze, challenging him, yet regretting it at the same time. She melted as his penetrating emerald gaze bore into her, as though merely looking at her would tempt her to say more. She clenched her jaw to keep from speaking.

"If ye'll excuse me, I must tend to ma horse and be sure ma men settle into the barracks." Michail nodded to the trio, but his eyes never left Blythe's until Cunnart's head nodded, as though he agreed with his owner. It broke the connection, so Michail led his steed away.

"Blythe," Evina whispered. "What was that?"

"What was what?"

"The way you looked at one another. I thought your flirtation with him was over. It seemed far more—intense."

"It is over. He isn't the mon I thought he was. His arrival reminded me of that."

"I think he's charming," Evina giggled. "And certainly braw."

"You can have him," Blythe offered.

"No. He's just nice to look at and talk to once in a while. He's too reckless for me," Evina countered.

"And that is why he isn't the mon I thought he was." Neither woman missed the irony in Blythe's evaluation, since they'd all just raced past the MacLeods like the hounds of hell were on their heels, and Blythe was the ringleader as always. She watched Michail enter the stables, wondering how she could avoid him for however long he remained in Stirling. She knew she was a glutton for punishment because the very next thought was whether he might ask her to dance that evening. She doubted he would, and it was for the best. But she couldn't help but wish he would. *You henwit. He'll disappoint you all over again.*

"We need to hurry if we're to change before the evening meal," Sileas pointed out. "And I'm worried aboot what Michail said. I need to look for Calder and find out if he knows what's happened. Edgar will tell me naught if I send a missive home. Perhaps he's told my betrothed something." Sileas prayed Calder Urquhart knew what her cousin planned because she feared Edgar would lead their clan to ruin. They'd been too close too many times in Sileas's life.

The women arrived at the chamber they shared. Blythe had shared a chamber with her sister Emelie until she left to marry Dominic Campbell. Evina had been Caitlyn Kennedy's roommate before she married Alexander Armstrong, then she shared her chamber with Catherine MacFarlane until she married Rab MacLaren. The three ladies wheedled the Mistress of the Bedchamber, the woman in charge of all the ladies-in-waiting, until they convinced her to allow them to room together. They squeezed an extra bed into Evina's chamber, and Blythe and Sileas moved in.

They chattered while their maids helped style their coiffures and laced their gowns. Despite taking part in the conversation, Blythe couldn't keep her mind from wandering. It always seemed to make its way to a certain red-headed man. Her heart ached as she scolded herself for having a single soft thought about the man who'd broken her heart and abandoned her. She refused to think about what else occurred between them, except for one memory that always returned, always made her pause.

Just about two years ago, Blythe had hurried to her chamber after her morning walk with the queen and the royal's retinue. Henry Pringle, who demanded to know where Emelie went, had cornered her. It hadn't been a secret that Emelie and Dominic Campbell married and left Stirling with shocking haste. Pringle claimed the Campbells hadn't allowed him to see Emelie at Kilchurn. Henry and Emelie had a brief but disastrous liaison, and while Emelie wished to sever ties and move on, Henry was not of the same mind.

Henry threatened Blythe and had even shaken her before putting his hand around her throat. Like an apparition, Michail appeared and yanked Henry away from Blythe, wrapping his own hand around the smaller man's throat. Michail pulled Henry onto his toes and tightened his hold until Henry turned purple, explaining Henry should have a better idea of what death by strangulation was like before he ever thought to touch Blythe again.

Michail had left the lists and seen Henry drag Blythe into a tucked-away corner of the building. It was clear she didn't want to go with him. He couldn't hear what they said, but he hadn't hesitated to help Blythe. Once Michail freed Blythe, he'd escorted her back to the queen's solar. Before they reached the chamber, they slipped into an alcove and shared a passionate tryst. They'd been interested in each other years earlier, but it had soured. Blythe had held a moment's hope that they were going to overcome what pushed them apart. If only she'd remembered what had happened years earlier.

"Are you coming?" Evina asked.

"Yes. Just thinking aboot Emelie and Dom. Their visit wasn't nearly long enough. Now that Emelie's had her second bairn, Fergus, I doubt they will travel soon. Nic is barely more than a year. Laurel is also carrying again, so they'll want to be near her and Brodie." Blythe didn't enjoy lying to her friends, but she would never share her thoughts about Michail to anyone, not even the man himself.

They made their way to the Great Hall, where they took their seats. Blythe looked around and sighed. Their meals lately had been peaceful and uneventful, which was just how Blythe needed that evening to be.

"Isn't it wonderful that we don't have to listen to Sarah Anne or Margaret anymore?" Evina asked, sharing the same thought as Blythe.

"I don't pity either mon who married them, but I pity the clans they joined. May the Lord and all his angels preserve those people," Sileas said, making the sign of the cross. But her unrepentant grin broke through.

"No clan deserves them being foisted upon them. But their dowries were substantial," Blythe commented.

"They had to be." Evina snorted. "That was the only way their father could get rid of them. He had to buy them husbands."

The conversation carried on around Blythe as she watched Michail walk toward the dais. He placed his fist over his heart and bowed to the royal couple. He exchanged words Blythe was much too far away to hear. She was unprepared for Michail to turn toward her, failing to avert her eyes in time for him not to see her watching. Servants were already placing the first course on tables, so it forced Michail to weave through the moving people to reach the table his men chose. She wondered if he'd told them where to sit, or it was merely for the devil's enjoyment that he now sat directly in her line of sight.

Blythe ate more than she intended, but it kept her attention away from Michail and made it difficult to join the conversation. Both suited her until the music began. She took her place in line for a country reel. She changed partners twice before she found herself with Michail's steely arm around her waist as he twirled her. She nearly didn't let go when it was time for them to exchange partners again. The set brought them together four more times, and Blythe was certain each time Michail tightened his hold slightly more, bringing their bodies closer together.

"Blythe," Michail whispered as they came together for the last time. "Are ye truly well?"

"Why wouldn't I be?" Blythe raised an imperious eyebrow.

"Because ye're at court."

"Where I have been for several years."

"Where I once found a mon with his hand around yer throat. Do ye think I've forgotten?"

"I don't know." Blythe shrugged one shoulder, her attitude blasé.

"Ye do. Ye remember as well as I do. He terrified ye. I doubt ye will ever forget that. I will never forget the rage I felt."

"And I thanked you for rescuing me. I—" Blythe exhaled when the music forced them apart. It disconcerted her that he brought up the very memory she'd recalled while preparing for the meal. It made her wonder if he thought about it as often as she did. She'd seen no one look so lethal as Michail had, and she'd grown up along the border where skirmishes were part of daily life when living within spitting distance of the English.

Blythe smiled coyly when Fletcher Drummond approached her and asked for a dance that would keep them partnered through the entire set. She glanced over his shoulder to find Michail watching her. She offered Fletcher her most charming smile, giggling when he drew her closer. She'd flirted with the man for months, even sharing kisses and caresses under the moon. As she moved around the dance floor, she could nearly forget Michail. But she caught sight of him dancing with a newly arrived matron, a woman with a reputation for warming any man's bed but that of her geriatric husband. Blythe glared at Michail until she realized he was watching her. She once again cocked her eyebrow, her eyes darting to the woman in his arms. She looked down her nose at him before turning her attention back to Fletcher.

Michail hadn't wanted to accept Lady Leslie Lindsay's obvious invitation to dance, but she positioned herself so he couldn't escape without forcibly moving her. As he said her name in his head, he wished to roll his eyes. He knew she neither picked her name nor her title, but it sounded ridiculous to him. But when he wrapped his arm around her waist, he realized his body didn't find her as objectionable as his mind had. He hadn't bedded a woman for longer than he would admit. He'd been drunk too many nights over the past three years to have even considered bed sport, knowing he likely would fail to perform or would merely fall asleep. Leslie's voluptuous form made his cock take notice.

He smiled down at the pretty blonde, enjoying the view of her cleavage. He knew she recognized his appreciation when she rolled her shoulders forward, pressing her breasts together and making her gown gape at the neckline. He was about to say something he prayed was charming and witty, but he caught sight of Blythe. The look of utter disgust she shot him cooled his ardor. When he looked at Leslie again, hair that had appeared like a halo of gold a moment ago now seemed mousy and drab after looking at Blythe's white-blonde locks. He'd fought, and barely succeeded against, the temptation to wrap one of her curls around his finger when they danced. His hand had brushed over the satiny strands each time they came together. Now he wished to extract himself from Leslie's hold even more than he'd wished to avoid her in the first place.

The song ended, allowing Michail to bow and step away from Leslie at last. But it was at that moment he watched Fletcher whisper something in Blythe's ear. Her smile made her attractive face stunning. Whatever Fletcher said pleased Blythe, as she nodded to go along with her encouraging smile. Michail's stomach knotted as Fletcher sneaked a kiss on Blythe's neck as he leaned over again to whisper to her. It was an act far too familiar to have been the first time. Since Blythe did nothing to stop him or remonstrate him, Michail realized she wanted Fletcher's attention as much as he seemed eager to bestow it upon her.

Michail turned back to find Leslie, but she'd already moved on to another partner, a man with whom who she was clearly very comfortable. The couple had moved together rhythmically somewhere other than the dance floor. Michail sighed as he tried to decide what to do beyond moving out of the way of the now-dancing couples. He watched Blythe and Fletcher dance a second time together, fearful that they would force him to watch them a third time. If they danced together thrice in one night, it would be tantamount to a betrothal announcement. Michail felt ill until he watched Blythe return to her group of friends before they followed the queen from the Great Hall, retiring for the night. He beat his own hasty retreat to his chamber.

~

Blythe thanked her maid before climbing into bed. When she closed her eyes, she couldn't rid her mind of Michail. She tried staring at the ceiling, but her memory refused to be silent. She'd reveled in every moment they'd danced together, and it irked her. She'd eagerly accepted Fletcher's attention, since she liked the young warrior. He was attractive and funny, but he lacked a forcefulness that she'd grown accustomed to with Michail. She reminded herself that she wasn't looking for the recklessness that came with Michail, and part of what she found appealing about Fletcher was his staid nature. Fletcher was the type of man her parents wished her to find after Isabella married Ric and moved to the Highlands and after Emelie eloped with Dominic. She felt she owed her parents peace of mind.

But try as she might, she continued to compare Fletcher, and every other man she knew, to Michail. They inevitably came up short. As much as she told herself that she didn't like Michail's daredevil streak, it appealed to her own wildness. She'd once imagined he was courting her when he would invite her along for rides in the surrounding meadows just beyond Stirling Castle's gates. They'd teased one another and raced at breakneck speeds. Blythe had ridden next to Michail during a hunt, determined to prove he wasn't the only person who could ride and fire a bow and arrow at the same time. They'd even slipped away to a few local taverns while dressed as peasants, Blythe's remarkable blonde hair well covered. She'd accepted his bets that she couldn't drink the drams of whisky he'd put before her. Not only had she matched him drink for drink, she wasn't the one who woke up the next morning with a sore head. She'd thought they were building a relationship to last.

She'd come to dislike him because of their falling

out, but she still respected most things about him and admired him in many ways. She'd seen his devotion to his clan when he came to court to represent them. She knew how close he was to his family from the missives Isabella sent her. She'd also heard of his bravery and honor in battle. It was his honor, however, that was a sticking point with Blythe. She wished she'd witnessed that instead of the opposite. She wanted Michail to be himself, but she also wished fruitlessly that he would be as dependable as men like Fletcher. But she knew, with Michail, she would never have it both ways.

Blythe tossed and turned for most of the night, unable to settle her mind. She abandoned her bed and moved to the window embrasure, where she sat and gazed at the stars. She was dozing there when Evina and Sileas woke.

CHAPTER 6

Michail clamped his jaw closed, keeping himself from spewing the vile curses that came to mind as he stood in the Privy Council chamber listening to Robert the Bruce. He couldn't believe what his sovereign said to him. He was certain his ears must deceive him. It was impossible King Robert would consider siding with the Mackenzies. After all, the MacLeods were the victims in all of this. They were the ones who had their villages raided and burned to the ground. Instead, King Robert made it sound as though the Mackenzies sought vengeance on the MacLeods. When the king noticed Michail's disdain turn to disgust, then morph into rage, he paused. He wondered if perhaps he didn't have the full picture. He only knew what Ulrich sent in a missive.

King Robert picked up the piece of parchment that lay before him and reread the letter from Laird Mackenzie. He was certain there must be more to the story, but he had believed Ulrich when he said Torrian encroached upon his land and stole more sheep and cattle than ever before. The Bruce watched Michail and noticed the younger man clenched his fist around a piece of parchment that he was yet to hand over.

"Give me what your father has sent," King Robert commanded. "I can see that you have a missive for me."

Michail handed the sealed letter to the Bruce and waited. He prayed what his father wrote would vindicate them and make the king change his mind in front of all those who stood there glaring at him as though he were the villain and not the victim. He watched as the king scanned the letter more than once. He felt more at ease as he watched King Robert grow ever more flustered, nodding his head as he reviewed the words. Michail studied the aging warrior, trying to guess what the monarch might say next.

"It seems your father has provided me with information I did not previously have. Given what I know of your father and Laird Mackenzie, I'm swayed in favor of your clan now. I know you have never had reason to lie to me before, and your allies would never continue their support if you made a habit of lying to the crown. I'm certain far more truth lies in your father's missive than the one I received from the Mackenzie. Tell me what you know."

"I was with the Sinclairs when the raid took place, but Adan rode to Dunbeath and explained what happened. He passed close enough to smell the smoke in the air while Ward rode directly to the villages. From what I understand from Adan, Mackenzies targeted our eastern villages. They pillaged and plundered like Norsemen, stealing and burning our villages after abusing and assaulting the women."

Michail paused as he continued to study the Bruce. He doubted his next piece of information was part of Ulrich's missive.

"Seamus and Magnus Óg were at Dunbeath when Adan arrived. They were there to hear what happened, and it was obvious they kenned naught of their father's plan. When they heard of the raid, they realized Laird

CELESTE BARCLAY

Mackenzie's ulterior motives sent them to Dunbeath. They believed they'd gone to see Siùsan and to visit with the Sinclairs. Instead, they realized their laird sent them so that he could raid our villages without either of the brothers standing in his way. I've come to learn Seamus may be laird sooner than any of us suspected because their clan council grows tired of their current laird's behavior. In fact, Seamus may already be laird."

"What?" King Robert bellowed.

"Aye. While I rode here, the Sinclairs, the Mackays and the Sutherlands rode home with Seamus and Magnus Óg. More than likely, just the sight of so many warriors riding upon them will have been enough for the Mackenzie to step aside. If it wasna, then the clan council will probably vote him out and will swear in Seamus. It may have already happened."

"Bluidy hell. Your father was not jesting when he said there might be a war in the Highlands. That's the last thing I need with those three clans involved. Which of the lairds took it upon himself to organize this little escapade?"

"It was Seamus's idea to have the other clans ride with him. He asked Tristan and Liam if they would accompany him. And he asked if someone would ride for Hamish. I dinna ken for certain that the Sutherlands went with them, but I ken that they requested their help. I canna imagine Hamish would turn down Liam."

"And what does your cousin think of her brothers riding against their father?"

"She likely believes it's a good idea. Wouldnae ye if ye were in her position?" Michail kept his voice bland. But he knew he was backing the king into a corner. He would either get the answer he sought, or he would find himself in the dungeon that night.

"If I were her, I would keep my neb out of politics."

"Which Sinclair woman do ye ken who keeps her

neb out of politics? They offer the sagest advice to the men in that clan. I believe they have even offered sage advice to this court."

"Aye, well, it was never a well-kept secret that the Mackenzie treated his daughter poorly. I wouldn't blame the lass if she never wanted to see the mon again."

"She already pledged that she never would, and Callum has pledged that she would never have to. It was the Sinclairs who trained Seamus to become laird, nae his own father. Even I feel as though I can put some of ma faith into Seamus, kenning he has become more of a Sinclair than a Mackenzie when it comes to leading a clan. He pledged to end the feud when he and I lead our clans. He made that pledge in front of the Sinclair siblings and their mates. Even if he was of a mind to lie to me, he would never do that in front of any Sinclair, let alone all ten of them. He made the same promise before Liam as well. I take nay comfort in kenning Seamus may now be laird of the Mackenzies, but I feel more confident an end to this feud is in sight without Ulrich leading his clan. Ma father will probably be willing to find an amenable way to end the fighting."

"You take no comfort in this, yet you would make it sound as though ye trust Seamus."

"What comfort is there to be found when I ken members of ma clan are dead, and ma brothers are seeing to their funerals? But I can look to the future and hope that we can finally put our feud to rest. If Ulrich is nay longer laird, there is nay reason to continue this. Ma father misses his sister, and Siùsan misses the mother she never kenned. But Seamus and Magnus Óg would never do aught to hurt Siùsan, nor would ma father and I."

"But you have been feuding for decades now. Were you not concerned aboot your cousin then?"

"The feud started well before Siùsan, Seamus, Magnus Óg, and I were even born. It was Laird Mackenzie who continued it. Ma grandfather fought because Laird Mackenzie had a hand in Lady Rose's death, ma aunt and his only daughter. The Mackenzie was as much to blame for her death as the Gunns. Why did he have his pregnant wife riding at such a speed on horseback? If he had really cared, why wasna ma aunt in a wagon? And it was Laird Mackenzie's decision to remain allied with the Gunns despite how his marriage to Lady Mackenzie was a disaster. Now the Gunns have turned on us and wish to draw us into battle. Seamus and Magnus Óg pledged to help us since their mother returned to her clan of birth rather than stay with them."

"She did what?" King Robert's mouth bunched into a tight line, clearly not liking this news in front of his advisors. It was one thing to find surprising news in a missive that he read silently. It was another thing entirely for the king to be blindsided twice with plenty of big ears and loose tongues around.

"I suspect she's aware the clan council plans to remove Laird Mackenzie and put Seamus in his place. She either doesnae care enough to stay as Lady Mackenzie, or she realizes her life would be better if she wasna left to her sons' decisions for her. She could manipulate her husband, but I dinna believe she can manipulate her sons now that they are men. But she's obviously manipulating Edgar, since he sent men to spy from within ma home. They are our guests right now in our dungeon. We caught the men trying to sneak into Ardvreck. They werenae vera good, since we easily caught them. Ma mother recognized three of them from when she still lived at Clyth Castle. They are the sons or grandsons of men she kenned and apparently bear great resemblance to other men in their families. Mayhap Edgar believes Ulrich or Seamus would support him against us. Little does he ken."

"And I suppose the Sinclairs have already promised to fight alongside you against the Gunns. And just like always, that means the Mackays and Sutherlands are at their sides."

"Naturally, Yer Majesty."

"If only there weren't so damn many of you," King Robert grumbled under his breath before he looked back at Michail. "I suppose I can consider the matter resolved before it even starts. There is little chance Edgar will drum up any support for the Gunns against that many clans, because, of course, we can't leave out the MacLeods of Lewis, who will come to your aid, anyway. They're tied as much to the Sutherlands as you are to the Sinclairs."

Michail opted to remain quiet after that observation. Everyone in the chamber knew that was true. The alliance that existed in the northern Highlands excluded the Gunns. It meant that they were at those clans' mercy, of which there was none. It always shocked Michail when the Gunns did anything against a single clan in that alliance, let alone something that affected more than one. Michail believed Edgar didn't wish to live a long life. He would follow in the last few lairds' footsteps. Michail had a pang of sadness for Sileas, but it heartened him knowing she was nearly married and wouldn't have to return to Clyth Castle once she was. As long as she remained in Stirling, she would remain out of the fray.

"You may inform your father to cease his threats, which I do not appreciate. I will consider this matter resolved, since it is unlikely that by the time you return home, Ulrich is still laird. It would surprise me if the mon is even still alive. You may let your father know that. His issues with the Gunns shall easily be resolved, either by your allies arriving with swords drawn or by my instruction. I will send a contingent of men to see to it."

"Ma humble gratitude, Yer Majesty." Much like the night before, Michail covered his heart with his fist and bent low. He waited until Robert the Bruce flicked his fingers before he rose. He looked around the chamber one last time, then turned to walk out. He wondered what he should do with himself now that the issue was resolved. His audience with the king came much sooner than he expected. It meant he had little reason to linger in Stirling, which meant he had little reason to see Blythe. He found he didn't like that idea at all.

CHAPTER 7

"He wants me to remain! Why?" Michail demanded of the page standing before him. The boy was eight or nine summers and could only shrug as Michail looked back down at the slip of parchment in his hand. King Robert demanded his presence at the archery tournament that day. Michail had planned to leave before the tournament began, but now the king would force him to remain in Stirling. He had no interest in participating in the tournament, but he knew he would have no other choice. If not by the king's order, then by the Lowlanders' pressuring the Highlanders, including himself, to defend their names.

Michail sighed and returned his belongings to the chest in which he'd put them when he arrived, emptying his saddlebag. He picked up his bow and tested the string before he looked at the arrows in his quiver. He nocked one and pulled the string back, as though he might fire it into the wall. Instead, he stretched the bow several times. He leaned his head from one side to the other, a satisfying popping sound filling the room. When he was convinced his weapon was ready for him to compete with, he left the chamber in search of the other Highlanders he'd noticed his first night there.

He reached the archery field and recognized Calder Urquhart, his cousin's betrothed. He came to stand beside the man, gripping his forearm and shaking as they greeted one another and examined their competition. He was glad to know there was someone he recognized and with whom he was on good terms. He liked the man Sileas was set to marry. He recognized several other Highlanders, but he was not so quick to start a conversation with them. It gave him peace of mind, however, that they were there. He didn't look forward to being amid a swarm of Lowlanders.

All the targets were in use, with many taking stray arrows from a gaggle of chattering ladies-in-waiting since there was at least an hour before the tournament began. Michail waited in the shadows with Calder until a target became available. Despite checking the weapon in his chamber, habit had him stretching the string back on his bow several times, checking its tautness before drawing his first arrow. He was just about to loose the first one when a loud cackle startled him, and the arrow sailed a few feet before falling flat on the ground. He drew in a silent breath, his nostrils pinched, as he pulled another arrow from his quiver.

He successfully fired a dozen arrows in quick succession, each hitting its mark in the center of the target. The range master called a halt so the archers could reclaim their arrows. Michail pulled his last arrow free when one went whizzing past his shoulder and into the woods. A second followed soon after, but this one lodged in the loose fabric of his sleeve.

"Bluidy hell!" Michail roared. He continued without bellowing. "Who the devil is trying to kill me? What bluidy buggering arse doesnae ken it isnae time to fire? Show yer fucking face so I can bury it in ma shite!" Michail didn't lose his temper easily, but two careless arrows that could have killed him were not a laughing matter. What was worse, someone shot from behind him. He looked around, but no one stepped forward. "Fucking coward! Do ye nae ken what the word halt means?"

Several men sniggered as they pointed to the other side of him. His gaze swung in that direction where several more men pointed toward the last three targets. It was where the group of ladies-in-waiting stood, aghast. He pulled the arrow loose that was still in his sleeve, noticing the nick it caused was bleeding more than he supposed. He then retrieved the arrow that sailed past him into the tree line. It was worse than he imagined. No one had shot him from behind.

Whichever woman fired was so inept that it had traveled more sideways than forward. He stalked toward the women but forced himself to curb his anger. Terrifying the queen's handmaidens wouldn't endear him to anyone. He intended to remind them calmly that they needed to take care when they aimed. When he drew close enough to make out their faces, he noticed Blythe standing behind one of the women holding a bow. Her hands covered her mouth and nose, but her eyes were wider than he'd ever seen them. She didn't seem to blink once as he came closer. Michail watched her eyes dart to his sleeve, where the material had a deep red mark.

Blythe had stifled her laugh when she saw Michail misfire his first arrow after one lady in her group squawked like a goose. Then she'd been so impressed with his precision that she'd grown distracted and forgotten she was supposed to be monitoring the women before her. She was certain her heart stopped for the time it took the two wayward arrows to sail toward Michail. When the first flew past him, she exhaled her breath. But when the second snagged his leine, she was furious. She'd already blistered several ears, but

Michail's expression as he drew closer made her want to hide. She watched as his mien changed from anger to calm, and she knew he wouldn't berate the women. But she would. Her temper flared all over again as she watched him clench his jaw to keep from saying to the women what he would have liked to say to any man as careless as they had been.

"You bluidy fools," Blythe hissed at two of the women cowering in front of her. They darted their gaze between Michail and Blythe, uncertain who to fear more. "If you can't aim better than a leper with barely a club for a hand, you don't belong practicing among the adults. I will take you back to the targets where the weans learn. But that's after you spend the afternoon gathering every stray arrow on this range. You both swore to me you knew how to shoot. I was supposed to be correcting your aim, not being your bluidy nursemaid. You lied to me and Queen Elizabeth aboot your skills. I will not easily forgive or forget this. You could have killed MacLeod!"

The other women surrounding Blythe and the guilty archers collectively stepped back as Michail came to stand beside Blythe. She was bristling with anger on his behalf, and he choked to keep from laughing. From a distance, she looked and sounded like an angry badger as she scolded the women. Two days earlier, she'd directed her iciness at him. He preferred someone else being on the receiving end. When he cleared his throat, she cast him a scathing glance. She'd recognized the sound of him trying to swallow his laughter.

"I don't know why you suddenly think it's so funny that these two bampots nearly shot you," Blythe rounded on him.

"And I dinna ken how ye can keep up with loathing me one moment, then coming to ma defense the next."

"It isn't my fault you can't keep up. Mayhap that first arrow didn't miss and knocked something loose in your head." Blythe wasn't sure if she was still angry at the women, or now just Michail for teasing her about losing her temper. She'd been seriously frightened. She turned to the women and barked, "Leave."

She'd never been so rude to her fellow ladies-in-waiting, but she'd never been so infuriated, either. She'd agreed to supervise the archery over her better judgment. The queen pressed her into taking the inept archers out to practice after they lied about their experience. It had terrified her watching the arrows flying toward Michail, then her failure to supervise them properly mortified her as he spewed curses for everyone on the range to hear. But when she could tell he was attempting not to laugh, her temper exploded. She waited until the women were out of earshot before she swiped up the bows and quivers and pushed past him.

She glanced over her shoulder at Evina and Sileas, who bravely remained behind after the other women scurried away. Neither woman had witnessed Blythe's temper, but they'd both heard stories from Emelie, so she didn't surprise them. They followed Blythe and Michail back to where Michail left his own bow and arrow. He reached for them, but Blythe stayed his hand.

"I'm sorry, Michail. It was as much my fault as anyone else's. I was supposed to supervise them, but I got distracted. I assumed they were better than they were, and because I wasn't paying attention, they nearly shot you." She reached for his injured arm. "Will you let me look?"

"It doesnae hurt, Blythe. I'm certain it's already stopped bleeding. It was just a scratch. It bled more than I expected, but it's nae bothering me," Michail assured her. "What distracted ye?"

Blythe's cheek radiated heat. "You," she whispered.

"Me?" Michail howled.

"Bluidy bleeding hell, Michail. Keep your bluidy voice down," Blythe hissed. "Aye. I noticed when your first arrow didn't make its mark, but then you fired off another dozen, and they each hit the center. I wasn't the only one on the range watching you. That's probably why those two twits missed their aim."

"They were a might distracted by you," Sileas commented. "I think most of the ladies were."

"Michail," Evina smiled. A fellow Highlander, she teased Michail when she dropped her courtly speech. "These lasses dinna ken what to do when such a braw Highlander steps before them. They arenae used to a mon in plaid. They arenae used to a mon who owns fewer clothes than they do. It makes them swoon. Dinna plan to get through this eve without every one of those lasses trying to partner with ye. I wouldnae walk in any dark passageways alone, or ye might be getting married in the morn. Because of them compromising ye and all." Evina winked.

"Shite," Michail muttered. It was his turn to blush as he looked at the three ladies before him. "I beg yer pardon, ma ladies."

Michail bowed to the women and returned to his target next to Calder. He couldn't help but notice Blythe remained with Sileas and Evina when they shifted to watch Calder. Michail struggled to keep his attention on his target. It was one thing when he had two incompetent archers to blame for his misses, but he would make a fool of himself if he couldn't focus. He had no desire to do that in front of Blythe and half the court. He fired another round, all hitting the target's center.

When the range master called another halt, he went to retrieve his arrows a second time. He turned back to return to the firing line, but he noticed Fletcher standing beside Blythe. Her smile was more familiar than Michail wanted to accept. Only minutes ago, she'd been defending him and chewing out the other ladies on his behalf. Now she seemed to forget him. He was about to line himself up with his target once more when he noticed Blythe watching him from the corner of her eye. She tried to shift her attention back to Fletcher, but Michail was certain she'd been watching him. When she leaned forward with her breasts leading the way to say something to Fletcher, Michail was certain she'd been watching. And he was certain she knew she was making him jealous.

The royal couple's arrival forced Michail to turn his attention back to the targets, blocking out the surrounding people. He waited as the king welcomed all the participants to the tournament. He listened further for the range master to call all competitors to the line. In just moments, he had nocked an arrow, brought the bow close to his ears, and waited for the signal to fire. When it came, everything around him ceased to exist. His vision tunneled as he aimed for his hay target. His arrow created a smooth swoosh as it flew and imbedded in the center of the painted circles.

Michail sighed as he looked around and noticed several other archers had done as well as him. When he leaned forward to look left and right, he realized the archers who hit the center of their targets were all Highlanders. There wasn't a Lowlander among the competitors who had done that well. All had struck their targets, but none so close to the center. Michail drew another arrow from his quiver once more as the range master gave the signal. This time he waited a heartbeat before releasing his arrow, letting the movement in his peripheral vision cease before he fired his. It flew with such speed that it entered the target at the same time as everyone else's. Once more, he'd struck the center and had scored more points than his neighbors.

"Cheater!" the man standing to his left hollered as he pointed toward Michail. Everyone turned to stare in Michail's direction, and he wondered what the man could mean. He hadn't cheated. He had done nothing wrong. He'd used an arrow that was within regulations, and his bow was made just like that of every other competitors'. He looked around, trying to imagine why the man would make such a claim.

"What say you?" The king asked as he approached. He looked between the two men, his russet eyebrows raised to his hairline. He had seen many competitions over the years, and he knew the Lowlanders were testy when the Highlanders began the competition well ahead of them. However, it seemed odd that someone should call foul so soon. It also seemed odd that they would choose Michail. He wasn't well known at court, and there was no one near his target who held a grudge against him or his clan.

"He cheated, Your Majesty," Michail's accuser said. "I watched him. He didn't fire his arrow until after everyone else released theirs. He cheated."

"If I had cheated, wouldnae I have released ma arrow before everyone else? Mayhap if ye were watching yer target rather than me, ye might have done better." Michail pointed toward the man's target, where everyone could see the arrow had landed in the outermost circle, barely catching the edge of the target.

"That's why you must have cheated. There's no way you could have made your arrow fly that far, that fast, if you had released after everyone else. You cheated."

Michail laughed, looking between King Robert and his accuser. "And just how did I cheat, pray tell? Did ye see me walk closer to the target? Did ye see me tamper with ma arrows? Or did I somehow convince a fae to carry the arrow for me?" Michail continued to grin as people around them joined in the laughter. He raised his shoulders in an arrogant shrug before turning away from the men and reaching for another arrow.

"Hold on, MacLeod. Cheating is no simple accusation. We shall examine your bow and arrows to be sure that there is naught amiss." King Robert shot Michail a warning stare as he reached for Michail's quiver, pulling out three arrows. Michail realized the king was silently defending him by testing Michail's weapons himself.

The Bruce held each arrow to the sunlight and looked at them. Pressing slightly on each end to test their flexibility, the king nodded his head. He bristled the feathers on one end as he checked to make sure that there was nothing odd about the fletching. When he handed the arrows back to Michail, he smiled. He reached out, palm up, for Michail's bow. He rested the bow against his thigh as he tested the string's tautness and how the bow arched as he added tension. When he finished, King Robert nodded once more, turning toward the crowd.

The Bruce declared, "I see naught odd aboot the MacLeod's weapon or his arrows. We shall continue."

Despite King Robert favoring Michail in the dispute, many others were now dubious about Michail's integrity as he continued in the tournament. The whispers grew louder, round after round as others fell out, but Michail and Calder remained. There was a veritable hum as one rumor after another developed and swept through the crowd. It only ceased when the Bruce cleared his throat.

In the last round, it was Calder and Michail, standing side-by-side. Before drawing his arrow from his quiver, Michail glanced over his shoulder, offering a reassuring smile to his cousin as she worried about for whom to cheer, her betrothed or her cousin. As he shifted his gaze from Sileas to the people she stood with, he noticed how Blythe's hands were fisted in front of her, as though to keep from reaching out. She leaned slightly forward, the weight on her toes as though she were eager to see the outcome of the competition. Michail wondered if she was rallying for him or for Calder. When his eyes met hers, he had his answer. There was hopefulness in them, and she offered him a soft smile before she caught herself. When she did, she looked away with a scowl.

"Good luck," Michail offered Calder as they both took aim for the last time. Given the signal, Michail didn't hesitate to fire. His arrow struck the center of the target with such force that the arrow vibrated, and the target wobbled before tumbling backward. Michail turned around in time to witness the shock on Blythe's face before it once more turned to a scowl.

"Show off," Blythe mouthed. Michail stood blinking, taken aback by the accusation. He'd been called a cheater and a braggart, and he didn't appreciate either. When the king presented him with a pouch of gold and silver coins, he accepted it with gratitude. He summoned his men, who'd been watching the entire competition. He gave each a silver coin before walking toward the queen.

"Yer Grace," Michail said after he bowed to Queen Elizabeth. He handled the coin pouch over to her. "Please give these out to the almshouses as ye see fit. I am nae in need of the purse, but there are plenty who are."

While his neighbors' accusation irritated him, he found Blythe's further disregard stung him more. He had hoped for a moment that she might have been proud of him, or at least pretended not to loathe him.

He refused to keep the purse, not allowing anyone to believe they were his ill-begotten gains. He quickly gathered all his arrows, bowed once more to the royal couple, and left the archery grounds before anyone could stop him.

"Michail." A hushed voice called to him. He spun around, knowing exactly who he would find, but shocked that she would chase after him. Blythe caught up to him and tugged at his sleeve as they moved into the undercroft. Surprised at how close she stood, Michail reached out for her. Blythe swayed forward, her body in control instead of her mind. When Michail slid his hands onto her waist, she stepped closer. She glanced around the deserted undercroft to ensure no one could see them. She hadn't intended to let him touch her. She didn't intend for her hands to rest on his biceps. When Michail bent his head, she lifted her chin. Their lips brushed against one another, but neither pressed for more. They merely gazed at one another.

"Congratulations," Blythe offered. When she said no more, Michail frowned. They stood together, neither speaking. When it grew uncomfortable, Michail eased his hold and nodded in appreciation and made to turn away, confused and disheartened. "Wait."

"What is it, Blythe? What do ye want? I thought ye couldnae wait for me to leave. The look ye gave me surely said as much. But now here ye are. Ye let me wrap ma arms around ye again. Ye let me kiss ye."

"What do you want from me, Michail? What do you expect? It scared me when I thought someone injured you. It excited me as you started. I was angry that anyone should question your honor. Then I was overjoyed that you won. There's still some type of rightness when you touch me. But that doesn't mean that it makes it any easier to look at you or talk to you."

"So ye dinna actually hate me. Ye just pretend to."

"I thought I did at first, but I find I can't. That doesn't mean I want to continue this game of cat-and-mouse when you leave, then return once more. Move on just as I am." Blythe pulled away, severing their connection, and ending the moment. She pressed her lips together, but it only brought the taste of Michail into her mouth. Her heart shuddered.

Michail opened his mouth to ask just who she was moving on with. To demand whether she meant Fletcher or some other faceless, unknown man. But he snapped his mouth shut, unwilling to sound desperate. "Vera well, if that's what ye want."

"We can have a few pints of ale or drams of whisky this afternoon. We leave for home the day after tomorrow. There is nay reason to linger, since the king has decided the matter is resolved, and that bluidy tournament is over. We will stay here one more day to rest before we set off," Michail explained to his guards as he led them into town. Despite his disdain for Stirling and the previous rush he'd felt to leave, he knew his men and their horses deserved another day away from the roads.

They chose the Picked Over Plum for a few rounds on Michail. The locals nicknamed the Picked Over Plum such because the whores who worked there were among the oldest in town. Michail knew he had no interest in any of them, nor did he want them to take any interest in him. While they would notice, they were less aggressive than other working women in the taverns in town. If his men sought company elsewhere that night, he wouldn't stop them. He merely wanted to drink, even though he intended to use restraint. He hadn't forsworn all alcohol; he'd only forsworn getting too drunk.

He and his men easily found seats in the tavern since it was only early afternoon. It was far too soon for most people to carouse, so only the most hardened drinkers were there. It gave Michail pause to think what that made him if he and his men were already there, and they were there by his order. Putting it out of his mind, he accepted the mug of whisky the middle-aged woman handed him. He took a slow draw, savoring the taste. It had been weeks since he'd imbibed any alcohol stronger than ale. He refused the offers while he was with the Sinclairs, and he found he missed the taste more than he thought he would. What he missed most was the burn as it passed along his throat into his chest, and it warmed his belly. It numbed everything it touched along the way.

A blonde woman passed their table, making Michail think of the one blonde who would not cease tormenting his dreams. He stared into his mug and suddenly wished for the oblivion he used to find with whisky. As soon as he did, he heard his grandfather's voice in his head, admonishing him for wanting to take the easy way out. The more he thought about indulging in more whisky, the more he heard his grandfather's voice. The more he heard his grandfather's voice, the more he wished to drink. It wasn't long before he found his head growing fuzzy, and he longed to rest it on the table to sleep. He shook his head and ordered a mug of ale instead, thinking it might help wash away the effects of the whisky. Just as he truly knew it would, it compounded the whisky's strength and made him drunker.

"Weeshould 'eave," Michail slurred, one word blending into the next. He stood, clutching the edge of the table to steady himself. His men looked at him before looking around the tavern. Michail laid coins on the table for the women who served them. He took a deep breath, closing his eyes for a moment, before making his way to the door, proud that he didn't stagger. When they reached their horses, he mounted with more ease than he expected, so he was certain he wasn't as intoxicated as he feared. He and his men wound their way through the town, but as they drew closer to the gates, Michail had an idea. "One crown sterling to any mon who can beat me to the top of the ridge."

Michail didn't wait. He spurred Cunnart on, looking over his shoulder for a moment to see if his men followed. At first, he assumed they rode with him because they had no choice. However, it didn't take long to see they were joining in his fun. A brief thought that perhaps they were enjoying the race at his expense crossed his mind, but he pushed it aside as he looked forward and squeezed Cunnart's flanks. He cared not if they only played along for the sake of winning the bet. The wind whipping across his face revived him, and he felt free of the oppressive weight that settled on his shoulders after learning about the raid and murders.

Michail and the half a score of MacLeod warriors with him charged through the gates and out across the meadow that surrounded the castle. It wasn't long before they reached the hill that would take them to the top of the ridge. He knew they would soon have a vista spreading over the Highlands. Michail drew his sword for no reason other than it felt natural to carry it while he was on horseback. He stood in his stirrups and circled the sword over his head before pointing toward the hilltop. He charged forward as his men fought to keep up. Each warrior rode a battle tested mount that was excellent horse flesh. But his daring nature urged him to push Cunnart faster than any of his men would do safely with their steeds.

He released a war whoop as they crested the top of the ridge, pulling Cunnart to a stop abruptly and allowing his men to catch up to him. He continued to stand in his stirrups, swinging his sword at imaginary foes. When he heard pounding hooves over his own bellows, he looked to see a group of riders with a woman in the middle. They charged past the MacLeods and into the woods. Michail was certain he recognized the petite rider within the center. It could only be one person.

With no warning to his men, he swung Cunnart around and chased after the Dunbars. He barreled down the hillside and followed the Dunbars as they entered the tree line. He scouted the surrounding area until he saw the horses. He urged his steed on, waving his men forward once more with his sword. Unfortunately, his blurred vision made it difficult for him to tell where the trees really were. When he nearly knocked himself from his horse as a branch swept across his forehead, it forced him to slow down.

Blythe!" Michail roared. "Blythe!" He squinted, trying to find the person he sought. It wasn't long before the horses in the distance shifted, and a petite figure stepped forward, leading her horse by its bridle.

"What the bluidy devil are you doing, MacLeod?" Blythe demanded. "Have you lost the tiny amount of sense you once had? Are you trying to get us all killed? We feared attack. Are you trying to kill Cunnart?" Blythe was certain even if Michail felt no guilt for terrifying her, he would regret risking his horse. She watched chagrin cross his face, but it was only a moment later that an unrepentant grin broke through.

"Worried aboot me, were ye?"

"Not aboot you, only aboot your horse. It would be a bluidy waste if you harmed that steed. If you can't care for him properly, I'll take him."

"Ye'd try to take ma horse? A wee lass like ye would have a hard time mounting this beast?" Michail waggled his eyebrows, only making Blythe flush red, not with embarrassment, but anger. There wasn't a man surrounding them who didn't understand Michail's innuendo.

"It doesn't look that hard," Blyth said, looking down her nose at Michail. Her retort only made the men howl louder.

"Come closer, and I'll show ye just how hard it is," Michail whispered for everyone to hear. He was unprepared for Blythe to accept his challenge and step in front of him. He was also unprepared for her to launch her full weight against him. Unsteady on his feet, he toppled backward. He reached to grab her for support, but he landed with his hands empty. Dirt smacked his face as Blythe kneed Cunnart, having easily mounted the enormous warhorse. Michail whistled, making Cunnart stop. It was Blythe's turn to spear him with an unrepentant grin. She hadn't made it far, but she'd proven her point.

"Like I said, not so hard." Blythe held Cunnart's reins tight enough that he couldn't turn but not so tight as to harm the horse. The beast wouldn't walk any farther away from Michail, but neither would he get any closer. Michail rose, scowling and brushing leaves from his *breacan feile*, or great plaid. He knew Blythe was forcing him to go to her, rather than how he'd wanted it to be the other way around. When he came abreast with his horse, he wrapped his hands around Blythe's waist and pulled her down. He had enough sense not to let their bodies touch in front of their men, despite how his demanded just that.

"You're drunk," Blythe whispered. "I already knew you were, but you reek of it. It's barely after the midday meal. How much did you drink?" Her lip curled in disgust as she jerked her head back.

"Enough to remember it all," Michail whispered against her ear. Blythe brought the heel of her hand up under Michail's jaw and pushed it away. Her knee went to his bollocks, leaving him doubled over.

"I hope you remember all of this, you arse. What a waste." Blythe rushed back to her horse, one of her guards standing beside her mount, prepared to lift her into the saddle. The Dunbars rode out of the trees while Michail sucked air into his lungs and tried not to howl in pain. He wasn't certain if she meant their brief relationship had been a waste or if he was the waste. He supposed she meant both. He closed his eyes as the pain subsided, but he winced when his bollocks hit his saddle as he settled onto Cunnart's back. It was a far more subdued MacLeod party that returned to the keep.

CHAPTER 8

Michail entered the Great Hall sober after soaking in a steaming tub until the water turned icy. He regretted the arse he'd made of himself when he encountered Blythe and her men. She'd been concerned for him when he was injured before the tournament began, but she'd made her position clear when they spoke in the undercroft. She'd been unerringly blunt in the woods. He remembered everything he'd said and done, realizing he'd likely done irreparable harm to the last threads of their relationship. She wanted to move on and intended to do just that.

As the music began, he glanced toward Blythe. She'd already made her way to stand by Fletcher's side. But before she turned to Fletcher, she welcomed another man who Michail didn't recognize. She offered a quick glance toward Fletcher before she accepted this strange man's offer to dance. Michail watched the couple twirl around the dance floor for the first set. Blythe's laughter floated to him each time they moved past where he stood, propping up the wall. Michail watched the same pattern with Blythe and Fletcher, then three other men, who he didn't recognize either. With each partner, she cast him a smirk.

She intends on punishing me, and I deserve it. It was one thing when I failed to be the mon she expected when it was in private. But the jests I made...They were hardly funny, and I made them in front of her men and mine. She kens I still want her. But does she understand it's more than lust? That it's always been more than lust? I've done a shite job showing her.

Finally, he grew fed up with his own sulking. He noticed Lady Leslie Lindsay staring at him much as she had the first night he arrived. Pushing away from the wall, he skirted the dancing couples and made his way to the voluptuous matron. Without a word, he stuck out his hand and offered to dance. She smiled and slid into his embrace as they made their way onto the dance floor.

Michail wasn't interested in conversation. He merely wanted to lose himself in a distraction. And a distraction is exactly what Lady Leslie intended to be. Frustration that the woman in his arms wasn't Blythe merged into unsated lust that his partner offered to assuage. She leaned forward provocatively, pressing her breasts against his chest in an easy to interpret invitation. As the music ended, she leaned forward and whispered.

"I find it rather warm in here this eve. Would you excuse me while I step out onto the terrace?" Lady Leslie turned away but then looked over her shoulder as though she thought twice of her suggestion. "MacLeod, would it be safe for me to go outside alone? Or do you think I should have someone accompany me?"

Lady Leslie arched an eyebrow at him, making it obvious who she meant. Michail gladly nodded his head, still having barely spoken a word to her. They made their way toward the door and slipped through.

As they entered the darkness, they descended the steps and made their way toward the garden. The fresh air was revitalizing to Michail as he watched the woman walking in front of him, her hips swaying. He considered accepting the invitation that his body most certainly wanted. He realized by walking outside, he'd already given his acceptance to her. His mind was slowly catching up with his body.

They found a space within the garden, tucked away from the lights that shone out from the Great Hall. Michail wrapped his arm around Leslie's waist and drew her close. He remembered how Blythe had felt that afternoon in his arms within the undercroft, then when he'd lifted her from her horse. His fingers itched to feel her body pressed against him rather than Lady Leslie's.

Michail forced his mind to return to the present, but it was his frustrated and unspent desire for Blythe that drove him. He inhaled the fresh, flowery scent as his lips brushed against Lady Leslie's neck. He kissed a line up her throat until he reached her jaw and then peppered kisses along it until he reached her mouth. He pressed his to hers, allowing the warmth and sweetness of the wine she'd drunk that night to enter his. He swept his tongue through the deep recesses of her mouth and nearly groaned as his cock strained within his breeks. Leslie sucked his tongue into her mouth as her hands roamed over his body. She wasted no time tugging at the laces to his breeks he'd worn to the evening meal and diving one hand beneath his waistband, wrapping her fingers around his turgid length.

It had been so long since Michail was with a woman that he nearly exploded. He was certain he would embarrass himself if he didn't take a deeper breath to slow his rapidly approaching release. He refused to make a fool of himself in front of this woman, certain word would travel. He attempted to distract himself from the sensations Leslie created with each slide of her hand. He tugged her laces loose and pressed the gown down her shoulders. He was just about to lower his head to suckle her ample breast when voices made him freeze.

∽

Blythe lost track of where Michail went. She'd felt smug while he stood against the wall, pretending not to watch her. She'd flirted with men she barely knew merely to annoy him. She realized she was being petty and spiteful, but she'd told Michail he should move on. She intended to prove that she could heed her own advice. When she watched Michail offer to dance with Lady Leslie Lindsay, Blythe stumbled and nearly knocked her partner over. She chided herself for being surprised Michail would return to the stunning woman. They made a striking couple, and it was Blythe's turn to be battered by waves of jealousy.

She felt an all-consuming regret that she hadn't let things go further with Michail in the undercroft and that she'd told him she wished to move on. She'd known it for a lie, and she suspected he did too. She'd expected him to argue, to counter what she said. Instead, he'd accepted it, leaving her feeling empty and angry at herself as much as she was with him. Then there'd been the scene in the woods. She'd missed their banter, but she didn't appreciate him being drunk or trying to humiliate her. When he'd lifted her from the saddle, she'd hoped their bodies would touch. When she realized Michail held enough honor not to further her embarrassment, both her body and her heart hummed.

She watched Michail and Lady Leslie twirl around the dance floor, their bodies far too close together.

Blythe's only consolation was that despite the ease with which they danced together, there wasn't the familiarity with Michail that she'd seen Lady Leslie share with men the entire court knew she'd bedded. There was still some type of formality between Michail and her. But when Fletcher whispered a naughty joke, she'd turned her attention back to him. He pressed a soft kiss behind her ear, as he often did when he whispered to her. The sensation sent a shiver along her spine straight to her core, but it fizzled the moment she realized she could no longer see Michail and his partner. She scanned the Great Hall, but they were nowhere to be seen.

"Blythe, perhaps some cool air would help you focus," Fletcher suggested. Blythe offered him an embarrassed smile, but she nodded. It wouldn't be the first time they'd slipped out for a dalliance. She'd never gone so far as to couple with her suitor, but they'd shared many heated kisses, allowing their hands to roam over one another. She'd discovered during their first tryst that he was a well-muscled man, and she enjoyed the feel of his body against hers. It filled a craving that was created long before she met Fletcher.

Blythe and Fletcher dashed into the gardens. When they were invisible to those on the terrace, they stumbled into one another's embrace. Wrapped in his arms, one hand tunneled in his hair and the other holding her skirts to keep from tripping, Blythe walked backwards. She trusted Fletcher to guide the way, despite them kissing. It wasn't until they heard a startled gasp that they turned around.

There stood Michail and Lady Leslie, whose gown sagged open while Michail yanked his breeks back in place.

"What're ye doing here?" Michail demanded.

"The same as you, from the looks of it," Blythe

replied, haughtiness and snideness dripping from each word. It was clear she hadn't put aside her earlier anger that he'd created in the woods.

"I doubt that. You're many things, but not a whore."

Another startled gasp filled the air as Lady Leslie raised her hand to slap Michail, but he caught her wrist. His expression held no guilt because all four people knew her reputation for being just that. She pulled away from him and attempted to right her gown as Michail stalked toward Blythe.

"Ye wanted me to see ye. Did ye enjoy seeing me? Kenning I was aboot to tup her?" Michail's embarrassment came out as anger, his voice mocking and harsher than he intended. The longer the two couples stood staring at one another, the more ashamed Michail grew from Blythe finding him. That was until he recalled she was there for the same purpose. As they glared at one another, all the long-repressed desire roared back to life. The sexual tension hummed between them. Each heartbeat made it crescendo.

"MacLeod," Fletcher stepped between Michail and Blythe. "Do not speak to Lady Blythe so."

"Why? Eager to get back to tossing her skirts?"

"Who I spend my time with is no more your business than who you're with is mine. You made that very clear a long time ago. I told you today to move on because I am," Blythe said as she stepped around Fletcher. Michail crossed his arms, the muscles bulging as he inhaled and expanded his chest. He was one of the largest men at court and resembled a colossus as he seethed. Blythe laughed.

"Snarl and posture all you want, but you'd never hurt me," Blythe asserted. "I'm as safe with you as I am my favorite hound."

"Lady Blythe, I—" Fletcher started.

"Go inside," Blythe interrupted as she stepped forward until her slippers nearly brushed the tips of Michail's boots. "We will have this out once and for all. We need no audience."

"But you need a chaperone," Lady Leslie insisted, speaking up for the first time.

"Worried my reputation will end up like yours?" Blythe sneered but didn't look away from Michail. "I know what you've said aboot me, Lady Leslie. I know you've tried to ruin me. You're lucky that I don't snatch you by the hair and slap *you*."

"You would never..."

"Are you daring me? Go back inside with Fletcher. Michail and I will have done with this, then I couldn't care less if I never see him again."

"Lady Blythe," Fletcher tried again, but she waved a dismissive hand over her shoulder, not releasing her locked gaze with Michail's piercing green eyes. The four nobles stood in silence, the anger rippling between Blythe and Michail. With a humph, Lady Leslie brushed past them, but Fletcher wasn't so quick to leave.

"He won't hurt me." Blythe softened her tone, making Michail flinch. He'd nearly killed a man with his bare hands for intimidating her. Michail had squeezed Henry's throat until he turned purple, then plowed his fist into Henry's groin. Blythe had never seen such anger before that day. But she'd known then, just as she did now, there was no one she was safer with than Michail. Angry as he was, he would never harm her. And as angry as she was, she still trusted him. At least with her safety.

Fletcher released a sound of disgust. "Tease."

Michail lunged forward, but Blythe pressed her hand on his chest. He glanced down, and in that moment, Fletcher spun on his heels and stormed off. The pair stood staring at one another.

"Ye never answered ma question. Did ye enjoy seeing me?" Michail taunted. "I ken what ye were trying to prove."

"You conceited mon," Blythe snorted. "I promise you, you were not who I was thinking aboot."

Michail seized her upper arm and practically dragged her into the depths of the garden. She had to jog to keep up. But it thrilled her, especially as he spun her around in front of him and pressed her back against the half wall that marked the entrance to the orchard. It reminded her of the passion they'd once shared.

Michail pulled her against his chiseled frame, then shifted to press her against the wall again. His whisper sent a shiver down her spine. "I ken ye were thinking aboot me as he kissed ye. I ken it was ma hand on yer breast that ye felt. Ye may have stopped us this afternoon, but I dinna doubt ye thought aboot doing just this. When I lifted ye from yer horse, I bet ye wished our bodies to touch, just as they are now. Do ye wish me to stop?"

Blythe froze, then slowly shook her head. Michail yanked at her laces, then used two hands to yank her gown open, pushing it down her arms until he could slide his hand over her chest until he squeezed her breast. It swelled in his hand with each shallow inhale.

"It was me ye were thinking aboot when he palmed yer arse." Michail gathered the yards of fabric until he slid his hand beneath her kirtle, his warm palm tapping her buttocks before squeezing. He kneaded her breast and bottom in an alternating rhythm. "It was ma tongue ye remembered as ye sucked his. He kenned ye ken how to suck a cock. And I ken how ye came by that knowledge."

Blythe's hands trailed over his chest and abdomen until one cupped his rod. Michail groaned as he thrust his hips forward, reveling in the feeling. Blythe knew there was no point in denying a single thing Michail said. If any other man dared speak to her as Michail did now, he'd be doubled over just as Michail had been earlier that day. But there was too much history between them. Too much unresolved need.

"Do ye ken how I'm so sure, Blythe? Because I was thinking aboot ye. It was yer breast, yer arse, yer dripping quim I was imagining. There is nay woman who can make me stop thinking aboot ye."

They came together with cataclysmic force. Blythe's hand grasped his hair, tugging until Michail's scalp tingled as she pressed his head to hers. Her hand rubbed his length, feeling each pulse and twitch through his breeks. His laces were still untied, so she pushed open his pants, freeing him as he ripped his mouth from hers and moved to devour her breast. He suckled, eliciting a moan that felt as though it came from Blythe's soul. His fingers delved into her entrance, swirling her dew before he sought her pearl. She wrapped her hand around his cock, stroking slowly, remembering what he taught her.

"It was you," Blythe confessed. "In my dreams, when I'm awake, when I touch myself."

Michail pressed his lips back to hers, and she opened without hesitation, welcoming his tongue in her mouth. When she felt her release starting, she stood on her toes, bringing the tip of his rod between her thighs. If she could just feel him for a moment.

Michail continued his torturous ministrations, rubbing in quick circles as Blythe clawed at the back of his leine. He knew she was close, and he wanted nothing more than to be inside her, to feel her climax around him. His free arm wrapped around her and lifted her from the ground. He carried her to a bench, easing her onto it, and following her as she reclined. But the moment his cock met the moisture at her entrance, he reeled back, stumbling as he put distance between them.

Blythe sat up, bereft of his touch, dazed. She watched Michail, his expression like a man waking from a dream and returning to real life. Horror washed over him as he took in her gown, sagging below her breasts, her skirts hiked up to her thighs. She looked like a woman well ravished. She looked exquisite. Temptation to finish what they started made his bollocks ache. He shook his head.

"I shouldnae have done that," Michail whispered. Blythe rose from the bench, hurt and anger warring within her chest.

"Why?" she demanded. "You were looking for a whore tonight. Am I not good enough? Or is it I'm too prim and respectable for your tastes? It didn't stop you the last time."

"Because I was angry."

"I know." Blythe's brow furrowed as he stated the obvious.

"I shouldnae have done that in anger. I should have sent ye inside, taken ye inside."

"You think I didn't understand what drove this? I was angry too. I still am. And I wanted every bluidy minute of that. More fool am I for still wanting it. I wanted to be taken, but it wasn't inside."

"Blythe," he hissed.

"Michail," she mocked. "You are conceited. You think you can decide for both of us as though I haven't the mind to decide for myself. You're arrogant to believe only your decisions are right. You were three years ago, and you still are today. You were the one to walk away, not me. Well, you're not my husband, and you made it clear long ago you don't want to be. Fear not. I might think of you when I'm with a mon, but it won't be you."

Blythe had fixed her gown while she berated him. She gathered her skirts and marched toward him, but he grasped her upper arm just as he had at the beginning of their interlude.

"Ye ken why I canna," he rasped.

"No, I don't because you won't share your thoughts. You just assume that I'll accept whatever you dictate. Fine. I accept you won't marry me, but I will marry someone. And he will be the one who buries himself inside me. It'll be him—his name—I call out. Think aboot that as you grow auld alone."

Stunned by the disdain and vehemence in her voice, he released her when she pulled away. He watched her walk away, his world crumbling around him. And in his misery, he knew there was only one person to blame. Himself.

Michail watched as Blythe made her way through the garden until she was halfway back to the keep. He burst into a sprint to catch her, wrapping his hands around her waist and pulling her back against him. He expected her to fight, but instead, her body sagged against him as though there was no fight left in her.

"I asked you earlier today, and I'm asking you again, Michail, what do you expect from me?"

"I dinna expect aught from ye, but there is plenty I wish for. I've made one mess after another since I met ye. I've wasted one opportunity after another. And now I doubt there is any left for me to have."

When Blythe didn't refute his assertion, Michail's shoulders slumped. He couldn't blame her. It was obvious physical desire still existed between them, and he supposed it might always, or at least until Blythe followed through with her pledge to find someone else. Michail was certain his feelings were unrequited. He'd extinguished any softer emotions Blythe might have held for him once upon a time.

Blythe sighed and shook her head. "What is done is done, Michail. There's naught left."

Michail nodded in resignation. They walked back to the keep in silence, each going their separate ways when they entered the passageway outside the Great Hall. Blythe fell into bed and cried herself to sleep. For the first time since the day he learned his grandfather had already been buried without him there, Michail fell into bed and did the same thing. He cried.

CHAPTER 9

Michail awoke just as depleted as he'd felt when he went to bed. The ache in his chest made him think about finding a dram of whisky. But then he recalled how he'd gotten drunk when he'd sworn to himself and his father that he wouldn't. And in his drunkenness and then his unspent lust, he'd only made matters worse between Blythe and him.

As he moved around his chamber, he knew neither his body nor his mind craved the alcohol to get through the day. It was entirely his choice. He could just as easily live without it as he could with it. Going to bed early and entering the lists as the sun rose was just as satisfactory an escape, so there was no reason to lose himself in mug after mug of alcohol. He'd decided before that he wouldn't continue drinking, and he refused to give into temptation now. He'd created the mess with Blythe, and there was no escaping it. He would have to learn to live with it. Sober.

Knowing where he belonged that morning, he set his sights on the training field. The only time he felt like his old self, the one he knew before his grandfather died and he destroyed his future, was when his weapons were in his hands. He found his guards crossing the bailey, so they entered the lists together.

"Do we still leave tomorrow?" Stanley, one of the youngest MacLeod guardsmen, asked.

"Aye. We can train and get a good night's sleep before we set off."

"And in which tavern will we be having that good night?" Stanley wondered.

"Ye may go out if ye wish, but ye will be here at sunrise. If I leave ma chamber and dinna find ye ready to go, then I will leave ye behind."

"That still doesnae answer which tavern? We can all stumble back and sleep it off here," Stanley pressed.

"As I said, ye can go out if ye please."

"I *bet* ye'll nay only join us, but ye willna drink as much as me." Stanley goaded, looking at the other assembled men. None shared his humor, some shaking their head. The young guard didn't know when to stop. "I also bet, looking at Lady Blythe's face, she'll come up with a better set down than ye can."

Michail swung around and spotted Blythe hurrying across the bailey to where a Dunbar warrior dismounted. He couldn't hear what they said, but he could see Blythe's distraught expression. Michail watched as she grasped her guardsman's arms as she swayed. Michail shoved his targe into Stanley's hands as he sheathed his sword. He hurried to Blythe, whose eyes filled with tears, and her lower lip trembled.

"Blythe?

"There's been an attack. My father..." Blythe looked to her guard to finish.

"Laird Dunbar was gravely injured four days ago. The healer isn't confident he will recover. I'm riding out in the morning to Kilchurn to tell Lady Emelie. Everett is riding to the Sinclairs to tell Lady Isabella."

The man nodded to another guard, who stood with the reins to two horses.

Michail watched Blythe as her guard explained. She seemed to shrink with each word. "Find a bed in the barracks and some food," Michail told the Dunbar warriors. He held out his hand to Blythe, who didn't hesitate to take it, but she refused to follow when he turned to the gardens.

"I don't want any of them to see me. I don't want to have to explain," Blythe whispered as she looked at the women gathered to accompany the queen on her morning constitutional. Michail offered a sympathetic smile and guided her toward the undercroft. She hurried to keep up with Michail's stride until they came to a storeroom. Enough light filtered through the window for them to see one another. Michail pushed the door closed with his foot and pulled Blythe into his embrace. Once again, she didn't hesitate.

"I'm not ready to lose my father," Blythe whispered. "For all his faults and poor choices, of which there are many, he loves my sisters and me just as he does our mother."

"I understand." Michail brushed hair from her face and cupped Blythe's cheek as she looked up at him, skepticism furrowing her brow. "I havenae lost either of ma parents, but I have lost someone I loved just as dearly."

Blythe nodded, a rock settling in her stomach. This wasn't when she wanted to learn he loved someone else. She knew she never wanted to learn that. She hadn't considered it, especially when they were passionately kissing in the garden just the previous night. But she understood there was much she didn't know about Michail.

"Ma grandfather, Blythe." Michail recognized what

she'd assumed, and he would disabuse her of that notion. "Ma grandmother died when I was too young to remember much. But I was extremely close to ma grandfather." He looked above Blythe's head and closed his eyes, swallowing to clear the lump from his throat. "It hasnae—I havenae—been the same since."

"That's what you meant last night. Michail, I didn't know, but you assumed I did."

It was Blythe's turn to cup Michail's cheek. She recognized the sorrow in his eyes, and her heart ached for him. She'd sworn she had nothing left to give after the previous highs and lows of the day before. But she suddenly suspected she understood the change she'd experienced in Michail. Her other arm wrapped tighter around his waist as she burrowed back against his chest and shook her head.

"I don't like that," she mumbled against the solid planes of muscle.

"That he died?"

"That too." Blythe leaned back. "There is naught weak aboot grieving, but it makes us vulnerable. I can't reconcile that with how I think of you. It makes my chest hurt to think of the bravest mon I know, ever feeling vulnerable. It feels so wrong."

"Brawest mon?"

"Yes. You're fearless and reckless and strong. To know you aren't invincible is hard for me to accept. I don't like that. And I don't enjoy knowing that you're hurting. When did it happen?"

"I dinna like seeing ye hurting either, Bly. Three years ago." Michail kissed her forehead, then her temple as he guided her back against his chest. He felt her ragged sigh as she relaxed against him. Neither noticed he used a pet name he hadn't said out loud in three years.

"You shoulder much, don't you? Perhaps the Lord made them too broad. It's too much." As Blythe listened, she realized the start of Michail's grief coincided with when their budding relationship fell apart. Michail gazed down at Blythe, whose eyes were closed as she thought aloud. Her hand dropped to rest against his heart, so he covered it with his own.

"They're broad enough to bear some of yer burden today." He kissed her crown and leaned his cheek against her head.

"Don't let me go yet," Blythe whispered.

Never.

Rather than saying aloud his desire, he tightened his arm around her waist and held Blythe until her tears abated. She took a shuddering breath and nodded her head, but neither of them pulled away.

"What will ye do?"

"I don't know. I can barely think straight right now, let alone decide."

"Ye dinna have to decide aught right this minute. But I will do what I can to help if ye need it."

"Thank you, Michail. I—I'm glad you were there to turn to. I—I—No one else." A sob tore from Blythe's chest as she admitted to herself what she couldn't articulate: no one else would make her feel safe. And there was no one else she wanted near her as she struggled through her fear and sorrow.

Michail swept Blythe into his arms and carried her to the table pushed against a side wall. He eased himself onto it until his back rested against the wall, his legs hanging off the front edge, and Blythe's dangling over the side. He tightened his hold, and she curled into him. He stroked her hair and rubbed her back as she fought to regain control of her emotions. Michail's touch was so gentle she found it lulling her to sleep. She suddenly felt exhausted after the rush of emotions only moments ago.

"Nay one saw us come in here, Bly. Sleep if ye wish. I ken the exhaustion ye feel after the fear and panic."

"Thank you." Blythe closed her eyes, but she didn't fall asleep. She listened to Michail's steady heartbeat beneath her ear. She sighed before pressing a kiss to his collarbone where his leine's neckline hung loosely above the ties. She eased away from him and offered a watery smile. "I don't want to leave here and face the world. But I must. I need to find the queen and tell her what's happened."

"Do ye wish for me to go with ye?"

Blythe hesitated, knowing if she arrived in the gardens with Michail at her side, it would only stir gossip. But her body felt so weary, she wasn't sure she could walk that far on her own. For all their problems, she felt braver having him at her side. "Yes, please."

They left the storeroom and made their way through the undercroft. They paused and looked around before stepping out from the secluded area. They'd broken their physical contact when they rose from the table, but they both felt closer than they had in years. They met Queen Elizabeth de Burgh as she and her ladies left the gardens. Blythe glanced up at Michail with a tight smile.

"I can do this," Blythe whispered.

"I'll be here if ye need me." Michail watched as Blythe curtsied to the queen. He listened as the two women spoke, but one of Blythe's guards approached. He remembered the man's name was Harry.

"MacLeod," Harry greeted him as he, too, watched Blythe and the queen. "Did either of the men tell you who did it?"

Michail furrowed his brow before shaking his head.

"I dinna recall a name. I just ken Laird Dunbar was injured four days ago."

"Aye. It was the Earl of Salisbury," Harry whispered. Michail released a Gaelic curse Harry didn't understand, but he didn't need to since he recognized Michail's tone and the fury on the younger man's face. "You've heard of him then."

"Thomas of Leicester and Lancaster? Who hasnae? He was the English king's cousin. All the bluidy Plantagenets are the same. They all believe they can rule Scotland. He didna like his cousin any more than he did us, but he was a greedy bastard. He fought for Longshanks just so he could gain more land and wealth by stealing it from the Scots." Michail's lip curled in disgust. "But I thought he was dead."

King Edward continued to order his border lords to encroach upon the Lowlands, and Salisbury believed it meant he had free rein to wreak havoc. Thomas's lineage held as much blue blood as King Edward's. His father, Edmund Crouchback, was one of the sons of King Henry III, and his mother was Blanche of Artois, the Queen Dowager of Navarre and niece to the French king, Louis IX.

"You're confusing two earls," Harry corrected. "Thomas was Longshanks' cousin. William Montagu, Earl of Salisbury, is one of the king's closest confidants. They both terrorized our side of the border before Lancaster died. They're easily confused since they looked alike, shared the same foul temperament, and were often in one another's company."

"So it was William Montagu who attacked Blythe and Isabella's father."

"Aye," Harry answered. "The Dunbars have a long history with Salisbury, as I'm sure you know. The mon will never forgive Lady Dunbar for his failed siege years ago. This time, he lured Laird Dunbar from

Druchtag Motte by razing three villages north of Barsalloch Point. It's the farthest north the mon has traveled since the Wars. He made it look like Clan Innes planned it, so the laird was unprepared for men to attack from the southeast."

"Clan Innes? Why the devil would they travel across the country from the northeast Highlands to attack yer clan in the southwest when they can continue to harass the Dunbars who live next to them? What do ye mean from the southeast?"

Harry shook his head. "You know they're connected to the Kerrs through marriage. Salisbury made it look like the Kerrs were the ones who carried out the plot."

"The mon takes his revenge seriously. That's a lot of maneuvering to make it appear plausible since Clan Innes is so far away from ye. Clan Kerr has been trying to keep its neb clean after the nightmare experiences Brighde and Deirdre Sinclair had with them. They've been keeping to themselves, except for their squabbles with the Elliots."

"That's what made everyone suspicious and why the laird rode out. None of us imagined it might be Salisbury."

"What's become of the bastard?"

"Naught. He got away. He left Laird Dunbar to die, but he underestimated the auld curmudgeon. The Dunbar isn't ready to depart this life. Not until he's certain Lady Blythe is settled."

Michail wanted to shift his weight and tug at his leine's neckline. The best he could do was nod. He turned toward Blythe and the queen as they approached. He bowed to the royal and looked at Blythe.

"Harry, Queen Elizabeth has granted me permission to return with you. We leave in the morn if you and the men can be ready."

"Yes, my lady," Harry agreed.

"How many men do ye have?" Michail inquired.

"Half a dozen," Harry said hesitantly.

"Nay." Three sets of eyes turned toward Michail. "Ye canna travel to the border, where yer father was just attacked, with only six men. Ye're courting trouble."

"I'm not staying here. I'm going home," Blythe insisted, hurt that Michail would argue when he knew how she felt.

"MacLeod isn't wrong, Lady Blythe. He and his men will accompany you," Queen Elizabeth announced.

"Yer Grace, I must return to Ardvreck." Michail had only made an observation. He didn't intend it to be an offer. "Ma father must learn what King Robert decided, and I have duties there. Things arenae settled with the Gunns."

"Send a missive, MacLeod. You will travel with Lady Blythe and her men."

Michail stared at Queen Elizabeth for a moment before offering a deferential nod. There was nothing for it. He would travel south instead of north. When his gaze met Blythe's, he watched her hurt turn to anger. He understood she believed he was rejecting her, and in a way, he was. But he had one woman's needs to balance against the safety of his entire clan. What he needed—besides returning home—was to talk to Blythe alone again. The queen offered the group a tight smile before walking toward the keep.

"We need to talk again," Michail whispered to Blythe, shooting Harry a warning glare. He grasped Blythe's elbow and steered her toward the storeroom they'd entered earlier. Michail began talking before the door clicked closed. "Blythe, I'm nae rejecting ye, and it's nae that I dinna want to help. Ye ken I dinna want ye traveling home with so few men. But I came here because the Mackenzies raided three of our villages.

Before that, I went to Dunbeath to see the Sinclairs. I was there to train with them and Laird Mackay because the Gunns sent spies. We ken they've set their sights on us. I'm ma clan's tánaiste. I have duties there, even if I'd rather be elsewhere. Blythe, what I want and what I must do arenae the same right now."

"What is it you want?"

"I want to build a wall around ye to shield ye and nae let any harm ever come to ye," Michail barked, surprised at his own adamance. "I want to tuck ye away and never let ye near a battlefield. I want to help yer father and yer clan, so ye dinna suffer the grief I ken too well. I want to protect ye, Bly."

"Why?"

"Because…" Michail paused, trying to gauge Blythe's feelings. "Ye would have me say it just to reject me like ye thought I just did to ye."

"I am not you. That you think I would purposely hurt you means you don't know me."

"I didna purposely hurt ye either."

"You walked away without an explanation. You had to know that would hurt me."

"I told ye what happened."

"Barely. I knew you were close to your grandfather, but you could have told me. You didn't even say goodbye before you rode out. I learned you left from Sileas."

Michail inhaled as he gestured toward the table, wishing there were chairs. He waited for Blythe to ease onto it before he paced. "I want ye to ken why I walked away three years ago. I intended to have yer hand in marriage. I was courting ye in good faith, Blythe. It's the only reason I would have ever taken yer maidenhead. It wasna to use ye or to be dishonorable. But the day I sat down to write a missive to yer father, to ask for yer hand, was the day I discovered ma grandfather was dead."

Michail's voice cracked as he recalled the searing pain that shot through his chest as he read and reread his father's missive while sitting in the very chamber he currently occupied within Stirling Castle. His chest tightened as he spoke aloud for the first time what Blythe and he had done. They'd both thought they would grow old together, so they'd sneaked away for a picnic beneath the stars. Alone and with no prying eyes, they'd made love.

"I couldnae think of aught beyond the strangling guilt I felt when I sat here rather than being home with ma family where I belonged. I kenned I should've explained why I was leaving, but I couldnae think of aught other than getting back to Ardvreck. I told ye stories of how close I was to ma grandfather, but even while I spoke to ye of him, I didna understand and appreciate what he meant to me until he wasna there when I rode through the gates and walked into ma home."

Blythe slid from the table and held out her arms. He accepted her embrace as the tears that filled his eyes glistened in the sunbeams streaming into the storeroom now that the light had shifted. She slid her hands over his chest and wrapped them around his neck. With a gentle touch, she pressed his head to her shoulder in comfort. He took a shuddering breath before continuing.

"The past three years have been misery between losing him and losing ye. There's little left for me to live for. I've done ma duty by ma clan. I've done what I needed to take care of ma people as ma father's tánaiste and the future laird. But I need ye to ken something, Blythe. I likely should keep ma mouth shut, but I need ye to ken I havenae been with a woman. Instead, I've been burying maself in whisky. Do ye ken why? Because the only woman I can ever think aboot is ye. The way yer laugh made ma heart beat faster. The way yer smile made me feel invincible. The way we were when we were together. But then I always remember what I've squandered. All that plays through ma mind every day, all day. While I'm awake and while I sleep; there's nay end to it."

Blythe listened without interrupting, but her mind screamed one refrain over and over. When it was clear Michail finished, she spoke it aloud. "But you ran from me rather than letting me be by your side."

"I ken. Foul weather made it nearly a fortnight's trek home. They'd already held the funeral, unable to wait until I returned. There was naught for me but a headstone. I barely came out of ma chamber for a moon. I finally forced maself to return to the lists because I feared what others would say, that they would think me unfit. I went to Dunbeath to visit Siùsan, and it was just after Emelie and Dom married. Isabella told me, even showed me yer missive. I was happy for them and even thought mayhap there was a chance we could have that too. Ma father sent me back here to inform the Bruce aboot ma grandfather's passing. That's when everything happened with Pringle."

"You came to my defense. In that alcove… We did more than just kiss. I thought…"

"And I did too. Being with ye eased the pain; it let me forget. But when I got to Kilchurn, it wasna hard to figure out that Emelie's pregnancy was a wee too far along for when I kenned she and Dominic handfasted." When Blythe went still, he soothed, "Dinna fash. I willna say aught to anyone. But I couldnae escape fast enough as guilt and shame gnawed at me. That could have been ye. Ye could have wound up married to someone else because I abandoned ye. Twice. When nay word came that ye were carrying, I thought ye wouldnae want me anywhere near ye, considering how Pringle treated Emelie. I was even more ashamed when I realized that while I'd meant every moment of being with ye in that alcove, I'd used ye to distract me from ma problems."

Michail released one arm and swiped his hand over his face, wiping the tears from his eyes and the sweat from his brow. He hadn't realized he perspired from divulging everything to Blythe, but the room was stifling.

"I feared and hoped that ye might find someone like Dom because I kenned I couldnae be the husband ye deserve. I'd already started drinking too much and too often. As much as I still wanted ye, everything seemed so—so—I dinna even ken how to describe it. Ma grief was all I could feel and think aboot. The next time Siùsan came to Ardvreck, Isabella was with her. I heard them talking to ma mother aboot how yer father was looking for someone dependable to marry ye, someone who wouldnae act in haste like Dom and Ric had. That couldnae be more different from who I am."

"And we are back to you deciding for both of us. My parents want me to have as happy a marriage as my sisters have. I thought that was going to be with you, but you decided that neither of us could have the happiness we were so close to. Instead of talking to me, you ran away. Instead of explaining to me, you shut me out. Instead of letting me help you, you turned to whisky and dares. Och aye, I've heard of your reputation. It's more than recklessness. It sounds like a death wish. Small consolation it is that you aren't womanizing. It doesn't change how I felt and how I feel. It only makes me lonelier."

"I ken, Blythe, and it doesnae make it any better. But I dinna ken if I can be the husband ye deserve or even the husband that ye need. I'd sworn off drinking after the arse I kept making of maself at home, but then I let maself have too much yesterday. I made an arse of maself all over again. I'm surprised ye're even here, letting me talk to ye, letting me touch ye. It shocked me earlier that ye turned to me. The recklessness ye saw in me yesterday, how I rode up that ridge, then charged after ye, that's always been within me. Ye ken that. But nowadays, that side is the only part that makes me feel alive. The only part that makes life feel real and vibrant when all I want to do is crawl into bed and cry. Can ye believe that? A mon ma age, ma size, wanting to cry. It's there all the time. The choking lump in ma throat. The tears burning ma eyes because all I think aboot is how I must disappoint Grandda and how I've already disappointed ye."

Blythe released a shuddering sigh as she held Michail against her. She could feel his trembles, but she was certain he wasn't crying. He was still holding that within. He still didn't trust her enough to show that side, and it hurt. Not that she wanted him to cry; it was that he still held himself apart from her. It hurt to see him in pain through his grief, and it hurt to know he was unwilling to treat her as a partner. As someone who was on his side and would stand by him until her last breath.

Blythe leaned away. "Michail, you could have told me all that. I know you may have felt uncomfortable, but I need you to know that you could have, and I wouldn't have turned away from you. I would have stood beside you. I believed you knew that. Your grief and your recklessness. Those are not the things that would have pushed me away. It's you refusing to trust me. It's you refusing to believe I could help. You don't think you need a partner. You might want me in your bed, but you don't need me at your side. And that's what hurts the most. If my father is allowing me to pick my husband, I have the chance for a love match with a partner who desires me in and out of his bed. A mon who will respect me and who knows he can trust and rely on me. I don't have that with you. I guess I never did."

"Ye did. But ye also had a foolish mon who waited too long. I couldnae face ye rejecting me on top of the grief I already had."

"But it comes back to trust, Michail. You didn't trust me to understand or to be loyal to you. You caused yourself additional grief that never had to be. All the while, it's obvious I still trust you. I turned to you today."

"I didna realize it was a lack of trust. I didna think of that." Michail straightened and took a step back, but neither released the other. "I would have always sworn I trusted ye more than anyone, trusted ye as much as ma parents and ma brothers."

"Have you let them help you? Have you turned to them and let them help ease your loss? I doubt it. I don't think you trust anyone enough for that. I thought you abandoned me. I thought you got what you wanted from me, then you walked away. Twice. For a moment, I thought I'd misunderstood when you defended me against Pringle and then when we came together again in the alcove. I thought we were reuniting, but you rode away for a second time without a backward glance."

Michail sighed as he looked at Blythe's heart-shaped face. "What will ye do?"

"Go home to Druchtag Motte," Blythe answered in confusion.

"Nay. I didna mean right now. I mean, in the future. Does Fletcher ken ye're nae a maiden anymore? What if he doesnae ask for yer hand?"

"He figured it out on his own. I suppose I kissed with too much experience."

Michail wondered if Blythe had gained any more experience since they'd been together. He'd admitted he hadn't been with anyone else, but she hadn't said the same. His eyes widened as a thought took root, turning him cold. "If he kens, are ye sure he isnae just dallying with ye? Is he—careful?"

Blythe released him, needing space between them. The direction in which the conversation turned displeased her. She didn't want to discuss her personal life. It was easier when they were talking about Michail. Thinking about her future only made her think about her father and what he would say if he ever learned she was no longer a virgin.

"He's never bedded me. What you saw is the most I've ever done with him or any other mon. You've been the only one. No one other than Fletcher has figured out I'm no longer an innocent. I don't know if he will ever ask for my hand, and I'm not even sure that I would say yes if he did. But he is a good mon; he's reliable and steadfast. So no, I don't believe he's dallying with me. He's not that type." Blythe's words could have held an edge, but her voice was soft. It wasn't as though she spoke of a lover or a man for whom she had tender feelings. It was just practical.

"Any other mon?" Michail demanded, realizing his reaction was out of place since Blythe made it clear he had little place in her life.

"Fletcher is not the first mon I've kissed after being with you, or even the first mon I've let touch me. But it has gone nowhere near as far as things went with you. But I figure I have naught left to lose. I've already lost my maidenhead and the moment that becomes public, I will lose my reputation too, so that is as good as gone. I may as well enjoy my life since it didn't turn out the way I thought."

"Ye ken that's poor logic just as well as I do. If naught else, ye should protect yer reputation with sword and shield. Why would you risk so much when I've already taken so much?"

"Because I'm bluidy well lonely. My sisters left. They're married and have children. You left. All my friends, like Sileas and Evina, are betrothed or already married. The other ladies here are not my friends; they are barely not my enemies. That only leaves the men who pay attention to me. I'm always cautious. Never too far from the light or to scream for help. More than one mon at court knows what my limits are. They've received the same knee to the bollocks you did yesterday."

"Ye play a dangerous game, Blythe. I'm certain ye ken it. There are plenty of men here and in the world who willna listen when ye say nay. They will think ye're a tease and will think ye wish for them to take ye. Even Fletcher called ye one last eve, and he's a mon ye say ye can trust. If ye fight back, they will only enjoy it more. They will be bigger than ye and stronger than ye. What ye say terrifies me, Blythe. One of these days, ye willna come out the winner."

"But I'm not your problem to deal with." Blythe pulled away, her head suddenly pounding. They would only go around in circles if their conversation continued. "I will keep your warning in mind."

"That's it? Ye hear something ye dinna want to, so ye walk away. Ye wanted me to treat ye as a partner, to discuss things with ye. But the moment it turns to something ye dinna like, ye want to leave."

"How dare you?" Blythe hissed. "This is not the same, and you know it. I don't need your chastisement for my choices. They are mine to make, right or wrong.

You gave up the chance to have a say. Michail, I meant what I said yesterday. Move on. I won't lie and say I don't think aboot you, want you. But it's also obvious we're not good for one another. I pray you find the comfort you need for your grief. I will speak to the queen and make certain she understands why you must return home."

"Nay. Wait, Blythe." Michail met her at the door, pressing his hand against it before she could open it. "I'm nae wrong that I need to get home. But ma father and both ma brothers are there, and it wouldnae surprise me if at least the Sinclairs and likely the Mackays rode to Ardvreck after they left the Mackenzies. It willna be me single-handedly defeating the Gunns. But it also willna be ye traveling to the border with only six guardsmen. I will keep to maself and ma men, but I will travel with ye. Combined, I still dinna think there are enough men to protect ye. An entire army wouldnae be enough. But it's a far sight better than six. I will leave ye alone if that's what ye wish."

Blythe stared at Michail. She wanted to scream that being left alone was the last thing she wanted, but at the same time, having him near only reopened a festering wound. But for better or for worse, there was no man she trusted more to get her safely home. Michail was a seasoned warrior and a natural leader, and she knew he cared enough to fight to keep her alive. She didn't doubt he spoke the truth when he pledged to protect her. She nodded.

"I will see you in the bailey in the morn." Blythe hesitated, then strained on her toes to kiss his cheek. "Thank you."

Michail pushed back from the door and opened it for Blythe. He watched her walk away, and the burning hole it opened in his belly made him wonder if Blythe had felt that way when he walked away from her. He could think of nothing else to do than return to his chamber to draft a missive to his father explaining his delay. It was hours before the evening meal, but once he finished writing, Michail climbed onto his bed and was asleep as soon as his head hit his pillow.

CHAPTER 10

Michail checked his saddle's girth one last time before moving on to Blythe's horse. He was checking the stirrups when she arrived in the bailey. She looked around and spied Michail, realizing he arrived early to organize the men and to ensure her mount was ready. As she approached, her chest tightened. They'd left so much unresolved the day before, and it would be a four-day journey in proximity. She knew she was kidding herself to think it would be easy.

"Good morn," Blythe greeted the men. She kept her voice low as she stepped beside Michail. "Thank you for seeing to Midnight."

Michail offered a tight smile as he handed Blythe the reins to her all-black steed. "Think naught of it." He helped her into the saddle and launched himself into his. Blythe watched as Michail maneuvered himself into the lead as the MacLeod and Dunbar party left Stirling Castle. She watched his shoulders relax once they were through the town's gates, but she could tell he was ever vigilant as they made their way to the road that would carry them south. She observed how he canted his head when he thought he heard something out of place or how he leaned forward and rose in the stirrups if he thought he spied anything suspicious.

Blythe shifted her attention to the men surrounding her. They were all highly aware of their surroundings, but they weren't as wary as their leader. She listened to them banter with one another, but Michail never spoke. When they rested their horses for the first time, Michail nodded to her as he led Cunnart to the loch to drink. She tilted her head toward the trees and only received another nod. When she emerged from her moment of privacy, she found him once more checking her saddle. She didn't know if he'd already checked Midnight's hooves before they left the castle, but she watched him examine each horseshoe. She doubted he did the same for Cunnart, and it made her uneasy. She approached with caution.

"Is something amiss?" Blythe asked, startling Michail. She blinked several times, taken aback that he wasn't aware someone approached.

"I heard and saw ye coming, Blythe. I didna expect ye to talk to me."

"Why not?"

"Because I'm trying to give ye some space."

"By hovering over my horse?"

"I'm also trying to keep ye safe."

"Is aught wrong with Midnight? Now or in the bailey?"

"Nay."

"Then don't fuss. I'm safe." Blythe attempted to sound reassuring, but she feared she sounded ungrateful. "I appreciate your concern. I just don't want you to worry."

Michail looked around, watching the men as they prepared to mount again. "I will always worry. We're a day's ride from where the English attacked yer father. I dinna ken who might lurk along this road. The English,

Scots who dinna care for Highlanders, yer neighbors who dinna care for yer clan, or lawless men. There is always something to watch out for."

"I won't presume to tell you how to lead the men, but I don't want you on edge so much that you dread every minute of this journey."

"Blythe, I dinna dread aught aboot being on this journey. I dread nae being alert, and we're ambushed. Anyone who comes across us will notice ye. I want to be prepared if anyone gets the notion to take ye."

Blythe knew it wasn't uncommon, at least not in the Highlands, for women to fall victim to bride stealing. And any woman in her position, the daughter of a powerful border laird, would be a target for kidnapping and ransom. She offered Michail another smile before she turned to Midnight. She was unprepared for the powerful hands that wrapped around her waist but lifted her with the gentleness one would use with a babe. She looked down at Michail, but he'd already turned away.

This shall be an interminable four days if he continues to be so distant. I know it's what I said I wanted, but I'm miserable and he's miserable. I did this. He's respecting my wishes. I said what I thought should be said. But we both know I didn't mean a word of it. Even if he doesn't want to be here, he's still showing he's an honorable mon.

Mayhap the decision he made hurt me deeply, and I felt wronged. But now that I know the truth of what happened, I can't really fault him for his grief or his need to return to his family. But why couldn't he have just told me?

Blythe looked wistfully at Michail's back before turning her attention to their surroundings. The weather was still warm, and the sun shone overhead. The leaves rustled with the breeze that passed through them. And close to the road, a squirrel chattered and scampered up a tree. Blythe continued to watch as the ground passed beneath her horse's hooves. She spied a fluffle of rabbits. She assumed there was a mama rabbit and a papa rabbit, since she could also see many babies with them.

It made her wonder if one day she might have a passel of children. And if she did, with whom would she have them? Inevitably, her attention shifted back to Michail. He was the only man she'd ever considered. She knew she would marry one day because her clan expected it of her. She knew she flirted with Fletcher and other men, and they'd returned her attention, proving she had potential suitors. But Michail was the only man she ever saw when she closed her eyes and pictured her future with a husband. Reasonably, she knew her father might pick someone else, especially since she was making no progress on her own. But time and again, the only person she could imagine was a man who still didn't ask for her hand.

Three more hours passed before they stopped for the midday meal. It was meager, merely dried beef and bannocks that one man collected from the kitchens that morning. But it was enough to satisfy them. Michail announced they would rest for an hour before they would return to the road. Blythe knew the horses didn't need that long, since they hadn't been riding harder than a trot. She suspected he did it for her sake, knowing that, while she enjoyed riding and did so often, she was unaccustomed to such long stretches on the rough thoroughfare. It was yet another way he showed he both worried about her and cared about her. She was determined to be more gracious this time. She thought about when they would stop for the evening. Blythe intended to help the men, if for no reason than to keep herself occupied. She planned to snare a rabbit or squirrel as a peace offering. She suddenly needed to be the one who provided him with his supper.

"Do ye wish to walk around?" Michail asked suddenly. "Mayhap stretch yer legs for a while. We'll have several more hours on horseback before we stop for the night. If ye'd like a chance to move around and nae be in the saddle, then this is a safe spot place for ye to do so. The men have already patrolled the area, and naught appears amiss. Just dinna stray farther than the tree line. But ye can walk around the perimeter if ye want."

Michail's offer surprised Blythe. It wasn't the thoughtfulness, since for all his faults, he took her needs into consideration. It was the offer of freedom to move around. He said nothing about a guard accompanying her, and he made no offer to do so himself. She didn't know if he sensed she needed time alone with her thoughts, or if he truly believed she wanted some exercise that didn't include her legs clamped to her horse's flanks.

"How long do I have?"

"Quarter of an hour. Make the most of it, Blythe. It'll be a long and rougher ride for the next few hours. The terrain that's coming up, as you may remember, is mostly uphill."

"I will. I promise not to go any deeper in the woods than the first few trees. You should be able to see me the entire time." Blythe moved away from the men and wandered around the perimeter. She kept the guards in sight, even when she peered into the trees. She'd been walking for five minutes when she sensed there was something larger than a squirrel or rabbit nearby. She stopped and stared between the trees, trying to spot what was there.

A brief movement at the top of a bush made her think perhaps it was only a bird. She had the sense not to walk farther into the trees, so she turned back to call Michail. As she turned away, there was more rustling. She spun back around, certain she watched a man dash away from the shrubs in which he'd been hiding. The man wore a doublet and breeks. His haircut was shorter than most Scottish men. Blythe's heart raced as she realized she was likely watching an Englishman run away after he'd spied on them.

"Michail!" Blythe raced across the opening, lifting her skirts to leap over a stump. Michail spun toward her, hearing the urgency in her voice. "There was someone back there. An Englishmon." Blythe pointed to where she'd been standing. Michail drew his sword and gestured for three men to follow him.

"Blythe, stay here with Harry. Dinna move unless yer life depends on it. I'll be back." Michail paused for a heartbeat before he pressed a hard kiss to Blythe's cheek. "I'm coming back."

Blythe watched Michail race into the woods with three MacLeod warriors alongside him. It wasn't long before he disappeared among the trees, the trunks too dense for her to see him. She spun toward Harry, her skirts swirling away from her ankles.

"If he catches the mon, he'll learn what he can before making sure the mon carries naught back to his camp. If he doesn't catch him, then he'll scout nearby. We need to be ready to ride the moment they return," Harry explained. Blythe understood what went unsaid. The man wouldn't live if Michail caught him. She rushed to Cunnart, stroking the massive beast's nose as he chomped on tall grass. Just as Michail had done with Midnight, Blythe checked the saddle and ran her hands over the animal's flanks and legs. When she was certain Michail's horse would be ready when he returned, she checked her own steed.

The minutes dragged as Blythe waited to mount and charge out of the clearing. All the remaining guards had drawn their swords and stood near their horses. Harry led Blythe into the center of their circle, the men now facing outward, ready to defend her. She studied each man as he awaited some type of attack. More minutes passed and nothing happened. Blythe's stomach was in knots, and her heart pounded behind her ribs. She feared she might be ill as she grew more worried about why Michail hadn't returned yet. Harry had said he wouldn't go very far, but if he'd been running, Blythe could only imagine how many miles he must have covered by now.

Just as her hands shook with worry, Michail broke through the tree line and made his way straight to Blythe. Seeing her anxious expression, he pulled her into his embrace, and she melted.

"I'm back safe and sound, as are all the other men. We didna find aught. We couldnae even find his tracks. How do ye ken it was an Englishmon?"

"His doublet and breeks, and his hair was short. It reminds me of the Englishmen who used to cross the border to fight near my home." Blythe lowered her voice, so only Michail heard. "I was so scared. It felt like it took forever for you to come back. I thought something happened to you. I—"

Blythe couldn't say aloud the horrible scenarios her mind conjured as she waited for the men to return. She knew the guards were watching, but she cared not. She wrapped her arms around Michail's waist and buried her head against his chest.

"Wheest, Blythe. Dinna fash. We'll continue south, but we'll stay off the roads." Michail assumed Blythe would release him once she knew his plan, but she didn't move. He wrapped his arms around her tighter, giving her a reassuring squeeze. But she still didn't let go. "We canna stay here, Bly."

"I know." Blythe kept her arms around Michail's waist. "I know I'm being ridiculous, but my heart still hasn't stopped racing."

"I promised I'll protect ye."

"But who will protect you?" Blythe demanded in a hoarse whisper. She tilted her head back and gazed into Michail's emerald eyes. She knew it was fear talking, but she knew the only reason her fear for Michail's safety was so intense was because she cared deeply for him. He guided her to the loch's bank and urged her to splash the crisp water on her face and neck. She wiped her face with her skirts and accepted the waterskin Michail passed to her from his saddle.

"Blythe, I willna live forever, but I'm nae ready to die yet." Michail offered her a lopsided smile, hoping it would soothe her nerves. She nodded but looked unconvinced. "What's going on?"

"I love you," Blythe blurted. Her mouth dropped open, her ears felt as if they were on fire, and she stumbled back two steps. She hadn't meant to admit that. Michail pulled her against his chest with one arm as the other hand tilted her chin up.

"I love ye, Blythe. I have since I met ye. I've failed ye before, so I dinna blame ye regretting saying it aloud. But I should have told ye that many times over." Michail paused, looking at her upturned face. He read the fear in her eyes, her uncertainty that she could believe him. He had no other words to say to convince her, so he showed her. He slowly lowered his head, their gazes locked. When his lips were mere inches from hers, her eyelids fluttered closed. The moment their mouths met, she sighed. Michail held her in his brawny arms, but once more, he was as gentle as he would be with a bairn. This kiss couldn't be more different from the passion-filled one in the garden only two days earlier.

Michail was tender and giving, slow to intensify the kiss. As his heart swelled with love for the only woman he'd ever wanted, he imbued it into their kiss. She opened to him, to the familiarity and warmth. He swept his tongue against the satiny skin of her inner cheek before their tongues coiled together, then danced apart, repeating the movement over and over. He slid his hand into her hair and cradled her skull. He felt as though they floated together somewhere near the heavens and far from reality. As they broke the kiss, they rested their foreheads together.

"Blythe?"

"Mmm."

"I ken this solves naught between us, but I didna lie. I love ye and always have. I dinna ever want to love someone else."

"I couldn't even if I wanted to, which I never have. You're right, this doesn't solve everything. But it's the first time we've been completely honest with one another. Mayhap, if I'd told you how I felt three years ago, you would have trusted me. You would have known what you meant to me."

"I didna ken. I'm as much to blame. Telling ye then leaving would have been even more wretched of me. I should have made the time to see ye, to make sure ye understood how I felt, that I wasna leaving ye. I was leaving court. Once I came out of ma isolation, I didna think ye could love me after how I treated ye. I missed ye so damn much. When we had the chance to make love again in that alcove, I thought I'd finally found hope again. But then it all came crashing down when I saw Emelie. Ye could have been her, and I felt despicable."

"We're three years aulder and three years wiser. I don't want to keep fighting this, fighting you. It seems so pointless. We've kept our distance from one another the few times you've been back to court, and it's done naught but make us both miserable. I could have sent you a missive. I could have demanded you explain. I could have done any number of things to set things straight between us, but it felt safer to just blame you than hear that you didn't love me."

"I have loved ye since that first ride we took with the king and queen. It chucked it down. While men and women whined aboot the rain, ye stomped in puddles and splashed water at me. I'd been just as mardy as everyone else, but ye made me laugh. I nearly asked ye to marry me on the spot."

Blythe chuckled. "You seemed like this massive, ornery bear who'd woken before spring. Sileas dared me to splash you. I wouldn't have jumped in that puddle if she hadn't. But once I jumped in the first one, it reminded me of the fun I had with Emelie when we were weans. I thought you were going to chew me up and spit me out when I splashed you the first time. You just stared at me, so I did it again. Then you laughed. It didn't prepare me for you to jump into the puddle beside me. I splattered you. You created a deluge. After that, I couldn't think aboot anyone but you."

"We had fun together, but I should have realized we'd created something deeper together, that I could trust ye when things went wrong. I dinna want to make that mistake ever again, Blythe. I dinna ever want to walk away from ye again."

"What're you saying? I know I don't want to let go of you."

"Ye dinna have to." Michail flashed the lopsided smile again for a moment. "I mean, ye will when ye get on yer horse. But I willna be out of reach, nae physically or emotionally. Blythe, I want to marry ye. I want ye as ma partner as much as I want to be yer partner. I'm asking for yer hand, and I'm asking for yer forgiveness."

Blythe gazed into Michail's earnest eyes and saw the remorse, but she also saw the conviction. She felt the anger and bitterness slide away. She couldn't promise it wouldn't return, but it fled for the moment, and left her able to know she would make a grievous error to turn him down. "I offer you both."

Michail stood dumbfounded.

"Aren't you going to say something? At least, kiss me again."

Michail whispered, "Ye're going to be ma wife. I amnae dreaming this. Ye said aye." When Blythe giggled and nodded her head, he swept in for another kiss. They filled it with as much love as the first, but where that had been conciliatory, this was joy. He lifted her off her feet, her toes brushing against his shins. She wrapped her arms around his neck and looked down at his broad smile when they drew apart.

"I did say, 'aye.'" She cupped his jaw, swooping in for a kiss. This one exploded with the passion they'd shared in the garden, except there was no anger or resentment fueling it. It was the promise of a future together. When Michail set her down, she waggled her eyebrows. "Since I'm going to become a Highlander, can we handfast right now?"

"Now?"

"I'd like my wedding night tonight," Blythe announced. "I'm not interested in waiting a moon, and I don't know in what state we'll find things when we get to Druchtag Motte. I can't ask my parents—my mother—to plan a wedding when we might be…"

"Aye, *mo chridhe*. It wouldnae be right, but willna it upset yer parents more that I didna ask their permission? I ken they wanted a different sort of mon for ye, one who wasna as impetuous as Ric and Dominic."

"I doubt it would surprise them. Neither Isa nor Emelie were as impulsive as I was. I'm fairly certain they expect this of me, and I was never one to let my sisters show me up." Blythe grinned unrepentantly. "So can we handfast? I'm tired of sleeping alone."

Michail pressed his lips to the skin behind Blythe's ear, and he had a momentary flash of seeing Fletcher do the same thing. He nipped and licked, reclaiming her as his alone. "Nae only will ye nae sleep alone, we shall fall asleep with me buried in ye just like the first time we lay under the stars. Ye'd best be quiet this time because we arenae alone now."

"I couldn't hear myself over you." Blythe tugged at Michail's belt before slipping her hand behind his sporran to cup his steely length. "I shall hold you to it."

Michail grew serious. "Blythe, part of me wishes to keep this moment to just us. I want to exchange vows for our ears only. But it would be prudent to have the men witness our handfast. Nay one has sanctioned this marriage. Ye and I already ken ye're nay longer a maiden, but if anyone tries to contest our marriage, they'll also cast aspersions on ye for nae being a virgin. I dinna want anyone to be in doubt that we wed."

Blythe nodded before looking toward the clearing where the men were milling around. She was certain they must grow annoyed at being kept waiting. They'd been talking far longer than either expected when they walked to the loch's edge. Michail slid his hand into hers, his broad palm engulfing her smaller one. They walked back to the group, noticing many shocked faces.

"Lady Blythe and I planned to marry many moons ago, but life had its own plans. It's finally brought us back together, and we intend to go forth as a couple. We ask ye to witness our handfast."

The Dunbar guards appeared skeptical, none embracing the Highland tradition as readily as the MacLeods, who grinned and elbowed one another. Blythe pulled her lips in and ducked her head, trying to hide her own laughter. She peeked up at Michail, who offered her a devilish wink. He unpinned the length of plaid that hung over his shoulder and wrapped it around their joined hands. Together, they tied a knot.

"As our hands are now bound," Michail began. "So are our lives joined in love and trust. Like the stars, ma love will be a constant source of light, and like the earth, it'll be a fine foundation from which our life shall grow."

"May this knot of love remain forever tied, blessing us and our lives together," Blythe pledged. "May we have the strength to hold on during the storms of life, and may we remain tender and gentle as we nurture one another."

The couple stood entranced as they both absorbed the significance of their promises. They'd shared hope and heartbreak since they'd met, and hope had finally won. With their hands still clasped, they floated together, exchanging yet another type of kiss. This sealed their pledge and set their world to rights. There would be no more doubts that they belonged together or that they both pledged their fidelity and loyalty until their last breath.

"I love ye, Bly."

"I love you, Michail."

The guardsmen offered their felicitations as Michail freed their hands and wrapped his arm around Blythe's waist. She leaned her head against chest as they both sighed, the sense of rightness not missed by either of them.

CHAPTER 11

"I would have ye ride with me, wife," Michail purred the last word. "But it was imprudent to remain here as long as we did after ye spied someone watching us. We're lucky naught's happened. I dinna ken what we might encounter, especially since we didna leave in haste. I need to swing ma sword without fear of hurting ye. I need ye to ride in the center, but I will ride alongside ye."

"Whatever you believe is best, Michail. I won't lie and say I'm not disappointed I can't ride with you. I don't want to let go now that we're finally together. But I'll survive, and I'll appreciate it even more when we make camp."

"We have time to make up, so we will ride harder than this morning. But if it's too much, tell me. Dinna suffer because ye dinna wish to inconvenience anyone. We all understand ye arenae used to riding like we do."

"I will." At Michail's scowl, she knew he'd read her thoughts. She had no intention of complaining. Her shoulders slumped as she exhaled, a playfully shame-faced expression making her lips twitch. "I will."

Michail helped her into the saddle, then drew Cunnart to stand beside Midnight as he mounted. Harry led the party out of the clearing as Michail took his place beside Blythe. He was just as aware of their surroundings as he had been that morning. Blythe could tell being in the center made him uneasy, since he no longer had an unobstructed view of what lay ahead and to each side.

"Ride up front," Blythe whispered.

Michail cast a glance at her before continuing to scan the road and embankments. "Nay. I ride beside ye from now on."

"But—"

"These men are trained warriors who I trust. Yer men and mine. But there will never be anyone who will fight as hard I will to keep ye safe. Each mon would do the same if he rode with his wife. I stay at yer side."

Warmth suffused Blythe as she raked her eyes over her husband, her desire growing not just from his physical attractiveness, but from how precious he made her feel. Not given to flowery words, Michail's practical tone made his explanation even more valuable to Blythe. She realized he had considered no other option, as though it were a given.

"Blythe, I should have ridden beside ye this morning. I dinna want ye to think that ye're somehow more valuable to me now that I've staked ma claim as yer husband. Ye meant as much to me this morning as ye do this vera moment. I ken ye sensed I was anxious aboot setting off. I havenae traveled south in years, so I was uneasy aboot taking a route I dinna ken. That's why I rode up front instead of beside ye."

"That thought hadn't come to me, but thank you for explaining. I didn't realize that's what made you uneasy. I just assumed it was because we traveled in general."

"I'm always cautious when I travel where I dinna ken the land. I may ride like the devil, but it's only when I ken where I am and what's around me. I'm nae only responsible for yer life but the men who travel with me." Michail turned to look at Blythe. "Ma days of accepting ridiculous bets and dares are over. I willna say that there willna be times when I ride too fast or take risks in battle. But ma life is nay longer just aboot me. I'm accountable to ye, and ye deserve a husband who takes yer wellbeing into account. Ye deserve a husband who will live long enough to help ye raise our bairns and to be a good father to them."

Blythe studied Michail once more, surprised at yet another change and revelation. It was clear he'd thought about how his life would shift with a wife before that day. Blythe wondered if he'd thought about those changes with her as his wife. As she continued to watch him, she was certain he had, since the love in his eyes was clear to anyone. She also found a staidness she'd never seen there before. She appreciated his promise and his realization, but part of her rebelled at the same time.

"As long as you promise not to grow boring." She leaned toward him. "What if I'm the one issuing the bets and dares…in our bed?"

"Then ye shall see the devil in me is merely quiet, nae dead." Michail stole a quick kiss as he leaned to meet her halfway.

Their afternoon ride was uneventful, and they made camp at sunset. Blythe's bow and quiver were tied to her saddle. She snagged them and moved into the tree line with two Dunbar warriors who were used to her hunting. It wasn't long before they had a brace of quail and several rabbits to bring back to the cookfire.

"Which would you like?" Blythe asked Michail as she held up a bird and a rabbit in each hand.

"Rabbit, please."

Blythe made her way to a boulder, where she

skinned and dressed the animals to cook. She brought them to where a MacLeod raised a spit over the flames. She speared the game onto the crossbar and thanked the guard when he offered to tend the meat. She dug out a lump of soap from her saddlebag and made her way to the riverbank to scrub her hands. When she stood, she nearly jumped when arms slid around her waist, but she recognized Michail's solid frame wrapping around her.

"Thank ye for catching and preparing ma supper. Though I'd rather feast on ye."

"This morning, I wanted to hunt and catch something as a peace offering. Now I merely want to offer my husband something, as thanks for taking such good care of me." Blythe turned in Michail's arms. She as much leaned in as Michail pulled her against his chest. She sighed as she relaxed. He rubbed her shoulders and kneaded her back before his hand slid to her backside. At first, she thought he meant to arouse her, but once she realized how tight her muscles were, she welcomed his ministrations as he eased her discomfort.

"Ye did well riding for so long today, Bly. But I ken ye must be sore."

When Blythe heard the hesitancy in Michail's voice, she reached between them and ran her hand over his cock. "Not too sore, so don't think I won't claim my wifely rights on my wedding night. You shall have to get over your nerves because I won't be turned away, husband."

Blythe giggled as she teased him, but she squealed when he squeezed her backside, then hefted her over his shoulder. He marched farther down the river's shore until a hill protected them from prying eyes. Anyone who approached would have to either come down the hill or come from across the river. There was no way an intruder could attack without Michail seeing them coming, but they had the privacy the newlywed couple sought.

"I will bring ye back down here tonight, when the sun's set and nay one can see me strip ye naked. Then I will carry ye into the water and make love to ye just as we did our first time."

"That was really the third time," Blythe smirked. "The first time was on the blanket. The second time was against the tree on the way to the river. And the third time was in the water."

"I intend to keep ma promise and bury maself inside ye beneath our blankets before ye fall asleep. I shall make love to ye in the river after the men settle for the night. The only difference is, I'm going to make love to ye now against a hillside. We shall have to save the tree until morning."

"Promise?"

"Och, aye. As though ma life depends on it."

"It may very well." Blythe tugged Michail's leine from beneath his belt and plaid. She inched her hands under the linen and reveled in the feel of his heated skin. She closed her eyes as memories and the present mingled. She felt Michail lifting her skirts, so she pulled one hand free to push his sporran behind him, then to gather the hem of his plaid.

"I willna undress ye when it's still light out. But I am going to be sure ye enjoy this. I ken it's been a long time. I hated the pain I caused ye the first time, and I fear it might be similar this time. I'll go slowly."

Blythe stroked the hair back from Michail's eyes before tunneling her fingers into locks that shimmered with hints of blond and gold among the light red. She allowed him to guide her to lean back against the sloping ground. Neither hurried at first as they shared a kiss that soon drove them to claw at one another. Her hand drifted beneath his plaid and wrapped around his cock. She felt him shudder as she stroked. She gasped as two of his fingers eased into her channel. Her hips rocked forward as his digits worked her stimulated body. Their kiss became a melee of dueling tongues, each wishing to devour the other.

Blythe's free hand clutched his leine, but she soon abandoned the garment for the feel of his scorching skin against her palm and fingertips. She tightened her grip around Michail's rod as she ground her mons against his pelvis. She murmured, "More."

"Patience."

"I have none, and I don't want to find any."

"I was talking to maself," Michail whispered before nipping at her earlobe.

Blythe shuddered as a spike of lust shot straight to her lower belly and burned. She spread her feet wider, making room for Michail to settle between her thighs. She lifted one foot and pressed it against the ground, giving her leverage to tilt her hips and lift them from the grass upon which she laid. She realized her heart raced as Michail drew attention to her chest as he flicked his tongue over the exposed swell of her breast. He eased the gown over her shoulder, but her maid had laced it too snugly to free either breast.

"I shall lavish them with special attention later." Michail returned his mouth to hers as he lifted the front of Blythe's kirtle, and she raised his plaid. He was careful to ensure Blythe's skirts shielded her legs from sight. If anyone stumbled upon them, there would be no denying what they were doing, but he would afford his wife the little modesty they had left.

He brushed the tip of his cock against her seam and groaned. It had been years since he'd been with a woman. He'd never imagined in his youth that he would go so long without coupling, but it had held no interest for him. He'd nearly made a grave error when he considered coupling with Lady Leslie Lindsay, but it hadn't been the lusty matron he pictured when he closed his eyes. There was only one woman who he belonged inside, and that was the woman he now called his wife. When Blythe's hands gripped his buttocks and pressed, he thrust into her. Theirs sighs blended as they both marveled at the feeling of finally joining.

"God, how I've missed you, missed this," Blythe whispered. Michail's thrusts made her gasp and moan as he seated himself to the hilt, then withdrew, never all the way, just enough to surge into her again and again.

"Me too. I've dreamed aboot this every night, every time I palmed maself. Over and over, but naught in ma memories was as good as being here with ye now."

"I did the same. When I thought my need for you, my longing to feel you again, would tear me asunder, I would remember how it was. More nights than I could count, I slid into my bed and hiked up my nightgown to rub my pearl like you taught me. When I closed my eyes, I could almost smell you and hear you."

Blythe's words charged Michail's lust, making him piston his hips faster. She rolled hers to match his rhythm. Breathless but hungry, their kisses claimed their mouths when they had no more words to share. When Blythe felt her core tightening, the wave building, she ripped her mouth free and pressed it against Michail's shoulder. Her teeth nipped at him as she kept from screaming her release. His fingers bit into her backside, spurring her to match his thrusts until she climaxed again. She rubbed her pearl against him as he shuddered and spilled within her.

Michail eased them onto the sandy shore, turning to rest his back against the hillock. They panted and clung to one another, their bodies still one. Their kisses were tender caresses as they held one another. When Blythe settled her cheek against his shoulder and the bridge of her nose rested against his neck, Michail rested his cheek on her head. Both sat with their eyes closed as their galloping hearts slowed to a steady walk.

"I love you," Blythe whispered as Michail murmured, "I love ye."

～

True to his word, Michail led Blythe back to the river after the sunset, the first watch posted, and the rest of the men settled for the night. Blythe carried the lump of soap, a clean chemise, and a clean pair of stockings, while Michail carried a fresh leine. But unlike the first time they arrived alone at the river, there was no impatience. Instead, they slowly undressed, talking as they stripped.

"If we encounter anyone tomorrow, ride for the Stewarts at Crookston Castle. Theirs is the closest keep, and neither yer clan nor mine is on bad terms with them," Michail advised as he unfastened the length of plaid from his shoulder just as he had before their handfasting. He dropped the brooch into his sporran before loosening his belt.

Blythe observed her husband undressing, more interested in what he would reveal than what he said, but when he mentioned the Stewarts, she offered him a confused expression until she realized he didn't know. "Michail, I'm related to the Stewarts. Not that branch, but the ones at Garlies Castle. Laird Andrew Stewart is my half-brother. We share our mother. She was married to Andrew's father until he died. She remained at Garlies until my brother was auld enough to foster. She went back to her family until she married my father."

Michail held his belt in one hand and kept his plaid from falling from his waist with the other. He hadn't known the familial connection, but he was glad for it.

The Stewarts were a powerful clan, not only in the Lowlands but throughout Scotland. It was good to know they would ride through allied territory.

"If you wish, we could spend the last night at Garlies. My sisters and I are close to Andrew, so we could stay for as long as you felt we needed to. Isabella used to visit Andrew with the royal court, and she spent holidays there when she couldn't travel home. She eventually left a chest of clothes behind, and now Emelie and I wear them when we visit. It's much easier. Though, they're tremendously long for Emelie." Blythe snickered. "She looks like a lass wearing her mama's gown. I don't know how she ended up being so short."

"Aye. She and Dom are quite a sight. Did ye ken he calls her Sparrow, and she calls him Wolf? Seems fitting." Michail grinned as Blythe nodded her head, but he grew serious again. "I'd like to make it across the Stewarts of Darnley's land tomorrow and camp near its edge with the Hamiltons. Then we can make our way farther southwest to yer brother's. I want to keep ye as far from the border as I can."

"I would prefer that." Blythe said with a rueful smile. She'd slipped out of her kirtle while they talked, and Michail now stood in only his leine. She stepped closer and murmured. "I've missed seeing you."

"Mayhap even as much as I've missed seeing ye." Michail pulled his leine over his head, only to find Blythe already naked, having pulled the ribbons loose at her shoulders. There was no holding back now. They fused together like opposite pole magnets. The urgency they'd shared earlier that day returned tenfold. Michail lifted Blythe, guiding her legs around his waist. She locked her ankles as Michail raised her high enough for her to guide the tip of his sword to her sheath. "Ye're ready for me."

"Aye. I have been since the moment I spied you arriving in the bailey days ago. You know I'm always wet for you."

"I feared…"

"Never fear. Just as I never stopped loving you, I never stopped desiring you. I admit I worried too."

Michail waded into the river, careful not to lose his footing. He moved away from the shore until the water came to their chests. As the water lapped around Blythe's breasts, he assured her, "I spoke the truth the other day. I may have drunk too much, but I wasna a womanizer. Blythe, it's been three years."

Her eyes widened as she understood what he meant. "You've been celibate the entire time?"

"I didna want anyone else. I kept maself sotted most nights, so I had nay interest in finding a woman. Besides, the more I drank, the more I thought of ye."

"But what aboot…"

"We were both angry and jealous that night. I hated watching ye dance with those men, and ye'd told me to move on. When the invitation came, and I thought ye'd be offering yer own to someone else… I finally relented."

"I forgot aboot Fletcher the moment he walked away."

"I couldnae tell ye what color her eyes were. Blythe, since I met ye, it has only been ye. There hasnae been anyone else." Blythe hung her head and shook it, ashamed that she couldn't say the same. Michail eased her chin until he could kiss the tip of her nose. "I dinna hold aught against ye, Bly. Ye had every right to move on, to find a mon ye wished to marry. Ye were right to replace me. I chose whisky and dares as ma companions."

"I knew you'd been with other women before me, and it didn't bother me. I assumed you'd already moved on, or at least moved to someone else's bed."

"I held out hope until the vera end, until this morning. I was ready to accept I'd leave yer home without ye at ma side. That's part of the reason I was so uneasy as we left. I was trying to keep from bawling like a wean."

"Michail, no more keeping things from each other."

"The only thing I'm keeping is ye." Michail brushed his lips against Blythe's, and she opened to him immediately.

"Make love to me, husband." Blythe rocked her body against Michail's, feeling the strength he possessed as he guided her hips. His length slipped in and out of her channel. She wrapped one arm around his neck as the other roamed over his shoulder, neck, jaw, until her fingers grasped his hair. She didn't realize she tugged until Michail grunted and thrust harder, thinking she signaled she wanted more. She knew she did. She freed his hair, sweeping her hand down his back. When his cock pressed against an especially sensitive spot within her core, her nails streaked up his back as she fought not to scream her release. With another thrust and a circling of his hips, Michail once more found his release within his bride.

Breathless, they smiled at one another. They shared a series of quick kisses before Michail dunked them under the water. They realized neither of them had remembered the soap, so Michail brought Blythe to shallower water where she could stand before he dashed back to grab the lump of rose-scented soap. He playfully pursed his lips as Blythe cocked an eyebrow.

"I know you'll never stray, but I shall make sure every woman who comes near my braw husband knows he already has a woman. One who doesn't share."

"Ye're branding me with yer soap? Mmm. I rather like that. Will ye help me with ma bath every night?"

"Yes. Does your family have one of those massive

tubs Isabella told me aboot? She was so surprised when she first arrived that she spent half a missive telling Emelie and me aboot how the Sinclairs have several tubs and that half a village could fit in them. At the time, she mentioned she was glad the Sinclair men were so big because it meant the tub was large enough for Ric. Now I know she was glad it was big enough to fit them both."

"And how do ye ken that?" Michail snickered.

"Because if you have one of those massive tubs, that's exactly how I intend to use it. I know my sisters. We all think alike."

"Aye, ma bonnie bride. We have one of those large copper and wood tubs. But ma parents and brothers will soon find they'll need a new one. I willna give it back once I get ye in it." Michail passed the bar of soap over Blythe's body before making her hair sudsy as she washed him. He massaged her scalp, and it was so soothing that she closed her eyes and nearly dropped the rose soap. She was at a disadvantage when it was her turn to wash Michail's hair. She giggled when he crouched low enough for her to reach. Knowing it was uncomfortable for him, Blythe didn't linger like he had. They hurried to dry themselves and slip back into their clothes. Once they were back in camp, with the guards not on watch soundly sleeping, they tucked their blankets around them. Spooning her, Michail bunched Blythe's skirts and his plaid until he could slip inside her. They fell asleep with him buried hilt deep, just as he'd pledged.

CHAPTER 12

Blythe awoke with a start as a ground-shaking clap of thunder clattered above their camp and a deluge poured upon them. She and Michail scrambled from their bedrolls as the men did the same. There'd been no hint throughout the night that a storm brewed.

"Hurry," Michail ordered. "The river shall swell its banks in a few minutes. We need to be packed before it washes aught away."

Blythe rushed to pack their bedrolls as Michail carried her saddle to Midnight. She finished with their bedding before Michail finished with her mount, so she struggled, but carried Cunnart's saddle to the horse. The leather seat was far heavier than hers, so there was little chance she could lift it onto the enormous beast that stood at least three hands taller than her own gelding.

"Thank ye." Michail's voice rumbled beside Blythe's ear. He hauled the saddle onto his horse's back, but rather than see to its fastening, he pulled a spare plaid from his saddlebag. He was quick to fold it into an arisaid and wrap it around Blythe. She didn't have a belt, so he coiled a length of rope he carried around her waist several times before knotting it. He pulled the wool over Blythe's head, then turned back to saddling Cunnart. "I would have ye ride with me, but it wouldnae be any safer. It's going to be impossible to see soon, but we must move on. I'm going to give Midnight's reins enough slack for ye to hold on to, but I'm tying them to Cunnart's saddle. I dinna want us to get separated if we canna see clearly."

"I won't be able to ride fast that way."

"Nay one will do more than a trot. The road is turning to sludge, and I'll only push us to that speed until we're safely away from the flooding." Michail guided Blythe to Midnight's side and lifted her into the saddle, helping to cover her leg on one side while she adjusted her gown on the other. He fastened Midnight's reins to a ring on Cunnart's saddle before he finished readying his horse and mounted. The men fell into formation around Blythe and Michail. The deluge forced everyone to keep their heads bowed against the wind and rain, even the horses.

They rode for fifteen minutes before Michail called them to a stop. The road was unrecognizable as a path, just a wide river of mud the horse's hooves sank into. He looked to the southwest and caught sight of even darker clouds. The eye of the storm was in the direction in which they needed to travel. He looked directly to the south, then southeast. He prayed that if they continued on a straight path that they could avoid the worst of the storm since the skies to his left weren't as menacing.

"We'll have to travel farther due south." Michail's throat strained as he tried to speak over the torrential rain, the battering wind, and the cacophony of thunder. One clap came immediately after another with barely a moment between, just long enough for lightning to streak across the sky. They trudged on, all soaked through and quickly freezing. The river water had been brisk but not unbearable the night before, but the raindrops were like icy pinpricks poking through the wool and pummeling their faces.

Michail looked back at Blythe, who huddled into her MacLeod plaid. In any other situation, Michail would have been overwhelmingly proud to see his wife wearing his clan's pattern. Instead, he was overwhelmingly proud of how she endured weather that would soon get the better of even the warriors, who were seasoned travelers and used to spending long stretches patrolling in winter.

Just as Michail was about to order everyone off the road and into the trees that ran along one side of the now mud-soup thoroughfare, a bolt of lightning struck a tree a dozen yards ahead of them. The wood splintered, and the massive maple tree crashed to the ground, sending a wave of sludge toward them. Michail looked at the meadow on the other side of them. It was a wide-open space, leaving them exposed. At least the trees offered some cover, so it was the better of two poor options.

"We must get off the road." Michail's voice floated away on the wind, so the others only saw his mouth move. He pointed toward the trees. The horses dragged their hooves as they struggled, but several whinnied in relief when they entered the trees. Michail slid from his saddle and tossed his reins to one of his men. He rushed around Cunnart and Midnight until he could reach Blythe. He noticed her lips were blue and her teeth chattered. He carried her back around to Cunnart and whistled. The horse lowered himself to the ground. The other finely trained horses followed suit, leaving only Midnight swinging his head back and forth. It was clear the other animals' actions confused the horse. With little grace, the beast made his way to the ground.

"What's happening?" Blythe shivered. Michail unpinned his plaid and wrapped them in the extra material. He eased Blythe to lie sandwiched between him and Cunnart. Blythe peered over Michail's shoulders and spied all the men huddled against their horses.

"They'll remain warmer for longer than we will. If we stay close to our mounts, they'll buffer the wind and help keep us from freezing. I ken ye're cold, *mo chridhe*. I wish there was more I could do."

"I'm only a wee chilled." Blythe's teeth chattered, betraying her bravado. Michail brought her hands between them, pressing his around hers, and breathed warm air on them. "What aboot you? You're the only one who isn't against a horse for heat. Midnight's laying down too. I can go back to him, and you can have Cunnart."

"Nay. I have far more meat on ma bones than ye do. Ye're already soaked. I'm scared ye willna make it without ma heat too."

"And when you've no heat left to give because you're an icicle?"

"I'm nae going anywhere, and neither are ye, wife." Michail's words and cocked eyebrow made it sound as though he issued a command, but Blythe saw the humor in his eyes. She knew he was trying to distract her from the predicament in which they found themselves.

"As your biddable wife, I will heed your demand. But once this storm is over, and all is back to normal, I shall make my own demands."

"And, what, pray tell, will ye demand?"

"There is one part of me that is overheated, even now. Mayhap I'll need you to blow on it."

Michail choked as he tried to stifle his laugh. He closed his eyes and shook his head. "By God, I love ye, Blythe. As yer biddable husband, I will gladly follow yer orders." Michail pressed a brief kiss to Blythe's lips before he pressed her head against his chest and curled around her further, his own head bowed against the onslaught.

~

It was at least an hour before the thunder and lightning ceased their battle over their heads. The wind and rain continued as the gale refused to give up its hold on that stretch of land. But without the fear of lightning striking them, the MacLeods and Dunbars set off again. It forced them to remain within the trees, leading their horses on foot rather than riding. Blythe and Michail walked between their horses with his arm wrapped around Blythe's waist, pinning her to his side as they continued to share the extra length of Michail's *breacan feile*. Harry and Durham, Michail's second-in-command during their journey, led the group. Even though it was only midmorning, it was nearly as dark as night among the trees. The men carried their swords, prepared for any surprise, be it man or beast. It surprised Michail when Blythe withdrew a wickedly sharp *sgian dubh* from her pocket. He'd never seen the knife before. He knew she carried one in her boot, and she had her eating knife fastened to her thin cord girdle.

"You grew up in the Highlands, but I grew up along the border. My father ensured I knew how to use this before I was auld enough to ride beyond the wall with only my guards. He made Emelie and me prove we remembered all his lessons before she and I left for court."

"Will ye show me what ye ken when we reach home?" Michail didn't understand the furrow between Blythe's brows. "I didna mean to sound as though I dinna believe ye ken what to do. I'm curious."

"I wasn't thinking aboot that. I realized I didn't know which home you meant. Then it dawned on me you meant Ardvreck. It's the first time I've thought of anywhere other than Druchtag Motte as home." Just as Michail worried she would reject thinking of his home as theirs, she turned a beaming smile to him. It was the only bright spot in the dismal surroundings. "Will you tell me aboot our home?"

"Ye ken it sits on Loch Assynt. There was once a castle on a small isle within the loch, but Ardvreck has been our home for several generations. It's a rectangle with a turret that looks out over the lake and the fields. Ma brothers and I used to race each up those stairs to be king of the castle. I dinna ken how we didna break our blummin' necks. We drove our mother barmy."

"Is that what I have to look forward to one day?" Blythe whispered against Michail's side. "I hope so. The weans, not the being barmy, or anyone breaking their neck."

"I hope so, too." Michail kissed the top of Blythe's head and held her a little tighter. "The keep has four floors. The Great Hall has a vaulted ceiling with crossbeams. I used to tell Ward that was where the saints sat to watch him, so they kenned what to tell God. He was the best behaved of the three of us. It wasna until I was much aulder that I realized I terrified him by making him think God would ken if he didna finish his neeps and tatties."

"Hmm. The plight of the youngest child. I know it well," Blythe giggled.

"Aye, well, dinna think he's an angel. He grew out of that and causes his own trouble now."

"That I'm certain you help him into."

"Only sometimes." Michail winked when Blythe leaned away to shoot him a playful scowl. "Anyway," Michail tickled her, "the wall walk is crenellated, so if ye're ever up there when there is snow or ice, be vera careful. If ye can avoid it, dinna go up there."

"Michail, I have to get familiar with the entire keep, including the battlements. One day I will oversee our home. If you're not in residence and something happens, I can't just hide inside. Will you take me up to the wall walk and give me a tour? I won't go up alone until you feel I'm ready, but you can't keep me from part of my domain."

"That's fair. It's just the one place where I take the danger vera seriously. Adan nearly fell through a crenellation a couple years ago in the snow. He slipped on a patch of ice that he couldnae see. As he fell forward, a gust nearly pushed him over sideways. It was Durham who was standing close enough to pull him back, but nae before they both nearly went over the side. It's the only place I never accepted a bet or a dare, even before Adan almost died."

"Will you take me swimming in the loch?"

"Aye. On the two days of the year where it's warm enough." Michail's laughter rumbled in his chest. "Ye're lucky that I'm able to make love to ye. The last time I took a dare to swim out to the isle, I thought ma bollocks had shriveled up and fallen off."

"We can't have that. I rather like them." Blythe moved her hand over his plaid and behind his sporran to cup his bollocks. "I'll help keep them warm. I just won't touch them to do it."

"Wheest, *mo chridhe*. None of us can afford me dragging ye off behind one of these trees like I said I would."

"Fair enough." Blythe canted her head. "I've never asked you what *mo chridhe* means. You used to call me that, and you do now."

"It means 'ma heart.'"

"If only I'd known Gaelic back then." Michail heard the wistfulness in Blythe's voice and realized she wasn't wrong. If she'd known what she meant to him, they could have avoided so much of their discord. "What can I call you?"

Michail's grin matched Blythe's when she'd asked him to describe their home. He wondered if it would ever interest her to learn Gaelic. Even if she never became fluent, he appreciated she wanted to learn at least the terms of endearment.

"*Mo ghràidh* means 'ma darling,' and *mo ghaol* means 'ma love.' 'Sweetheart' is simple; it's *leannan*. *Mo bhean* is 'ma wife,' and *an duine agam* is 'ma husband.'"

"I think I will stick with *mo ghràidh* for now, since even that is a challenge. Remind me of the others once I master that."

"It willna take ye long since I intend to say all of them often." Michail nudged Blythe with his hip. "There are some others to teach ye too, but I dinna want anyone hearing."

"Keep talking like that, and all of me shall overheat. There'll be more than one place to blow on."

"There is a tree trunk with yer name on it wherever we camp this eve."

"Mmm. And is there anywhere that might have you overheated?"

"There is. But I fear yer warm tongue will only overheat me more."

"I'm certain it will—*an duine agam*." Blythe gazed hopefully at Michail, who struggled to smother his laughter.

"Almost." At Blythe's playfully miffed expression, his steely arm lifted her off the ground as he continued to walk. He pressed a hard kiss to her cheek before setting her down. "I shall reward yer efforts, and part of me hopes it takes ye a while to learn."

Blythe grinned and waggled her eyebrows. But they both fell silent as the group emerged from the trees to find a raging waterway in front of them. It made the river they'd abandoned appear like a stream. Blythe groaned. When Michail looked down at her, she shook her head with an annoyed sigh.

"The River Dee only gets wider as it flows southwest. It's usually swift and deep, but horses can swim it. It only narrows and slows to the east. A long way to the east." Blythe pursed her lips and twisted her mouth in thought. "If it's like this here, it'll be impossible to cross it to the west without turning too far north. We can likely ford it if we turn east, but not for at least twenty miles."

"How much worse would it be to the west?" Michail asked.

"Significantly." Harry joined their conversation. "It would lead us to Clan Montgomery and Clan Cunningham. They're amid a feud that makes Scotland and England look like long-lost friends. We can't take Lady Blythe into that. They're fighting almost every day along their border, and they're raiding well into each other's land."

"Our only choice is to go through Douglas territory," Michail noted. He watched as several Dunbar guards shifted uneasily. Michail had noticed all of Blythe's guards must have been senior warriors within their clan, since they were all nearing an age where they could be Blythe's and his fathers.

"All of us were on a campaign against the Douglases when Lady Dunbar was newly married to our laird. The Douglases and Stewarts aren't friendly. The Dunbars aided the Stewarts during several battles. None of us can go near them. Between our time spent on their land and Lady Blythe's hair, they'll recognize us as Dunbars immediately."

Michail nodded. He was aware of the clan dynamics in the Lowlands, but he wasn't aware of which clans were actively fighting. He also didn't know the geography as well as he did the Highlands. He would trust Harry and the other Dunbar guards. "What would ye have us do?"

Michail's request for advice took Harry aback a moment, but he quickly answered. "We try to head east. There's a narrow corridor of land that is slightly the Douglas's but mostly the Cunninghams' once we pass through Hamilton territory. These Cunninghams are disinterested in their distant cousins' feud, except for when they're called upon to fight. They keep to themselves mostly, so if we stay on their land, we should be fine. If we keep traveling south, that'll put us in Maxwell territory. From there we head west across the Hannays' territory until we reach our land."

"How many days will that add? What if we made camp and waited out the weather?" Michail prodded.

"I've seen this river like this before, but it was when the Montgomerys and Cunninghams weren't at each other's throats. We'd be here at least ten days, then we'd still have two days of travel. If we could head west, it would only add one day, but I can't advise the risk. If we head toward the Maxwells, that'll add five days in this weather, but it's likely the safest choice."

"If that's what ye believe, then we follow yer suggestion." Michail swept his eyes over Blythe, concerned about her continued exposure to the elements, but he knew waiting a week and a half for the river to cease swelling its banks was not even a consideration. He wouldn't lead her intentionally into a war zone, either. Their only option was to continue east, then south, and pray. "How close to the border must we travel?"

Blythe shot Harry a nervous glance, knowing there was no avoiding the answer and no avoiding Michail's refusal. Blythe admitted, "Five or six miles."

"Nay. Absolutely nae. We find an inn and ride out

the weather there. The English traveled much farther north than that to fight yer father." Michail's crossed arms and resolute mien told Blythe this was not the time to argue with her husband, and she would much rather wait out the foul weather in a room with a bed. Especially since she now had a husband with whom to share it.

"We still need to get across the river. We can look for lodging after that. If we don't head east, the river is likely to flood where we stand." Blythe sounded reasonable, and Michail knew she was right. He nodded, switching his attention from Blythe to Harry.

"Ye must lead the way still. I dinna ken this land and what to look out for. If ye sense even a hint of danger, be it mon, beast, or nature, ye speak up."

Harry bristled, but Blythe shot him a warning stare. She knew Harry would never lead her astray or ignore a risk to her. He'd been her guard for years, and he'd sneaked sweets to her sisters and her when they were children. But she also understood how apprehensive being so far south made Michail when he didn't know the land or the clans.

"We'll travel parallel to the river until we come to a bridge or somewhere we can ford. Then we turn south. We might even double back and regain some of the lost time." Harry awaited Michail's agreement, which came without hesitation. It assuaged the senior guard's indignation. The group finally mounted once more, even though their horses could only walk as the ground remained boggy and slick.

They'd only made it a third of the distance they'd hoped to travel before they set up camp for the night. They risked a larger fire than usual because they all desperately needed the heat. The rain had ceased an hour before they stopped for the night, so they each had sodden clothes stretched around the fire to dry.

The Highlanders shared their extra plaids with the Lowlanders, barely hiding their smirks. Blythe and Michail sat together, but neither felt talkative. They were both fatigued, and neither was given to chatter in the best of weather. Blythe was asleep within moments when Michail curled around her. But she remained awake from the moment Michail slipped from their bedroll until he returned from his hour of watch. Once they burrowed beneath the covers together once more, they both gave way to their exhaustion.

CHAPTER 13

The next four days were nothing but trudging through rain and mud. They made less progress than they hoped each day, traveling a quarter of what they normally could. They found no inns along the way; they didn't even see a croft as they continued to travel beside the river. At times, it forced them back north when flooding prevented them from remaining close to the waterway's expanded diameter. It was midafternoon on the fifth day when they finally reached a place where the guards agreed to try crossing. Durham volunteered to take his horse across first, since the steed was among the least affected by the inclement weather.

Before man and beast entered, Michail threw a stick into the water, and they all watched the rapid current push it downstream. Durham continued several yards farther up the riverbank before nudging his steed into the rushing water. It was almost immediate that everyone watched the churning current force the horse to swim. But the animal regained its footing halfway across, coming out in line with the rest of the party waiting on the northern shore.

"Ride beside me, Blythe," Michail stated.

"No. We have to go one by one. If we try to cross together, whoever is on the left risks their horse pushing the other. It's too risky that one will spook. I can do this, Michail. Midnight has forded rivers before. You know he's as much like me as Cunnart is like you. He'll enjoy the challenge. I'll even wager him some oats on how fast he makes it across." Blythe tried to jest, but it fell on deaf ears as Michail watched the river.

"I dinna like it, but ye're right. It isnae safe for two at a time. Wait for Harry and me to cross first. Let Midnight watch two more horses go before him."

Blythe nodded before glancing behind her, then looking across the river. "How much rope do you and the men have?"

"Plenty I would imagine. If yer men are like mine, they all travel with a few yards. Why?"

"Could we tie the lengths together, then tie them to those two trees?" Blythe twisted to point to the tree on their side, then at the one near where Durham stood. "If it's taut enough, it might keep the horses from being pushed downstream. And if any of us slip, we can catch it."

"It's worth the try."

"I'll ride across with the rope," Harry offered. He and Michail exchanged a look over Blythe's head that she didn't understand, nor did she appreciate.

"I think it's better if I ride behind ye instead. In case aught happens, I can get to ye easier." Michail turned to give his men orders before Blythe could respond. She pulled the length of rope Michail gave her as a belt from her waist. She folded her new plaid and shoved it into her saddlebag before handing the rope to Michail. He opened his mouth to argue, but he merely nodded and turned back to the men. It wasn't long before they tied the ropes together, then coiled and knotted it around the tree. Harry and his horse waded across with a struggle, but crossed successfully. He and Durham worked quickly to secure their end.

Blythe looked at her husband, and fear finally crept into her heart. "I love you."

"I love ye. Go as slowly as ye and Midnight need when ye enter the water."

"We will. Be careful."

"I will." They exchanged a quick, hard kiss before Michail helped Blythe into the saddle.

Michail watched with his heart in his throat as Blythe and Midnight entered the water. The horse released a short whinny, but Michail would have sworn it was in glee, not fear. The horse swam like a seal, gliding through the water as though there were no current at all. Michail gawked as the horse gained its footing and veritably pranced out of the water. Blythe looked over her shoulder with a grin and a shrug. But it faded as she watched Michail hang back, allowing the other men to go ahead of him. Once the last man crossed, Michail untied the rope from the tree. He threw it into the center of the river, leaving Harry to tug it back in, then he mounted Cunnart.

"Come on, lad. Ye canna let Midnight show ye up. The horse doesnae even have his bollocks anymore. Where are yers?" Michail guided his mount to the water's edge and eased the warhorse forward. What he didn't tell Blythe, but what Harry sensed, was Cunnart loathed water that came above his belly. Michail had never figured out why, since there'd never been an incident to frighten the horse. Even in the calmest and warmest of water, the horse's eyes rolled, and he shook his head, jostling the reins in Michail's hands. The MacLeods knew about Cunnart, so the bets and dares issued to Michail involving water always excluded the beast.

He'd been willing to urge his mount into the water

when he feared Blythe crossing without him. Now he hoped Cunnart watching the other horses would make him braver, but such was not the case. The beast shook his head and snorted, pawing at the water before rearing. Michail fought to stay in the saddle, prepared for Cunnart's reaction. He whispered to the horse, soothing and encouraging words mixed with stern commands. Cunnart refused to budge, forcing Michail to swing down from the saddle. He held the reins in his left hand while his right hand took hold of the horse's bridle. He glanced across the river, immediately regretting it when he spied Blythe's pale face and wide eyes. He waded into the water, tugging Cunnart behind him.

"Dinna fash, Bly," Michail called out. "Once he's in, I'll mount and be across in two shakes of a lamb's tail." Leading the way, Cunnart finally entered the water. Michail shook his head. *At least the daft beast trusts me.*

The pair made it into the raging current, but Cunnart panicked. Disliking the sensations of the rushing current and not being able to feel land beneath his feet, he attempted to pull away from Michail. With a serious of Gaelic oaths, Michail maneuvered himself onto his horse's back, but he couldn't hook his feet into the stirrups. He struggled to control his steed with his thighs as the water pulled at the reins, further confusing the horse.

"Michail!"

Michail looked across the river as Blythe waded in, wildly pointing upriver. He was about the yell to her to go back when his peripheral vision caught movement. He turned to look where Blythe pointed. A massive tree trunk hurtled toward him. He knew there were branches submerged that no one could spy. The speed with which the tree moved was misleading. It looked, at times, to bob along like a stick in a stream, and other times it looked like a surge engine preparing to batter him.

"All right, Cunnart. We dinna have a choice. I canna ride ye across, so I'll get off. But ye must swim, lad. I dinna want aught to happen to ye. Ye trusted me enough to get in the water. Now I need ye to trust me enough to move yer arse."

Michail slipped from the saddle, nearly sucked under his horse's floundering legs. He placed the reins between his teeth before kicking as hard as he could. Fighting the current, he moved beyond Cunnart's head. He thought they'd reached the point where the river suddenly grew shallow, so he lowered his legs. A wave knocked him beneath the surface when his feet met nothing. He kicked his powerful legs and broke through the surface. As another wave washed over them, this time submerging the horse's enormous head, Michail was quick to pull the reins over Cunnart's ears. He tried to lead the horse across the rest of the river's width.

"Come on, Cunnart. We dinna have time to wait. Look. That bluidy tree is—" Michail sucked in a mouthful of water as a submerged branch struck his belly. He had imagined none were long enough to strike him yet, but he'd underestimated the size of the tree. His feet tangled with the leaves and twigs, dragging him under once more. He reached around in the murky water as it burned his eyes. His hand brushed the saddle horn. He grabbed it and yanked himself upward. He popped out of the water just as the trunk twisted direction, bringing its end around to plow into Cunnart. The horse shrieked but finally focused on making it across. Michail struggled to hang onto the reins as Cunnart raced toward the shore, his hooves meeting the ground long before Michail's feet could.

"Michail!" Blythe had pulled her skirts up between

her legs and tucked them into the rope belt she made from a length Harry gave her while Michail struggled through the crossing. She waded farther into the water until she grasped Cunnart's bridle. She crooned at the animal, praising him for his bravery, and promising him every apple in the Lowlands and time with any mare that took his fancy. Once they reached the riverbank, Blythe maneuvered herself under Cunnart's head and wrapped her arm around Michail's ribs. He gasped in pain but sagged against his wife.

"What shall ye promise me if I behave and come on shore?" Michail's words came out as wheezes as he stumbled up the embankment. It relieved him when Stanley hurried forward and snagged Cunnart's reins. Michail pitched forward and sprawled on the ground once he rolled onto his back. He shaded his eyes as Blythe towered over him. "What?"

"What? What! You daft mon. You might have told me your horse hates the water. What were you thinking going without the rope? If anyone needed it, it was you. At the very least, you could have tied the end around your waist. Even if you had to tug Cunnart across, we could have helped you. You bluidy eejit. You could have died." Blythe sank to her knees, but she was more intent upon examining Michail's ribs and abdomen than she was in his response.

"I'm sorry, Blythe. I didna think of that, but I should have. Cunnart has never liked the water. Nay one kens why since he didna have any terrible experiences as a colt or during battle. He just has never liked it."

"Because he's not in control." Blythe ran her hands over Michail's rib, feeling for anything the tree might have fractured or any bumps. He caught her fingers before he howled.

"I dinna ken what ye mean."

"Cunnart. He doesn't enjoy being in the water because he can't see the bottom. He isn't in control of where he's going or what he's doing. Even when you're riding him, he's still picking his course and can see where you're headed. He can't do that in the water. He's like his owner. He likes to be in control. You do the ridiculous dares and bets because you think you can control fate. You couldn't control what happened to your grandfather, so you think to get back at fate by risking your life and coming out the winner."

Blythe spoke with such a pragmatic tone that it gave Michail pause to think. In the back of his mind, he knew what Blythe said was true. Such thoughts filtered through his mind in his drunken stupors, but he never would have attributed the same need to be in command of his life to his horse. He groaned as he turned his head to see where Cunnart stood calmly with the other mounts, as though he hadn't nearly died along with his owner.

"Can you sit up? I need to check your head and your back."

"I'm hale, Bly. Ma ribs and gut hurt, but the rest of me is fine. Naught else struck me. Ma feet got tangled. That's all. I need to check Cunnart."

"Durham and Stanley are doing it." Blythe jutted her chin in the men's direction. "Humor me. Let me be in control for a wee while. I need to be sure you're all right."

Michail gazed into Blythe's hazel eyes and realized she wasn't teasing him. He sighed before wrapping his arms around her waist and pulling her down to sprawl across him. She hissed his name. He tucked hair behind her ear and pressed a soft kiss to her lips. She cupped his jaw and rubbed her nose against his.

"Let me have one more kiss, wife. Then ye can see to me. All of me." Michail winked as Blythe playfully swatted at him. She gave him a quick kiss before she pushed off his chest, making him wince. She narrowed her eyes, unconvinced he was in pain. When she saw the humor in his gaze, she harrumphed and rose to her feet. She stuck out her hand, and Michail took it. They both knew he came to his feet in one graceful movement from his own muscular legs pushing him upward, but Michail kissed her temple. "Thank ye."

She walked around him, pushing his leine up as she examined his back and ribs. There were livid bruises forming across his belly and left ribs, but nothing more serious seemed to have happened. When it satisfied her that he had no cuts that needed tending and his ribs didn't need binding, she pulled her skirts loose and shook them out. She said nothing as she returned to Midnight and pulled out the plaid she claimed as hers. She fumbled as she tried to refold it as an arisaid. Before she grew frustrated, Michail took it from her, showing her how.

"I used to watch ma mother do it when I was a wean. I used to think it looked difficult until ma father tried to teach me to pleat ma own plaid. The mon has the patience of a saint, and he had three sons to teach. I've never given him enough credit. I always thought ma mother was the saintly one."

"Saint Michael in a *breacan feile*," Blythe grinned as she pictured the commander of God's saintly warriors.

"I shall tell him that." Michail chuckled as he helped Blythe secure the woolen wrap.

"Are you truly well enough to ride?" Blythe kept her voice low, the humor gone. "I can say I need longer to recover."

"Nay. I can ride, and I believe Cunnart is ready to get away from the sound of the river." Blythe stared at Michail, her lips turned down. Michail placed her right hand over his heart. "I'm sorry I scared ye. But I'm nae lying. I'm all right to ride. I dinna need to hide behind ye. If I couldnae, I would speak up. Lying wouldnae do any of us any good if I dropped off ma horse's back."

"Very well. You're already my hero. You don't need to prove aught."

"I'm yer hero, am I?" Michail waggled his brows. Blythe rolled her eyes before she lifted her foot into the stirrup. She bounced and was prepared to pull herself up when Michail's hands on her waist tugged her back against his solid frame. "And who will save ye when I ravish ye tonight?"

"I won't need saving. But you may need a nap to rest up. I have those wifely demands, remember?"

"Ye'll have to jog ma memory."

Blythe twisted and kissed Michail's cheek. "Let's get going, so we can be away from this blasted river. The sooner we move, the sooner we can find somewhere to camp."

It had taken nearly two-and-a-half hours for the party to cross the river, and none looked back as they rode away. As their horses walked along the road, Michail was certain Midnight pranced. The jet-black steed appeared to peek at Cunnart every few steps. Michail was certain the gelding was taunting his stallion.

"Nay one likes a showoff," Michail grumbled as he leaned toward Midnight's ear, which twitched. The powerful steed nodded his head, as if in agreement, but Michail was certain the horse only lifted his feet higher with each step. Blythe's laughter filled the air.

There was a collective sigh when the scouts spied an inn and rode back to tell the group. They guided their horses to a stop in a village large enough to host a market day where people avoided puddles, and mud splattered everyone's clothing. The inn sat at the edge of the village and proved to be clean and warm. Michail handed his reins to a MacLeod and instructed Harry to stay with Blythe until he was certain he could secure accommodations. He was away only a few minutes before he returned with a smile.

"There's room for us, and the owner says the men can sleep inside. It'll be on the benches in the main room, but a far sight warmer and drier than the stables. There's a chamber for us, and the tavern keeper's wife is preparing a bath for ye, *mo chridhe*. I asked that they send up a tray as well. I want ye dry and well-fed before we think aboot aught else. If the weather is foul in the morning, we'll stay for the day and let everyone rest. We might do that even if the weather is fair. A couple nights of proper sleep and a few hearty meals will do us all some good."

"I won't complain at that. I stink of river water, and I dare say there are no warm places left on me."

"We canna have that." Michail led Blythe inside, pointing to where the owner told him their men could eat and sleep. He hurried Blythe up the stairs and along the passageway until he reached the door to their chamber. He was glad to have a key, knowing he could secure the portal for the night.

When they entered, there was already a steaming bath set up and a tray overflowing with food. Neither talked as they nibbled on heels of bread as they shed their sodden clothes. With a wheel of cheese split between them, Michail helped Blythe into the tub. It would be a struggle for Michail to fit in it alone, so sharing a bath was impossible for the newlyweds. They ate what was easy to manage while Blythe bathed. She hurried so the water would still be warm for Michail, but she winced when she realized how filthy she'd left it.

"Dinna fash. Half of those buckets are empty. The innkeeper's wife must have guessed. Help me empty the tub, then we can use the water that's before the fire to refill it." They worked in silence, both moving slower than normal from fatigue and still being chilled. It wasn't long before Michail was drying himself with a linen, and Blythe kneeled against the tub, scrubbing their clothes. They wrung them out and spread them on the floor to dry. They'd both had to launder all their attire since nothing escaped the river water, even what was inside their saddlebags. They climbed into bed with the tray between them. They each devoured a bowl of pottage along with more bread. They washed it all down with pints of summer ale before splitting an apple.

"We didn't make it very far today," Blythe mused.

"Actually, we made it farther than I expected. We rode a good five miles before we could cross. And I would say we did another six or so once we did. It wasna as far as I would like to travel in a day—really only half of what we normally would—but it was better than naught."

"True. Where do you think we are?"

"I think we're among Cunninghams, but I canna be sure. I didna ask Harry."

"We haven't heard a brawl erupt downstairs, so either we are among Cunninghams, or our men have said naught aboot us being Dunbars if we're amongst the Douglases." Blythe glanced up at Michail as she considered what she said. "Michail, you know I think of myself as a MacLeod now, don't you?"

"Aye. Ye agreed to marry me, and ye wear ma plaid."

"And I didn't do that just because it's warm. I did it because I'm proud that you're my husband and that I'm now part of your clan."

"What has ye bothered, Bly?"

"Just now, when I said any of us are Dunbars. It makes it sound like I think of myself as still a Dunbar, not a MacLeod."

"*Mo chridhe*, ye are both and will be from now on. Ye canna change yer clan of birth, and I would never want ye to renounce them. I didna think aught of it."

"I'm glad for that. But I also want you to know that since I feel like I'm part of your clan now, I also feel you're part of mine. You'll never bear the Dunbar name, but you're my family, which makes you a part of this clan."

"I like that notion, Blythe. Thank ye for welcoming me into yer family and yer clan. I'm proud to be a part of both. I'm proud to be yer husband." Michail placed the tray on the floor before they burrowed beneath the covers. Their naked bodies came together, a tangle of limbs as Michail sank into Blythe's heat.

"Mayhap not all of me is cold after all." Blythe clenched her core around Michail's cock as he moved languidly. Neither was in a rush, since they didn't fear anyone stumbling upon them. Despite their need to sleep, they lavished one another with attention. Michail suckled Blythe's breasts as she arched her back. Her hands roamed everywhere she could reach: his chest, his back, his buttocks. She favored that more than any other place, aroused by the marble-hewn muscles beneath the satiny skin. She'd giggled three years earlier when she discovered how pale Michail's backside and upper thighs were compared to the rest of him. "Your arse is still a beacon in the dark."

Michail growled as he kissed her neck and behind her ear, flexing his hips over and over. Blythe pressed against his shoulders, and he rolled onto his back without more urging. Blythe followed, straddling him. She rose, then sank onto his rod over and over before switching to a rocking motion. She held her body hovering over Michail's with her hands beside his head. As her breasts swung with each movement, Michail kneaded them until Blythe's channel ached with need. His tongue swirled around her nipple before enclosing his lips around it. With renewed urgency, Blythe increased the pace until they both soared over the precipice to land softly in a tangled heap on the well-stuffed mattress. Their exhaustion led them to sleep deeply, but only in spurts, both waking the other to make love thrice more that night.

CHAPTER 14

Michail eased from the bed, watching a sleeping Blythe, and wishing he could stay abed with his bride rather than be a responsible leader. He padded to the fireplace, where their clothes dried overnight. He pulled on his leine, then bent to pleat his *breacan feile*.

"Can I ask you to remain like that all day? That's the best view in the Lowlands," Blythe's husky morning voice filled the room. Michail swayed his hips in response, eliciting a giggle from Blythe, who crossed the chamber to gather her own clothes. "You're up early."

Michail's gaze followed Blythe's. There was no denying either of her meanings, so he shrugged unrepentantly. "That's what happens when I have the bonniest woman in the world in ma bed with me."

"But we're not in bed. Which is where we should be." Blythe pouted.

"I ken, and it's where I want to be. But I must check on the men. We still dinna ken whose land we're on. I'd rather ask some discreet questions instead of us scrambling when a guard is pounding on our door." Michail rose after he wrapped his plaid around his trim waist.

He fastened his belt, then held his arms open to Blythe, who nestled against him. "If I'm quick, and there is naught to worry aboot, I'll bring us a tray. I'll even climb back into bed with ye."

"But in the meantime, I suppose I should dress in case we must make haste." They both stared at her kirtle, neither making a move to gather it. Finally, Blythe picked it up and shook it out. Michail helped her with the laces as she coiled her hair into a bun. She used a hair ribbon from her satchel to secure her hair in place. "Should I come down with you?"

"Nay. Lock the door behind me. If naught is amiss, I'll come back and take ye belowstairs. Or we can break our fast in bed like we'd both prefer." Michail kissed Blythe behind the ear before she followed him across the chamber. He handed her the key as he slipped through the door. He listened to the lock turn, then he made his way to the ground floor. The MacLeod and Dunbar men were in various stages of wakefulness, some sitting up and others rubbing their eyes, while a few still snored.

Michail spied Harry and Durham sitting together, neither with their back to the doors or the stairs up to the sleeping chambers. He nodded his head toward the door leading outside. He whispered to one of his men to stand sentry at the base of the stairs while he was outside.

"Do ye ken which clan's land we're on?" Michail kept his voice hushed.

"Yes. Douglases", Harry answered.

"Between half of us being Highlanders and the other half nae getting along with our hosts, we all kept quiet and slept with one eye open." Durham frowned. "Nay one asked who we were. None of us volunteered, but it was odd. Either they have far too many guests who dinna wish to share their names, or they already ken who we are and didna need to ask."

"I suspect the latter," Harry offered. "No one was rude or aught. They kept their distance, but it felt as though the tavern keeper recognized us. I'm certain I've never been here before."

"Could it have been Lady Blythe? Her arisaid covered her head, but I ken people could see her hair. People might nae ken it's her, but they'll ken she's one of the three Dunbar sisters." Michail stared at the door as he spoke to the two experienced guardsmen.

"Lady Blythe isnae traveling with an English-sounding mon, so everyone will ken she's nae Lady Isabella," Durham pointed out.

"And most people who know of the sisters also know Emelie is a nearly a half-a-head shorter than her sisters, which makes her tiny next to most men," Harry elaborated.

"Perhaps it doesnae matter, since I paid with gold coins." Michail shrugged, but he felt uneasy. He doubted the English would be foolish enough to step foot on Douglas land after how James Douglas earned his moniker "the Black." His bloody slaughter of English soldiers who'd invaded and captured his home was the stuff of legends. His reputation on the battlefield solidified why most people kept their distance from the man and his clan. But this very reputation made Michail unsettled. He didn't need Blythe caught in the Black Douglas's sights. "We eat and ride out. We need to get back to Cunningham land."

"At least we know both clans are ever loyal to the Bruce. The English won't tread a foot near here." Michail didn't think Harry looked as convinced as he tried to sound. The three men hurried back inside, Michail taking the stairs two at a time. He hurriedly explained what he learned as he and Blythe packed their meager belongings. The party ate and was ready to ride in a quarter hour.

~

The morning bled into the afternoon, which bled into early evening. The ground was still saturated, but the rain had ceased the night before. They spent an uneventful night on Douglas land, and they all breathed a collective sigh when they realized they crossed onto Cunningham soil. Blythe asked how they knew they'd passed the border, and Michail explained most of the men had seen the tree etched with two different notches. It was the boundary marker. She'd seen nothing, but all the men nodded when she looked at them. She slept better that night than she did the previous.

But tension rose to an unprecedented level two days later when they entered Clan Hannay's territory. The clan had been suspicious of Robert the Bruce from the beginning. They pledged their allegiance to John Balliol, since he descended through his mother, Lady Davorgilla, from the same ancient Galloway princedom from which the clan grew. Like many clans, their name appeared on the Ragman Rolls. But where most of the Lowland clans eventually came over to the Bruce's cause, the Hannays remained loyal to Balliol, which meant they remained loyal to the English king, Edward Longshanks.

Michail continued to ride beside Blythe within the center of the circle the guards formed. They had a Dunbar scout riding two miles ahead. There'd been nothing of note since they left Cunningham territory and entered Hannay lands. Michail continued to swing his gaze back and forth, often looking behind him at Durham, who usually rode half-turned in his saddle to monitor the road they'd traversed.

"Are you just being cautious, or do you sense something?" Blythe whispered. "You seem more anxious."

"I am. I dinna ken ma way around here, and neither do ma men. If aught happens, none of us ken where to ride. I trust yer men, but there arenae that many of us. If I'd imagined we'd have to take such a detour, I would have insisted royal guards travel with us. Ma ten and yer six willna be enough if they send a war band after us."

"Do you think they would?"

"We're a large enough group to make them question why we're here. They're also surrounded by clans who support the Bruce. To add half a score of Highlanders to the mix to boot may prove more than they're willing to ignore."

"If we must ride to anyone, then we go to the MacLellans. They welcomed Ric when he first came to Scotland. They know he married Isabella, so they would know who I am. I believe they would give us sanctuary."

"How do we get there?"

"They're slightly southeast of the Hannays." Blythe's brow furrowed as she acknowledged the inconvenience.

"So they're in the opposite direction from where we're going."

"They are, but from here, their keep is closest to us. Otherwise, we ride for the Gordons."

"I only ken Ewan and Eoin. They arenae these Gordons."

"I don't know this branch well either, but I can't think why they wouldn't help us."

Michail waved Durham forward and explained what Blythe and he discussed. Once Durham was back in formation, Michail moved outside the circle and nudged Cunnart to ride alongside Harry.

"I agree with Lady Blythe. The MacLellans are the best choice by distance. But the Gordons are in the direction we need to go."

"Vera well. We continue as we are, but we have a plan in place." Michail let the other riders pass until he moved back into the circle beside Blythe. After talking to Blythe and the two warriors, his mind was only slightly more at ease. He appreciated the guards' opinions, along with Blythe's explanation. But he disliked being unfamiliar with the landscape. He couldn't shake the notion that if Blythe's father was ambushed, and he knew the land and the clans, then this group was little more than moving targets.

"Michail, there's naught for it." Blythe reached for his hand, their fingers entwining before she squeezed his. They let go to return to guiding their horses. "I'm glad you insisted I didn't travel with so few men. You were right. Whatever happens, we'll sort it out as it comes. We've done what we can."

Michail offered his wife a tight smile, but he continued to survey their surroundings as they plodded along. Despite Blythe's reassurance, he couldn't shake the sense of impending danger that settled over him. He, like other warriors, trusted his intuition. It kept him alive in battle and even in his more daring endeavors. A shiver ran along his spine as he glanced at Blythe.

I dinna have the second sight. I dinna ken something is going to go wrong. Why canna I relax? The weather has improved, and we arenae at risk of drowning. We didna have trouble on the Douglases' land or the Cunninghams'. There is just something unsettling aboot this journey. Other than at the inn, we havenae even crossed paths with another traveler. Why havenae we? The Lowlands have far more people living near one another with more clans jammed together. It's nae like the Highlands where ye can ride for days on the same clan's land. That's what feels off. Where is everyone?

Michail tried to cease his restlessness because he feared scaring Blythe. But then he recalled his wife was from the very area in which they traveled. As he watched her from the corner of his eye, he realized she was just as attentive as he. However, she was far more subtle. He took heart knowing his wife understood the dangerous path they rode. Recognizing Blythe's situational awareness meant it shouldn't have surprised him when it was she who sounded the alarm three hours later.

"Michail." Blythe's hushed voice didn't hide her urgency. "I saw something shiny flash to the left."

Michail shifted in his saddle to look past Blythe, riding on the opposite side in case he should need to draw his weapon. He didn't want to slice or spear his bride if he had to swing his sword. Michail could see nothing, but he didn't discount Blythe's observation. "How far away?"

"I don't know. Before that thicket."

Michail judged the dense group of trees to be at least three miles from them. There was time to flee, but he wondered where. He squinted at a shimmer he noticed. "How do we change course for the MacLellans? I saw it too. That was sunlight off a sword. Where there is one, there are bound to be many."

Michail signaled Durham to ride alongside Blythe while Michail nudged Cunnart to move forward within the circle until he and his steed were just behind Harry and his mount.

"You saw it too?" Harry continued to face forward.

"Aye, Lady Blythe spotted it, then I did. How do we get to the MacLellans? I'm nae wasting the time to send a scout or to dither aboot whether we continue."

"Where there is one, there are bound to be many."

Michail grunted. "That's what I just told Lady Blythe. We need to hurry before we add to the distance we must travel and give them more time to approach."

Harry canted his head toward the meadow to their right. It was several miles wide, which meant they were easy targets, but there were no obstacles to navigate. Once Michail was next to Blythe again, he raised his hand and signaled their change of course. The eighteen riders swung their horses around and charged toward the meadow. They laid over their horses' withers and each rider squeezed their mounts' flanks to remain in the saddle during their mad dash. Michail looked at Blythe every hundred yards, impressed that she held on. Then he remembered how they'd encountered one another during his most recent visit to Sterling. She'd been leading her guards, along with Sileas, Evina, and their guards. She'd been a furlong ahead of everyone else and hadn't thought twice about skirting his guardsmen and him to continue racing to the keep.

"I'm all right," Blythe called over the rushing wind. "Just mind where you're going, so we both make it home in one piece."

"I should have asked how far it is." Michail rued forgetting that singularly important detail when he discussed their options with Blythe and their men.

"A couple hours," Blythe admitted. Everyone knew they couldn't run their horses at that pace for several hours. Their steeds would drop from beneath them.

"Is it flat most of the way?"

"Yes. They'll see us from a few miles away since their keep sits on a hill. If we're racing toward them, they'll send men out."

"Aye. If we're still being followed, then we'll need them." Michail glanced over his shoulder again, having noticed more than one reflection the last time he checked. This time, the glint of steel was nearly at the place where they switched course. He could barely make out horsemen atop their mounts. It was the shiny metal that gave their pursuers away. As he turned back to face forward, an arrow whizzed past him and imbedded in a MacLeod's throat. Michail drew Cunnart closer to Midnight and leaned his body over Blythe's as another arrow whipped through the air and knocked another MacLeod from his horse. The men closed their formation, and those riding closer to their invisible menace drew their targes. Michail handed his to Blythe.

"Until I can get to the other side of ye, ye must carry this. Slide it up yer arm as high as it will go." Michail counted on Blythe's slim arms being far narrower than his. She struggled to manage Midnight while pulling up the shield. But her slender arm meant the targe covered most of her side and left both hands free to control Midnight.

"What aboot you?" Blythe was glad for the protection, but not at her husband's expense. "And don't you dare say, 'dinna fash.'"

"Unless I stop to grab one of the fallen men's targes, there is naught I can do. We hope to outrace them." The couple exchanged a momentary glance, and both knew the likelihood was none that they would escape this attack without more men dying. Michail fumbled but unfastened his bow from his saddle and drew his own arrow from his quiver. "Stay down."

Michail fired off five arrows in quick succession, but he couldn't see where they landed, nor could he locate who fired at them. The best he could do was send them in the direction from which their invisible enemy attacked.

"Harry!" Blythe gasped. Michail watched as the head guard wilted from the saddle, an arrow pieced his chest and back. Unfortunately, the already-dead man's foot caught in the stirrup, causing his horse to drag him.

Blythe turned her head and squeezed her eyes shut. They traveled at least another mile before Harry's limp body came loose, and his horse left him behind. Blythe struggled against the threatening tears. She knew it was hardly the time, but she'd known the man nearly her entire life, and he was the one guard who'd remained with her during her entire tenure at Stirling Castle. He'd been like a thoughtful and amusing uncle.

Regret coursed through Blythe as she realized the impossibility of offering Harry or any of the fallen men a proper funeral. There was no choice but to continue if they wanted to make it past their attackers. Their need to arrive at the MacLellans' keep outweighed anyone's desire to bury their dead. She prayed someone might come along to give them a proper Christian burial, but she knew that was highly improbable. It was merely a dream to assuage the wave of guilt for both being alive and for leaving them behind.

She adjusted the shield on her arm before she turned her head and watched her husband fire off another round of arrows. The volley flew over her head and made its way into the distance. With this round of soaring projectiles, they heard muffled screams from men Michail struck. Hearing their leader's success had the other men drawing their bows and arrows to add to their defense. But despite their amplified effort, it wasn't long before the hidden threat picked off more MacLeod and Dunbar guards. A handful of men remained to guard Blythe.

The shrunken group of warriors brought Durham closer to Michail and Blythe, but he still brought up the rear, twisting and firing arrows behind him every so often. By the time he drew close enough to hear Michail speak, there were only seven men, plus Michail left. He had to accept the slim likelihood of their group outriding the archers and warriors pursuing them. Michail and Durham exchanged a look before Michail nodded. He called the group to a halt then turned to Blythe, not wanting to share the silent decision the two men made.

"Our greatest chance to survive is for us to stop." At Blythe's look of horror, Michail shook his head. "I ken it seems insane to stop while we're ahead of those who chase us, but we willna make it past their archers. We'll lose more men, and then they'll take ye, regardless. If we stop now, there's the chance they willna kill Durham or me. Ye'll still have us to protect ye. The last thing I want is for us to get separated. That's most probable if we dinna surrender now."

Blythe swallowed the gorge threatening to seal her throat. She knew the men wouldn't consider surrendering if she weren't there. They would put up a fight until they each drew their last breath, but she understood Michail's reasoning. It was the only chance any of the men had to survive the ambush.

"Keep the circle around Lady Blythe." Michail nudged Cunnart until his horse walked out of the group. He kept his hand wrapped around the hilt of his sword, but he laid the massive weapon across his lap. It left him prepared to fight, but he wished to look less threatening. As the remaining MacLeods and Dunbars waited, the archers rose from the tall grass and approached on foot with weapons raised.

Michail and Blythe watched in horror as an archer pointed a nocked arrow at each of them before releasing it into Durham's chest. Michail lunged to catch his friend, but the man plummeted from his horse, already dead. There'd been no reason to shoot any of them, expect for entertainment and to assert dominance. Blythe trembled with a desire to rip the archers head from his neck. She'd grown fond of the MacLeod senior guard. Her heart ached for Michail's loss since she knew they were friends.

It was another fifteen minutes of heart-stopping tension before the riders caught up. A collective gasp passed through the Scottish group as they watched men in chain mail approach.

"Fucking Sassenachs," Blythe muttered. Michail swallowed his laughter, knowing it was the least appropriate time to find anything humorous. The English mounted knights led their group of foot soldiers, who jogged behind, slowing their progress. A single knight on the finest horseflesh among their attackers urged his horse forward a few steps. He lifted the visor to his helmet and peered at them. Blythe noticed he had the eyes of a dead fish. There was no warmth, no vibrance to them. Instead, they were beady and hostile. She held still and waited for him to speak. She suspected she knew who he was, but she would give away none of her revulsion when she finally heard her name.

"Lady Blythe." The nasal English accent grated on every Scots' nerves as the knight directed his attention on Blythe. "You are a long way from court, are you not? And what brings you south among these barbarians? Could you be headed home to see your dear father on his deathbed? Did you hear that he and I met and only one of us came out the better?"

Blythe met the older man's gaze but refused to speak. She would let Michail decide how their group proceeded, and she didn't trust herself to say anything that wouldn't worsen their situation. Instead, she clamped her mouth shut and tried to ease the tension in her hands, not wanting Midnight to shift restlessly under her. Instead, all her anxiety and fear rested in her jaw and between her shoulders.

When Blythe didn't respond, the Englishman looked at Michail, the obvious leader of the group. "You're a

Highlander. What are you doing so close to the border?"

Michail remained silent, just like Blythe had. He would volunteer nothing until the man sitting on a horse two yards from him introduced himself. He would make no assumptions about who chased them. The knight looked past Michail and once more caught Blythe's gaze.

"Does the barbarian not speak English?"

Blythe continued her silent standoff against their nemesis. She refused take the bait and defend Michail when she knew there was no reason. Everyone present knew Michail was a Highlander and knew the reputation that gave him. Some might call Highlanders barbarians or savages, but there was no one on either side of the border who doubted a Highlander's ability to fight. Blythe hoped the English didn't antagonize Michail to where he demonstrated his skills. She didn't shift her stare, but Michail's stoic presence reassured her he would never act in haste. She chided herself for even doubting him. Whatever Michail did, Blythe knew it would be strategic.

"Since none of you are prone to speak, I shall introduce myself, lest the English gain a reputation for being as heathenish as the Scots. I am William Montagu, the Earl of Salisbury." Once more, the man awaited a reaction from the Scottish contingent. Unused to being ignored, the earl furrowed his brow. Blythe wanted to laugh, looking at the man as though he were a frustrated child who didn't receive the attention he wanted. She supposed it infuriated him. He looked like a toy man seated upon his horse. If only he were small enough to pick up and toss aside like a wooden carved figurine.

"If you know who we are, then you know why we travel." Michail's refined speech surprised everyone.

He'd once told Blythe his childhood tutor trained him to sound like a Lowlander, but he just chose not to adopt the pretend accent. Now he would use the refinement to his advantage. He hoped it would confuse the English into believing he might wear his *breacan feile*, but he wasn't a Highlander who fit the stereotype. No one among his party doubted that he fit that stereotype. He was a skilled warrior not given to long negotiations, and he held a grudge as well as the next man from the north. He wouldn't easily forgive the earl for endangering Blythe, and for that, he would punish the Englishman.

"Ah, he speaks, and not just in grunts and growls," the earl taunted. "I know who Lady Blythe is, so I know half the men who travel with you. Such a shame there aren't as many as there was an hour ago. But you wear that savage man-gown along with the other half of these men. Who are you?"

"I am Lady Blythe's husband. I do not appreciate you detaining us while we make our way to her clan's home."

The Earl of Salisbury snorted. "You don't appreciate me detaining you. Will you appreciate me taking your head from your shoulders? Shall I do to you what I should have done to Laird Dunbar? I shouldn't have ridden away until I was sure the devil was dead."

"Are you certain he's the devil you sought? Because I am the devil you found."

"Brave words from a man who shall soon be a guest in my dungeon. That is, assuming you make it that far. And while you enjoy those accommodations, I shall enjoy your wife."

"Then you must plan to die in your sleep."

"And why is that?" Salisbury's inflection was whiny and antagonizing.

"Because my wife is very protective. I doubt she'd

appreciate you doing me any harm. I may be a Highlander and you'd be right to fear me, but there are few people on Earth more dangerous than a Scottish woman defending her family.

"A woman defending her family," Salisbury scoffed. "All I need to do is bind her hands and stuff of rag in her mouth. Then I can toss her skirts and do as I please. Mayhap I'll even have you watch to prove who is more dangerous."

"You clearly don't know many Scottish women. Perhaps your English women are wilting roses, but our Scottish women are strong as thistles. They survive the land and the weather here and thrive. Not a single English woman ever joins any of you as you try to steal our land. The only women who do have been your king's wives, and they're not even English. Why is that? Can your women not handle the hardiness of this land? Must you leave them behind as they cower? As they rely on the comforts of their home. I've always wondered that." Michail appeared thoughtful, as though he pondered his own questions.

"A woman's place is within her home. What do I have need of an Englishwoman when there are plenty to take and have here?"

"I believe my mother would agree that a woman's place is within her home. It might even be in the kitchen, where she bakes a loaf of bread to send to her neighbors." Blythe cocked an eyebrow, challenging Salisbury and reminding him of his encounter with Blythe's mother, "Black Agnes," the Lady Dunbar.

"That bitch," Salisbury snarled before catching himself. "And where will your mother be while you're my prisoner at my home? Still tending your invalid father at his bedside, counting the moments until he dies?"

"Did you know I was there during that siege? The nine-and-ten moons we lasted comfortably, sleeping and eating within our home while we forced you to sleep under the stars in the snow and rain. My memory is long and sharp. While my mother may have dark hair, and I do not, we are much alike, and I remember what she said when she strategized. Perhaps her lessons will finally come in handy. I have no loaf of bread to offer you, but we may still have some wine."

Michail listened as Blythe goaded Salisbury, knowing she was giving Michail time to survey their situation. He prayed, much as she had, that his spouse wouldn't antagonize the earl too much. It amused him to listen as Blythe casually reminded the experienced knight of his humiliating defeat to a woman. As Blythe spoke, Michail assessed the men in the English entourage.

The mounted knights wore heavy chain mail while their mounts sported barding. It relieved him to see none of the horses' armor were caparisons, the full-body chain mail for the steeds that bore the earl's heraldry on the cloth cover. Only some wore peytrals to protect their necks and chests. He spied no croupieres to shield a horse's hindquarters or any flanchards that covered a horse's flanks. Only William's horse wore a chanfron, a metal helmet for animals. Michail concluded the earl poorly equipped his men, or, more likely, assumed the Scottish riders would put up an insignificant challenge. So far, the latter appeared true. However, the Scottish warriors had proven more than once to the English that they would knock the knights from their mounts by taking them out from under them. With little armor to protect the animals, they became larger targets than the English.

William watched Michail before attempting to draw him back into the conversation. "Admiring our horseflesh. Among the finest you will find." When an English horse whinnied, Cunnart neighed and shook his head before turning it away. Michail grinned, his horse clearly disagreeing with the earl's assessment.

"If only you didn't have to play dress up to make them so," Blythe chirped.

"Little girl, you play a dangerous game."

"Is this meant to amuse?" Michail interjected. "I find I grow bored. Shall we be on our way to Carlisle?"

William swung a suspicious gaze at Michail, unprepared for him to guess their destination. "Why would you think we shall drag you there? Mayhap we will kill you on the spot."

"You shall take us there because it is obvious those men," Michail pointed to the ones whose horses wore peytrals, "are fresh from the jousting fields. The dents in their horses' armor are new. There is a tournament there as we speak. These jaunts across the border to harry us are costly. You hope to win a purse or two." He recalled his conversation from weeks earlier with Ric while he was at Dunbeath. He'd taken a leap in making his assertion, and from the knights' surprise, he guessed correctly.

"That they are. But do you know what pays better than a tourney purse?" Salisbury waited, but neither Michail nor Blythe showed any interest. "A ransom."

Blythe wished to spit at the man and slap him like she'd seen Catherine MacFarlane do to Agnes Buchanan.

A shame the bitch shares a name with my mother, but how satisfying that was to watch.

She kept her hands loose around the reins instead. She didn't doubt her parents would pay a ransom for her, but she was unconvinced they would do so for Michail. She wasn't sure he would live long enough for Salisbury to demand one.

"We've wasted enough time here," Salisbury announced. "Kill the guards and bind the couple." He lifted his hand to shoulder height, only two fingers straightened, and waved nonchalantly before maneuvering his horse away from Blythe, Michail, and their guards. It tempted Blythe to fight when a man approached with rope in his hands. She turned panicked eyes to Michail, who gave a barely noticeable shake of his head. He didn't fight the man who took his sword, then bound his hands. When the man walked away, and the one binding Blythe's wrists bowed his head in concentration, Michail moved his foot in his stirrup. Blythe realized he reminded her he had a dirk in each boot and several others stashed on him that only she had seen.

"If you do away with our guards, you'll have less to ransom." Michail shrugged a shoulder when William turned back to him. "I suppose I should tell you I'm Michail MacLeod, tánaiste to Clan MacLeod of Assynt." When Salisbury appeared confused, Michail rolled his eyes. "For the time you've spent here, you would think you'd learn something of our ways. My father is our branch's chieftain. I'm his heir."

"Assynt? Does that make you related to the MacLeods of Lewis or Skye?"

"We all come from the same line."

"Are you the ones with the Fairy Flag? Will you call upon the wee fae to protect you?" Salisbury infused a poor imitation of a Highland accent when he mentioned "the wee fae."

"I don't need the flag to summon Titania, queen of the '*Ben-shi*.' She is a guardian to my people. She and her legion of fae are not to be underestimated." Michail spoke with no hint of jest, but he offered a condescending expression to those who listened. With his left brow raised and his lips pursed, he shrugged as if daring the English to learn whether he could bring forth the mythical goddess. He watched the men behind Salisbury, noticing which seemed susceptible to superstition.

Salisbury said nothing more, but neither did any of his men move to kill the remaining Dunbar and MacLeod guards. Instead, they circled the mix of Highlanders and Lowlanders, before the English and Scottish riders retraced their steps, then headed south.

CHAPTER 15

After two days with their captors, the remaining MacLeods and Dunbars reached the Firth of Solway. The Scottish and English party rode mostly in silence. It surprised Blythe and Michail that William allowed them to sleep beside one another. The chill night air caused Blythe to shiver, even with Michail's warmth wrapped around him. They deduced Salisbury realized the danger that Blythe might freeze or fall ill if he didn't grant her the extra warmth. No ransom would be paid if there was no woman held captive.

It shocked Blythe to see boats waiting for them within the firth as they dismounted. It came to her how the Earl of Salisbury could travel so far undetected. Rather than going overland and passing through Douglas, Cunningham, and MacLellan territories to reach the Dunbars, Salisbury sailed and brought himself practically to her clan's back door. The only advantage Blythe saw was that it would save them another three or four days of hard riding. They could sail across the waterway and ride for a day to Carlisle.

"This is how he reached Barsalloch Point with no one noticing. But my question is, how did he know we were traveling? Was it merely luck? Or did somebody see us and tell him?"

"Ma bet would be a mixture of both." Michail maintained his courtly accent any time the English could hear. But he slipped back into his burr when Blythe and he whispered together. "He discovered by chance that we were traveling, and that chance was likely a Hannay patrol informing him. We never saw them, but that doesnae mean they didna see us. I'm certain they are still in bed with the English, despite how long the Bruce has now been on the throne."

"I'm scared, Michail. If we cross the border and wind up in England, how will we get back? I don't believe he'll send a ransom request to my father. Instead, I fear he'll kill us both and then brag of it to my father. Your clan is too far to reach us in time to do aught. Are we sailing to our death?"

"It pains me to agree. But ye have stated the obvious that we both may need to accept. But ye must also ken I will fight to ma vera last breath to get ye away from this madmon. There is naught I wouldnae do to protect ye, Blythe."

"Just don't go getting yourself killed if you can prevent it. I would rather go to the Lord's Heavenly Kingdom together than you leave me behind."

"Blythe, dinna say that. Ye're young. Ye have an entire life ahead of ye."

"Do you believe I would replace you so easily? Do you believe I would create a life and a family with someone else?"

"Ye werenae wrong before. It would be time to move on if I'm nay longer yer husband."

"If you keep spewing such rubbish, I will be the one to put you in an early grave. I do not want to hear you giving me permission to share my life and share my bed with another mon even if I were left a widow."

"That's hardly what I want, but, Blythe, there's the chance that ye could already carry our bairn. What then? Yer life canna end when we have a future, even though I might nae be there for it. Ye will always be welcome at Ardvreck, regardless of whether ye bear us a child. But it's unlikely yer father or the king would allow ye to remain without remarrying. The choice may nae be yers."

"This is not what I want to be thinking aboot right now, Michail. I don't care if what you say is true. It's only upsetting me, and I refuse to allow that mon to see me cry."

Rope still bound their hands, even though they had control of their own horses. With no way to wrap his arm around his wife, Michail leaned against her side and twisted to find her hand. Blythe tilted her head and rested it on his shoulder. It was the small touches they shared that offered them the comfort they missed. It hadn't been easy to sleep with their wrists encircled with the coarse fibers, but at least they had slept together. Blythe pressed against Michail's chest as he hunched his shoulders around her.

"Once we reach Carlisle, we need to be prepared for Salisbury to separate us." Michail brought them back to what they really needed to discuss. "He may give ye a chamber abovestairs, but I will find ma accommodations in a dungeon just like he promised. Nay matter what happens to me down there, I need ye to remain alert. Remember what ye see, what you hear, what happens around ye. It may be yer only chance to escape. It's all information yer father will need to get me out or information ma father needs to secure ma release."

"If I could get free, it would still take at least another fortnight for a missive to reach your father. Do you believe Salisbury would keep you alive that long?"

"I believe he's a greedy mon who wants to prove his

superiority over the Scots. If there's a chance that he can goad ma father into a battle or strip him of his coin, then he will. But the only way to do that is to keep me alive. If word reaches ma father that I'm dead, there is naught for Salisbury to gain."

"Wouldn't your father fight him if he killed you?"

"There would be nay fight. Salisbury would merely never take another breath. Ma father would have him killed with nay battle needed. Blythe, that's what I was doing at Dunbeath. Tristan was training me with skills his father gained as a mercenary in France. All the men who were with me at Dunbeath and trained alongside me also accompanied me to court. But I dinna doubt ma father could call upon Tristan and the Mackays. If ma father couldnae kill Salisbury with his bare hands, then he kens who to send to do it on the sly."

"It's small comfort to me to know your father might send mercenaries to avenge your death. But at least I know Salisbury will not survive this battle. Be it one of wills or on a field."

"Just promise me that if the chance comes to escape, ye'll take it. Dinna wait for me. If ye do, then neither of us may have another chance."

"I don't love that you're right. But I can't ignore what you said before. I might carry our child, so I must remember that if I am, it's no longer just aboot me and just aboot what I want, or even just aboot you. But know that if I get free, I will do everything under the sun short of raising the devil himself to get you out of there."

"If Salisbury does aught to hurt ye, he will discover the devil is already within his home. I will bide ma time as I need to, so I do naught to endanger ye. Bly, I willna accept going into that dungeon of ma free will, even if I dinna put up a fight. It may nae be the right time, but when it is, I understand that might mean using ma mind rather than ma brawn. The winner is usually nae merely the strongest, but the smartest."

Men pushing them onto the boat and steering them toward the stern cut their conversation short. The Englishmen shoved them to the deck, forcing them to sit cramped together. But it allowed them to continue whispering. It surprised them that they'd shared such a long conversation near the dock, but Salisbury had been busy arranging for their trip. His soldiers were disinterested in the Scots. They merely turned their nose up at their enemy and walked away.

"What is the first thing you wish to eat once we reach my parents' home?"

Michail chuckled at Blythe's unexpected question, taking note that she no longer considered Druchtag Motte her home. He realized they had reached the end of their previous conversation. There was nothing left to say until they gained more information, or they knew what Salisbury would do next. "I think I would like a pot of honey." Michail waggled his eyebrows. "Something I havenae tasted in years."

"I know how you savor the sweet taste of honey. I will be sure there is plenty for you."

"What would ma bonnie bride like as her first meal?"

"I believe I crave some meat and taters."

They both struggled to keep their laughter quiet, not wanting to draw more attention, but their jests lightened their mood and eased some of their fears. There was no way to ignore the danger in which they found themselves. But the moment of lightheartedness allowed them to regain some of their courage as they faced this uncertain future together. Once more twisting, Michail found Blythe's hands, and they held them despite the awkward angle. The silent reassurance they offered one another was proof of the deep connection they had created so many years before. The connection they both feared they'd severed by misunderstanding and miscommunication. Instead, it grew with each moment they relied upon one another, trusting that their partner loved them and would do any and everything to protect them and fight for their future.

As the ship got underway and bobbed across the water, Blythe found her eyes growing scratchy and her eyelids were heavy, but she fought the urge to shut them. Finding it surprisingly comfortable leaning against Michail, she wanted nothing more than to catch a couple hours' sleep, but she refused to lower her guard despite her strong and silent husband's presence. She knew he wouldn't accept the chance to rest, knowing he had to protect Blythe. She rejected the luxury of taking a nap while someone else had to remain alert. She would do her part, just as her husband did. She realized she might not put up the same fight as he, and she didn't have the weapons she knew Michail still possessed, but she could be alert, and she had tenacity. She believed those two things alone were worth remaining awake to use.

"I ken ye're tired. Why nae shut yer eyes for a few moments and just rest? I ken ye refuse to fall asleep, but that doesnae mean yer body couldnae do with a reprieve. I'm here beside ye. Let ma shoulders lift the weight. Ye're nae used to this type of physical strain. Ye havenae been in battle before, and ye're nae accustomed to remaining awake for such long lengths after such physical exertion. If ye dinna rest, ye'll exhaust yerself and make yerself ill. That's the last thing either of us need. So please do as I say, just this once." Michail offered her a charming grin.

She could admit the soundness of Michail's suggestion and explanation. The last thing she wanted to do was to become a burden to her husband and the few guards who remained with them. She was tired, and she could feel her body weakening. While she hoped she didn't fall asleep, she would resign herself to Michail's request that she rest. She lowered her eyelids and released a deep sigh as she nestled closer to her husband.

Michail lifted his arms awkwardly but wrapped them over Blythe's shoulders, pressing her against his broad chest. Blythe released another sigh. But this one was from contentedness, not exhaustion. She inhaled Michail's scent. Despite the sweat and grime they both carried, there was still a lingering rose scent to his skin. It made her smile. She recalled bathing with him and saying that she intended to make every woman know her husband was taken.

Michail's long arms allowed his hand to rest on her hip. She found the slight gesture both protective and possessive, as well as endearing. She didn't mind in the least in that moment because that was what she needed. She never sensed Michail would be the type to keep her from doing what she wanted or being friends with whom she wanted. Just the opposite. So the small moment of possessiveness warmed her heart and showed how much he valued having her at his side.

Michail felt Blythe's body relax against him. Some of the tension eased from between her shoulders as her head became heavier against his chest. It was his turn to exhale a sigh of relief. He'd seen the shadows forming under his wife's eyes and could see the strain across her forehead. She had held up better than he could have ever hoped, but he knew the exertion was taking its toll on her. He was fatigued, and he was used to battle. Fights that stretched day after day. If he was aware of his exhaustion, he could only imagine how

Blythe suffered. She'd done nothing to complain, not even show a moment's discomfort. Pride swelled within his chest. But it didn't relieve his concern. It would be a disaster if she became an invalid and even more at Salisbury's mercy.

As both relaxed their bodies, if not their minds, he tilted his head and rested it on her crown, liking that the difference in height while seated wasn't so significant that he couldn't sit comfortably. He lowered his eyelids but did not close them. He focused on those closest to him, noticing the differences in how the men stood. These postures told him how aware the men were of what went on around them. He could identify those still alert and those who were complacent, believing nothing would go wrong now that they were aboard their boats and sailing back to England. If ever the chance came to get free, he would focus on the latter first. He shifted his attention to those farther away and already seated on the deck. Many reclined with their eyes shut, like how he appeared. There were still too many Englishmen for his men and him to put up a fight. But he learned much about Salisbury's men's dynamic among themselves by merely watching who lay in repose and who remained on the *qui vive*, or vigilant. After he assessed each of the Englishmen, he slid his lowered gaze toward his own men and Blythe's. He was certain they were doing the same thing. While each man seemed calm and resting, Michail sensed they were still as attentive to their surroundings as was he.

It saddened him to know that, one way or another, he would return home with fewer men than when he rode out. Durham and he had been friends since childhood, even though the guard had been slightly older than Michail. He trusted Durham with his life, and in turn, with Blythe's. Michail dreaded going home to tell the dead warrior's wife and parents that he would not return. He dreaded riding through Ardvreck's gates and having to pass that message along to several more families. It was the uncertain future every warrior and his family accepted, but it never made it any easier to be the bearer of bad news.

He considered how Harry's death must hurt Blythe. While she had never fought in battle alongside the man, he knew they were close. He recalled Harry had been with Blythe since she arrived at court. He wondered if he could ask her about that without causing her too much pain. Their relationship seemed familiar, but respectful, as though he were an uncle despite their disparate social stations.

Allowing his mind to wander once he felt Blythe's deep breathing, enabled him to relax and gain the rest he advocated she find. It also passed the time. It surprised him when the boat bumped against the dock in Silloth. He shook Blythe awake and helped her to her feet. Blinking her still-tired eyes, she looked at the dock as Michail surveyed their new surroundings. Neither of them knew what to expect. They still had a day's ride ahead of them to Carlisle.

Michail wondered if anywhere along the way there might be a chance to make their getaway. He needed the opportunity to speak to their guards and formulate a plan with them. If only the Dunbar guards spoke Gaelic as well. He was certain none of Salisbury's men, or even the earl himself, would speak the language of the Highlands. He could speak to Blythe's men in Scots, but he feared Salisbury had spent enough time across the border to understand that language. French was out of the question, since the earl would most assuredly speak that, and he doubted any of Blythe's guards would know the foreign language. He was aware his men didn't understand it either.

"Stay as close to me as ye can, *mo chridhe*. If they pull

us apart, I will make ma way back to yer side. Just remember I still have dirks on me. If we can separate ourselves from them, then I can slice our bindings. It's time for us to do as Salisbury says, without protest. He'll wonder why we're suddenly being so complacent, but if we can lure him into lowering his guard, then we may learn something for him. Or we may find our opportunity. But either way, the time for antagonizing the mon is over."

"I agree. I think since we're so much closer to his home now, he'll take his frustration out on either of us without the fear of us getting away or that it would be difficult to travel with either of us incapacitated. Now that we are in England, there is naught that can be done quickly to avenge us. He'll count on that. What we need to focus on is staying alive and staying together."

"I need to speak to the men. I was just thinking aboot how much easier it would be if yer men spoke Gaelic as well, but I will have to make the best of it. I may speak to ma men first without the Sassenachs understanding, then they can pass along ma message. The chances of them staying together are much stronger than me being with them or me being with ye. I also wonder what ideas they've devised. Mayhap one of them has come up with the solution."

"May we be that fortunate." Blythe turned toward Salisbury, who issued orders for them to disembark. Michail did what he could to steady her as they made their way down the plank to the dock. Michail positioned himself ahead of Blythe, and their guards soon created a wall from the rear. When they moved onto solid ground, Blythe observed the knights separate from the foot soldiers while everyone milled about. She watched as the knights stood near a cluster of bushes, and it gave her an idea.

"May I have a moment of privacy?" Blythe asked as they walked past Salisbury.

"You have one minute."

"That shall be rather difficult." Blythe held up her bound hands then shook out her skirts.

"I'm not untying you."

"Then you will have to accept I will be gone more than a minute." Blythe banked on Salisbury not releasing her. She needed her hands to remain tied to justify taking longer.

"Very well." Salisbury turned away, disinterested in Blythe and her needs. She moved to a group of trees away from the gathered knights. There were bushes in front of them that continued to where the knights stood. Michail followed her, his eyes narrowed, suspicious of Blythe's intentions. Neither of them had drunk anything but a few sips that morning. She offered him a reassuring smile that only made him more anxious.

"Dinna fash," Blythe murmured with her smile still in place. She tilted her head toward the armored men. "Keep an eye on them."

"Blythe—"

"One of us needs to hear what they're saying. There's no way for you to dawdle or go far enough into the trees to be out of sight."

"And ma clothes arenae likely to get caught in a bluidy bramble bush and give me away."

"Then I shall have to be careful."

"Bluidy hell," Michail grunted. "Now I ken how ma mother must feel when I pull foolish stunts."

"It'll only be foolish if I'm caught, and right now, we're wasting time I don't have. I'll be careful." Blythe slipped into the trees then gathered her skirts close to her and lifted them mid-calf. Michail's observation about the bramble bush was astute, and she didn't want the swishing fabric to alert the knights. She crept along the bushes, keeping her head well below their tops. On silent feet, she eased her way until she was behind the men. None investigated the trees, which made Blythe grin. Their arrogance was so great that they held no concern that someone might ambush them. Their bravado would serve her well.

"My forty days are over as of this morn," a middle-aged knight said as he lifted his visor. "But I'm stuck with this bastard because we're too far from home to just ride away."

"It's the same for all of us, Simon. Our days are over, and we should be enjoying ourselves at the tourney. You know he won't pay extra, and we're missing our chances to earn the prize purses." A young blond man with hair sticking out from beneath his helm made his armor clank as he put his hands on his hips. Blythe sucked her lips in to keep from laughing. He looked like a metallic scarecrow.

"We'll be back in Carlisle in a day. Cease your griping, Timothy." The chastisement seemed ironic since the middle-aged man began their conversation with his own complaints. From what Blythe could tell, the oldest man in the group was the one who she'd seen discussing something with Salisbury while they sailed. It made her curious to learn this man's connection to the earl, and why any of the men would dare complain in front of him if he had closer ties to their leader. The man shifted to look back at Salisbury, who drank deeply from a waterskin. "The last thing we need is for the fool to hear you. Bide your time. Once we're in Carlisle, there is little he can do to keep us together. He'll be within the keep, and you'll be garrisoned in the village. You can wench and joust all you want."

"But he expects us to give him the bulk of our winnings, Simon. I might wench the nights away, but I still have a wife and children to feed at home." Timothy's comments made Blythe's lip curl in disgust. He was hardly the first or only man Blythe knew who was unfaithful to his wife. That wasn't what annoyed her. There'd been strength in his objection to giving William any of his coin, but he hardly sounded committed to ensuring that money made it home. It was more likely he would spend it on whores and libations.

"I'm just done being soaked in this rusty bucket," a third man spoke up with his visor still lowered over his face. "How can the weather differ so much on those savages' side of the border from ours? We barely crossed into their shitehole, and it chucked it down. I want somewhere dry, where I can shed this bloody armor, and sleep in a bed. It was one thing when it was our days of service. But if I sleep in another downpour, I will leave. I have no family to care for. I will ride away and not look back. He will never find me."

"You're full of piss and vinegar, Will, but you haven't the bollocks to do a thing. Besides, you wouldn't survive on your own." Simon taunted the man whose visor remained closed. "You'd tuck tail and scamper back to your father. You like his keep too much, and you're too eager for his title to run away."

Blythe's eyes widened as she realized who stood before her. Salisbury's son and heir was part of the group. He would be an appealing hostage for them or for her father if he ever received word of their capture. She wondered if the lowered visor was to disguise his presence.

"And who has lived under my father's largesse for longer, *Uncle*?" Will taunted. Blythe couldn't believe her good fortune. If only they would say something about what would happen once they reached Carlisle. So far, all she knew was they wished to return to the tourney circuit, and both Salisbury's brother and son were on the journey.

"We shall live under John de Warenne's largesse when we arrive in Carlisle again. We'd all do well to give thanks Thomas of Lancaster isn't there. The feud between him and Lord Warden de Warenne was the last thing we needed to be amid." Simon turned the conversation away from the familial squabble. "Our lord plays a dicey game, remaining friends with the Lancasters while sleeping under de Warenne's roof. I should like to return home—with my head still attached to my neck. I'm not convinced my brother shares that wish."

In the secrecy of the bushes behind which she hid, Blythe cast the men a condescending look. William Montagu, the Earl of Salisbury, and Thomas of Lancaster had never been friends. Enemies to be more exact, but Salisbury had benefited from the friction between Lancaster and de Warenne since it distracted Lancaster from him.

The men continued to talk, but Blythe knew she had to return to Michail before he worried, and before her absence caught Salisbury's attention. She picked her way along the large shrubbery until she emerged from behind a tree, shaking out her skirts.

"If ever there were a time I wished I already spoke Gaelic, it would be now." Blythe spoke from the side of her mouth as she scanned the clearing for the earl.

"What did ye hear?" Michail shifted as though he blocked the sun from Blythe's eyes, but he obstructed anyone's view of her mouth. He didn't want anyone to guess what they discussed.

"That knight with his visor down is the earl's son and heir. His name must be William, too, since he goes by Will. The others were complaining aboot their forty days being over, but there's no sign of when they'll go home. The Lord Warden of the West Marches is in residence in Carlisle. The Earl of Salisbury and the Earl of

Lancaster were hardly close, but Lancaster was at odds with the Lord Warden. The men welcome Lancaster's absence. His death is convenient for them since it will keep the peace."

"I remember mentioning Thomas, Earl of Lancaster, to Ric. I confused him and William Montagu. I thought Lancaster was the one who attacked yer father. I didna ken he was dead, and William was made the Earl of Salisbury. I ken naught of the Lord Warden."

"Thomas of Lancaster became the Earl of Salisbury through marriage to Alice de Lacy. When her father died, he inherited the title. Once Thomas died, Longshanks made our captor, William Montagu, the new Earl of Salisbury. John de Warenne is the Earl of Surrey. Part of what makes this all so bluidy complicated is that they were all equal nobility. Thomas and John loathed one another because Longshanks favored John over his own cousin. John made it far worse when he did naught to his knight after the mon abducted Thomas's wife. When Longshanks turned on Thomas, John was among his accusers. John and William grew up as wards of the Crown, just like Ric. They must have known one another well."

"Mayhap that's why Ric thought we could slip over the border."

"What?" Blythe stilled, brewing anger simmered just beneath the surface. Michail knew he had a fine line to tread if he didn't want Blythe to erupt. He knew his thoughtless comment frightened her.

"Ric sensed there was growing tension along the border. Since I took to jousting easily and am good at it, he suggested I travel south with him and enter a tourney. I told him I had nay armor, and even if I did, I dinna ken how to put the bluidy pieces on. He suggested he would squire for me. Something aboot the situation kept him from worrying aboot people recognizing him as ma squire. I would wager it's de Warenne. Ric and the Lord Warden must be on fair terms if Ric doesnae fear rotting in Carlisle's dungeon."

"You didn't think to mention this plan?"

"*Mo chridhe*, there was nay plan. I didna consider it seriously, then news came of the Mackenzies' attack. I forgot aboot it in ma haste to travel to court. Once there, well," Michail gave a nonchalant shrug, "other things drew ma attention."

Blythe remained quiet but nodded. She didn't want to admit the idea of watching Michail in a jousting tournament excited a tiny part of her. But she didn't want him crossing the border to compete. She nearly rolled her eyes at herself as she recalled they'd already crossed the border. However, there was neither excitement nor a prize in the offering.

"I shall show ye one of these days just how I handle that lance." Michail's grin was infectious. Try as she might, given what Michail shared and where they were, she couldn't keep from returning his smile. They leaned in and shared a brief kiss.

"Bloody rabbits," Timothy, the blond knight, grumbled as he walked past.

"If only there were a chance for me to bed ma bonnie wife," Michail whispered beside Blythe's ear.

"I should like to learn how to wield that pole."

"How am I still surprised by the things ye say, lass?"

"I really don't know, husband. But at least I keep you amused."

"Hard as a bluidy poleax too."

"You keep me wet as—"

"Mount!" Salisbury bellowed.

Blythe smirked at Michail. "If only you knew."

"I'll ken the first chance I get to bury maself in ye. Dinna ye doubt that." Michail walked with Blythe to Midnight. With no freedom to move his hands apart, the best Michail could do was cup them and offer Blythe a boost into the saddle. Once she was settled, she watched in awe as Michail raised his foot to his stirrup and was seated in one fluid movement. The strength in one leg propelled him upward without him needing his hands.

"I often have a sword in one hand and ma targe in the other," Michail explained, guessing Blythe's shock. Blythe swept her eyes over Michail, her gaze heating as she thought about the strength she knew was hidden from everyone's eyes but hers. "*Mo chridhe*, ye make it bluidy uncomfortable to sit a horse when ye look at me like that."

"Why should I suffer alone?" Blythe tossed back as she nudged Midnight into a trot. When the Englishmen surrounded the Scots, she knew it wasn't to protect them so much as to secure their captivity.

CHAPTER 16

The final day and night of their journey to Carlisle passed with nothing of note happening. Blythe was unable to eavesdrop on any other conversations, and the men remained quiet whenever Michail accompanied them to the tree line to relieve himself. Since there appeared to be no benefit to Michail's refined speech, he opted to openly speak Gaelic with his men. None of the English objected, and those riding near them didn't strike him as well-tutored men. They wore the armor of a lowly knight, and he noticed their horses didn't have the superior breeding a true knight's mount would. He assumed these were men with enough money to afford the metal protection but not the training. He swept his eyes over their boots and spied no spurs. Once he realized the men around him didn't have the education to speak multiple languages, he switched to Scots. He repeated what he'd said to his men, so the Dunbars knew what Blythe learned. When he finished his story, he asked if any had suggestions.

"We heard complaints too," Stanley offered while Michail and Blythe listened. "The foot soldiers are hungry, and many fell ill during the storms. Apparently, as bad as it was for us, it was worse farther south. We were fortunate that the River Dee forced our detour. They lost a dozen men between a flood near their camp one night and the ague. Some of the remaining men lost fathers, brothers, and sons. Morale is low and discontent is high."

Michail glanced at Blythe, knowing she wondered if they could play the men's resentment to their favor. Michail doubted they could spur a mutiny, but they could make Salisbury's life difficult. He still accepted he would wind up in the dungeon, but he suspected Salisbury would insist some of his men stand guard in the cesspit, not trusting de Warenne's guards with him.

By early afternoon on the day following their sail across the Firth of Solway, the party arrived in Carlisle. It was Michail and Blythe's first time in England. To Blythe, it looked much like where she grew up, only on the wrong side of the border. For Michail, it was as though someone dropped him off in hell. He hadn't been eager to enter the Lowlands as a Highlander, but now he was an oddity at whom people stared and pointed. Once people looked past him and noticed his men, there was a buzz of whispers, and suspicion grew among the people they passed. He supposed he should keep his eyes forward, but instead, he returned people's stares. In Gaelic, he told his men to laugh as though they jested at the villagers' expense. The men's hearty and booming laughter had the desired affect: people fumbled and pushed to get away from the Highlanders.

"I thought we weren't going to antagonize anyone," Blythe muttered.

"We arenae going to antagonize Salisbury. Right now, I am ensuring nay one gets too close. If they come near me, then they come near ye. By riding at ma side, I'm making sure all of them, especially the men, ken ye are untouchable. There's nae a one among them so daft as to nae understand ye're with me, even if ye dinna have a ring on yer hand. If they're scared of me, then they'll be too scared to dare do aught to ye."

Blythe wouldn't argue with her husband's logic since it made sense to her, and she would accept nearly anything that kept her unharmed and away from the English. She surveyed the bailey as they entered Carlisle Castle. It was a bustling keep with various outbuildings teeming with people working. She spied the blacksmiths, the laundresses, and the fletcher with ease. She looked at the stables, impressed by their size. De Warenne either owned many horses or he expected many guests. She also guessed it meant he housed plenty of mounted knights. She turned toward the castle's steps where she spied a couple descending. She blinked several times before she realized who accompanied John de Warenne.

"It is true," Blythe hissed to Michail, who turned a confused mien to her. "That is not Joan of Bar, the king's own granddaughter! That's Matilda de Nerford, his mistress. I heard he doesn't live with his wife and is often in that woman's company. But the rumors must be true that he lives openly with his mistress."

Michail watched the scandalous couple approach. The woman appeared disinterested until she spied him and the other Highlanders. He recognized the interest in the woman's eyes, and Blythe must have too because Michail veritably felt Blythe bristle.

"Wheest. She willna visit any of us in the dungeon," Michail whispered.

"Who's that?" John de Warenne demanded, forcing the couple's attention back to the English. "Bloody hell! Which of Dunbar's daughters is that?" John pointed an accusatory finger at Blythe when she shook her arisaid from her head, and her hair tumbled loose.

"I'm Lady Blythe MacLeod, Laird Dunbar's

youngest daughter." Blythe refused to allow people to talk about her as though she wasn't there. She would retain her dignity and demand the respect that belonged to her title, if not her.

"MacLeod?" de Warenne questioned.

"Aye. I'm Michail MacLeod, tánaiste and auldest son of Laird Torrian MacLeod, chieftain of the MacLeods of Assynt.

"MacLeods of Assynt?" de Warenne muttered to himself before he exploded. "Salisbury, you bloody coxcomb! Do you know who you have?"

"Some filthy heathen." Salisbury responded offhandedly before turning back to his horse.

"No. Not some filthy heathen," de Warenne snarled. "This man is related to half the bloody Highlands." He marched forward and yanked on Salisbury's shoulder. "Dunbar will look like a yapping pup if you bring that lot down on us."

"They'll piss themselves before they step foot over the border."

De Warenne shook his head, and Blythe watched his fingers curl like claws in frustration. "How do you not know their alliances yet?"

"What do I care for them? One dead Scot is the same as the rest."

"Mayhap you recall that the Dunbars are allied with the Kennedys, who have close ties to the usurper. Laird Kennedy was also a mercenary before the wars. Do you know who's his godson?"

"Of course not."

"Laird Tristan Mackay. His father was a mercenary alongside Innes Kennedy. Do you know who Tristan Mackay is married to? Liam Sinclair's daughter. The bloody Earl of Sinclair. Do you know who's Sinclair's daughter-by-marriage? Lady Siùsan Mackenzie. His," de Warenne jutted a finger at Michail, "cousin and

Laird Ulrich Mackenzie's daughter. Do you know who else the man is related to? Laird Kieran MacLeod of Lewis. The man who is married to Maude Sutherland, the Sinclair's bloody niece. Do you know whose godchildren all the ruddy Sinclair and Sutherland siblings are? Robert the fucking Bruce."

By the time de Warenne finished rattling off Michail's family tree, his face was scarlet, and spittle collected at the side his mouth. It periodically spewed as he punctuated some words with extra venom. It most shocked Michail that the English noble knew the well-guarded secret that the Sinclair and Sutherland siblings were the Scottish royal couple's godchildren. Most people in Scotland didn't even know that.

"If you bring the Highlands down on me, I will string you up and roast you like a Christmas goose. The MacLeods, Sinclairs, and Sutherlands are also tied to the Camerons, the MacKinnons, and the Frasers, not to mention their links to the Kerrs and Johnstones. Yes. The border reivers who already harass us. You foolish, foolish man."

"While that's an interesting study in genealogy, that doesn't change that not a one of them will step foot across the border."

De Warenne spun away before turning back to Salisbury. "Did you miss the part about Kennedy and the old Mackay being mercenaries? They'll have men across the border before you realize you died in your sleep!"

De Warenne turned back to Matilda and grasped her hand and practically dragged her up the steps in his haste and anger. When he reached the stoop, he turned back.

"Get them out. They will not stay within the walls. I want naught to do with this death wish."

"De Warenne, cease your prattle. I need only a cell

in your dungeon where he can rot and be forgotten. No one will remember he's there by morning. I'll take her to an inn until her ransom comes. A bed there is as good as a bed here for what I intend."

De Warenne flew back down the stairs, drawing his sword along the way. A cacophony of sliding metal sounded as English knights from both sides unsheathed their weapons. Blythe and Michail looked at one another, unprepared for the impending bloodbath.

"Now I understand how that woman bested you. You truly are a simpleton. If you hold no wariness for aught I've said, remember who Lady Blythe's mother is. I will not have Black Agnes showing up on my doorstep. God help us if she laid siege to us."

Blythe dropped her chin and turned her head away to keep her laughter from the arguing men's ears. If only her mother could hear the fear she struck in de Warenne's heart. She looked sideways and noticed Salisbury merely stood staring at de Warenne. He had no rebuttal. Blythe figured there was none to be had. No one on either side of the Marches was unaware of Salisbury's failed standoff. Blythe remained quiet, letting de Warenne make her arguments for her.

"You had twenty thousand men at one point. You cost the Crown six thousand pounds. And one woman —one Scots woman—defeated you. What was it she said when she so nearly snared you in her net? When you were so daft as to consider supping with her? 'Farewell, Montagu. I intended that you should have supped with us and assisted us in defending the castle against the English.' You were nearly her captive."

"And now I have the bitch's daughter."

"You learned naught. This will not make you even. It will make you." De Warenne pointed at Salisbury before sweeping his finger in a broad gesture to encompass everyone within the keep's barmekin. "And the rest of us dead. I can't get my wife to bear me one bleating brat. But I have my children here, bastards they may all be, and I'm not losing the closest thing to an heir I have. Take MacLeod with you and leave. Lady Blythe remains. She is a guest of Lady Matilda's until such time as a ransom arrives."

"My husband stays and Salisbury leaves."

All eyes turned toward Blythe, who swept her leg over her saddle before sliding off. She prayed she landed on her feet and her knees didn't give out. She would have a difficult time sounding authoritative sprawled on the ground with her skirts around her ears. She breathed easier when she dismounted without trouble. She walked around Midnight to stand beside Michail, who'd dismounted from Cunnart while de Warenne bellowed at Salisbury.

"You'd do well to fear my mother *and* my father. She is a woman with a long memory. He is a mon with a short temper. Between the two, there is rarely much forgiveness to be had for anyone who dares threaten our family. You rattled off my husband's family tree quite easily. You're clearly aware of the clan alliances, and I dare say you're aware of how the Highlanders fight. You're more likely to come out of this alive if not a red hair on my husband's head is tousled. You will send a ransom for me. Do you know how I'm sure? Because you need the coin."

Blythe took another step forward, remaining out of reach of either English earl. She cast an assessing gaze over de Warenne, making her disappointment obvious before she cast Salisbury a scathing glare.

"Once my parents learn I'm here, they will learn Michail MacLeod is too. They will send a message to his family, and at every keep along the way, their messenger will inform that laird of what's happened. By the time my father-by-marriage hears of this, most of Scotland will have descended on you. Laird MacLeod will be lucky is there's even a scrap left of any of you. Never mind that I've just come from serving Queen Elizabeth de Burgh for nearly a decade. She will not be silent aboot this, which means you can expect King Robert to send his own men. Do you plan to be the cause of the next war?"

Everyone who could hear Blythe stood in stunned silence. She'd kept her voice even and matter of fact. Had she screeched or screamed, she would have been written off as a hysterical woman. But her coolness and articulate warning struck fear in all around her. She glanced at Salisbury and realized he second-guessed his decision. She thought she'd gained the advantage until he shook his head.

"Very well. We take leave and ride for West Country," Salisbury snapped.

"You'll get naught for your troubles," Blythe warned. "The time it takes to travel that far south is time wasted. What Scots messenger is going to chase down the length of England?"

Salisbury's scowl struck Blythe as that of a petulant child. His frustration reminded her of earlier when she'd thought he looked like a toy carved knight. If only she could snap him in half like she could a figurine. "You and your barbarian may spend the night here. We depart in the morn. No one but me shall know where we go." He didn't wait for any response, storming past de Warenne and not sparing a glance at Blythe or Michail. His men trailed after him in confused silence as they all passed beneath the portcullis on their way to the village.

Blythe and Michail stared at one another, neither certain what their status was. Or rather to whom they were a prisoner. They turned together to look at de Warenne, who once more stood beside Matilda. The woman glared at Blythe but turned a predatory smile on Michail. He caught himself before he hid behind his wife.

"Fear not, *mo ghràidh*. You know you're not the only one carrying a dirk. If she threatens you, I will tear her apart." Blythe winked at Michail, who found her attempt at the Gaelic term of endearment touching. He grasped the rope between her wrists and tugged her forward. His mouth descended to hers, and she opened for him. Their kiss was hardly subtle, and the passion was real. Relieved they'd survived their journey thus far, they cared not who watched. When they pulled apart, Blythe whispered against his lips. "I know that was as much for us as it was to prove a point to them. I don't think anyone is in doubt of how we feel. They'd do well to remember we're a love match. Neither of us will accept aught happening to the other."

"*Mo chridhe*, I ken ma honor is safe with ye as ma protector. Now to get us in the same bed." Michail returned her wink before they both faced de Warenne and Matilda once more. The disgust on the English couple's face made Michail and Blythe smirk. "At least she'll leave me alone."

"And I may not have to kill her."

"Enough," de Warenne huffed. "You can't stand there all day and into the night. Come inside. You are under house arrest. You will go to your chamber and remain there."

Blythe and Michail glanced at one another, both registering the word chamber in the singular. Once inside the keep, three de Warenne guards followed the couple up the stairs as a maid led the way. Once inside, a guard cut their bindings before they were locked within.

"At least we're still together, *mo chridhe*."

"Do you think we might be lucky enough to have a bath sent to us?"

"They've locked us in, but I'm certain there's a guard on the other side. Knock and ask, even if ye speak through the door." Michail followed Blythe to the door. He offered to knock for her, so he pounded loudly.

"What?" A voice called from the passageway, but no sound came from a lock turning.

"Please ask Lady Matilda if I can bathe," Blythe called. No response came, so they turned away. They moved to the window embrasure and peered outside. The chamber's height afforded them the opportunity to see the outlying village.

"There is a tourney." Michail pointed to several tents pitched just beyond the edge of the village. They couldn't make out people, but the jousting field was easy to spot. "There are the quintains near the list field's entrance. Since there is nay one out there on foot, I can only assume they have mounted melees. I can see the tilt." Michail pointed to the barrier that would keep the jousters to their own side.

"Are they all the same?"

"Nay. There's more than one type, and there's at least three competitors in two types. Elimination melees are weeding out the competition. Mayhap how many blows each jouster takes, or how they protect their crest, or a jouster bows out. Crest melees are like they sound. The jousters attempt to break or knock off their opponent's crest. A mounted duel is only two men. The duel is what Ric trained me to ride. The Sinclair men can joust since Ric's taught them too, but they dinna care for all the rules to a mounted melee. They see it as pointless after so many years of fighting in battles that are true melees."

"But you like it?"

"I like the single combat. But I also havenae worn all

the armor a knight wears. I've only donned ma leine, ma plaid, and Ric's auld hauberk. I dinna ken how I would do with all the extra weight. I dinna ken how Cunnart would do with the extra weight and his own armor. He took to jousting too, so mayhap he would be fine. He's a competitor at heart."

"Aye. The daft animal is as wild as you." Blythe offered a mockingly superior mien, including rolling her eyes and a quick shake of her head.

The lock jangling made them turn as a guard pushed open the door. A maid entered followed by half a dozen male servants carrying the tub and water. The maid was quick to place the linen lining before the men dumped the buckets. The maid stacked other linens and a bar of soap on a table. A guard arrived with Michail's and Blythe's saddlebags, which he dropped just beyond the threshold. Within minutes, the couple was alone once more. They undressed in haste, glad to shed their filthy clothes. Unlike the tub at the inn, this was just large enough for Michail to settle in before Blythe sat upon his lap with her back pressed against his chest. Their sighs mingled as they welcomed the hot water easing their sore muscles. They soaked in silence for five minutes.

"What happens next?"

"We make the most of having a clean and warm chamber. We bathe, I get ma honey, and we sleep."

"Your honey," Blythe giggled. "I wonder if your meat and taters will be the only meal I receive."

"I intend to make the most of our privacy, which we havenae had much of. I also want us to get as much sleep as we can. We dinna ken what they'll do to us, but we canna do much if we're too exhausted."

They scrubbed one another until they both felt refreshed. Just as Blythe did at the inn, she laundered their clothes. Michail pulled the grate back from the blaze he stoked before draping their garments over it. Blythe pulled her clean chemise from her bag while Michail withdrew a fresh leine. They'd barely covered themselves when the door opened once more. It surprised them both to find Lady Matilda standing inside the doorway. Her eyes skimmed over Blythe then feasted on Michail. He shifted behind Blythe, wrapping his arms around her waist. He felt her laughter rather than heard it. She covered his hands with hers.

"Delightful," Matilda scoffed. "You will join us for the evening meal. Proper garments will be brought to you. You will not appear upon the dais in that ridiculous blanket."

Blythe notched up her chin in indignation on her husband's behalf. "Disappointed that my husband's *breacan feile* doesn't shows as much as breeks?"

Matilda turned her nose up, but she didn't deny Blythe's accusation. Blythe would appreciate the tight pants on her husband as much as any other woman. However, she would miss the access his plaid offered her, and she resented sharing the arousing view. Yet she wouldn't deny she welcomed clothing that was neither dirty nor wrinkled.

"Thank you for your hospitality," Michail stated before tightening his arms around Blythe and kissing her behind the ear. He shifted his gaze to Matilda without moving. "Be sure the maid or guard knocks first." He spun Blythe around and kissed her, effectively dismissing their hostess. Blythe gladly leaned into the kiss, and both barely noticed the door slamming behind Matilda.

Once they were alone, they whipped off their clothing and flung them to the floor. Michail scooped Blythe into his arms and carried her to the bed. She quickly leaned and yanked down the covers before he lowered her to the mattress. He followed, bearing most of his weight on his forearms as he hovered above her.

"I am bluidy grateful we're alive and that you aren't in the dungeon."

"I feel the same. I want to hold ye and never let go. As appreciative as I am, I keep waiting for this to be ripped from us. I want to savor each moment with ye. I want to make up for the time we could have spent together."

"So do I. The past is the past, but I still wish to spend all my time with you. I feel starved for it. We've barely been alone since you arrived in Stirling. Our hurried moments together and these hours spent in fear are hardly how I envisioned the beginning of our marriage. But regardless of the danger, any time spent with you is what I crave."

"We have hours before the meal is served. I meant what I said before. I wish to make love to ye, wife. Then we should sleep." Michail shifted, sliding down the bed. Blythe widened her legs, making room for his broad shoulders to settle between her thighs. The first sweep of his tongue against her petals sent a shiver coursing through Blythe's body. She clutched the bedding when Michail's tongue swirled around her pearl. She lifted her head and shoulders from the mattress to watch her husband.

Michail's eyes were closed as he relished his first taste. It had been three years since he'd touched Blythe like this, touched any woman like this. The heady scent, a mixture of fresh soap and musk, filled his nostrils as he grazed his teeth over her sensitive skin. He peeled back the folds until he could see what he sought. His tongue delved into her entrance as his thumb rubbed slow circles over the bundle of nerves that made Blythe writhe. When he eased two fingers into her sheath, she lifted her hips off the bed and rocked them in time to his thrusts, knowing how it would feel when he replaced his digits with his cock.

Michail felt Blythe shift positions. He opened his eyes in time to watch her press her breasts together, kneading them as she tilted her head back. His free hand reached up and plucked one of her nipples. Her moan made his rod throb. He ached to be inside her, both for the physical release and to join them as one. He had never sought the emotional connection with his bed partners before he met Blythe. Once they'd made love the first time, he knew he wouldn't find it again with any other woman. It was one of the strongest reasons why he had no interest in being with someone else. He knew it would only remind him of what he'd believed he'd squandered.

"My love." It was the first endearment Blythe could remember using other than a couple of attempts at "my darling" in Gaelic. She used a few when they first began their courtship, but it had pained her too much to think of doing it again at the beginning of their reunion. Now she chided herself for waiting so long. It felt as natural as the next breath she drew. And it certainly wasn't as boring as only using his given name. "No more teasing. I need you."

Michail pushed himself up, kissing a trail along her belly. He swirled his tongue in her navel before encircling each of her nipples, first with the tip of his tongue then his entire mouth. He suckled as he aligned his sword with her sheath. His mouth met hers in a ravenous kiss as he thrust his manhood into her. Their passion erupted with a carnality that made their coupling primal. They clawed at one another, as though it were a feast after a famine, despite having coupled several times since their reunion. It was release from their fear and the unknown as well as a blending of their enduring love. Their physical desire for one another compounded their neediness as they each enjoyed the sight and the feel of their partner.

"The way ye feel. By God, there is naught like it. I want ye so much that I dinna think I will ever get enough."

"I expect you to keep trying," Blythe panted.

"Only the Lord can save anyone who tries to keep me from ye. I willna ever quit ye."

The telltale feeling built low in Blythe's belly, the sensation growing deep within her channel. With each slide of Michail's cock, each tilting of her hips, the collision of their bodies coming together, she surged toward her release. It consumed her, leaving her clawing at Michail's back. Blythe's muscles contracting around Michail's rod signaled his body to move faster. He pulled back, kneeling as he grasped her hips and lifted them from the bed. He pounded into her over and over, until Blythe screamed, "Yes!"

Michail's climax left him shuddering as his cock continued to pulse within Blythe, setting off another climax as his pubis rubbed against hers. She tugged on his shoulders until he relented and lowered his body to hers. She wrapped her arms and legs around him like a bear climbing a tree. They shared breathless kisses as Michail brushed hair from her damp temples and neck. She ran her hand over his reddish hair. When Michail's body no longer cooperated with either of their desires, he rolled onto his back. Blythe snuggled closer, her head resting on his shoulder as her hand covered his heart. He laid his over hers and kissed her forehead. Once their bodies cooled, they pulled the sheet over them.

"I never wished this upon us. But I knew you were the only mon I could rely on to get me home. I would be terrified if I entrusted anyone else with my safety.

We haven't made it to my parents yet, but I feel safe with you."

"This is why I panicked when I thought ye would ride home with only six men. I didna wish this either, but I'm glad I'm here. I couldnae bear the idea of aught happening if ye werenae properly guarded. I ken I said I wished to return home, but that was duty speaking, nae what I wanted."

"I understand that now. It hurt deeply until you explained. I wish we'd embarked upon a trip to our home instead of having to travel south. I'm scared that if we escape here, we'll arrive at Druchtag Motte, and my father will already be dead. I speak as though he will wage a campaign against Salisbury, but for all we know, my cousin Alasdair could now be Laird Dunbar."

"From how Ric describes Alasdair, he's the sort to rally the entire Lowlands to protect his family."

"He would. I don't doubt that whoever leads my clan will send warriors once they learn what's befallen us. I'm just scared I've missed my chance to say goodbye to my father."

"I understand that. I ken the guilt ye feel for nae being there. But dinna let it consume ye as it did me. I could never get ma mind to accept that ma grandda didna blame me for nae being there. He never would have faulted me because I was doing ma duty when it happened. Ye were at court doing yers, and this is hardly what ye asked for. Dinna let that guilt make yer loved one into a ghost who haunts ye. Let their spirit be a guide and a comfort. I didna understand any of that until I nearly drank maself into a grave beside his."

Blythe nodded, squeezing her eyes shut against the tears that threatened. Michail's hand ran over her back, soothing her. "I know you're right. I just need you to hold me."

"I will, *mo chridhe*. We need to sleep, but before we

can, I must get one of ma dirks." Michail rolled from the bed and hurried to gather the dirk that had been strapped to his thigh. He shoved his boots, which each carried a knife, under his side of the bed. He tucked his sporran beneath his plaid, knowing he had two *sgian dubhs* inside. It amazed him that once the English had the Scots' swords, they didn't search any of them closer. He didn't know if any of the Lowlanders carried more than one knife, but he was aware each of his men carried as many as he. He pushed the dirk under his pillow before climbing back into bed beside Blythe. Michail gladly obliged Blythe's request to hold her while they slept. Once they were nestled closer, they both drifted off.

CHAPTER 17

*M*ichail and Blythe woke to a loud knocking. As they realized what disturbed them, they looked at each other with a chuckle. At least, Matilda passed along the message to whomever that they shouldn't barge in on the couple.

Michail pulled on his leine and padded to the door. He put his ear against the portal and could hear little on the other side. "Who?" he demanded.

A feminine voice filtered through the wood. "I brought clothes for you and my lady, my lord."

"You may enter." Michail spoke as though he were in control of whether they unlocked the door and whether anyone could pass through. His air of command remained, regardless of their situation. In the presence of his captors, be they a servant or a noble, he continued to use his refined speech. He would give them no reason to continue labeling his as a heathen. It put him on closer footing as a noble peer.

He stepped away and allowed the door to swing open as a young maid entered. She was the same one who'd helped prepare their bath. She brought a gown, fresh chemise, stockings, and slippers for Blythe. There was a tunic and breeks for Michail. When Blythe spied his clothes, she sighed, grateful the tunic would fall to mid-thigh on Michail, assuming the clothing fit. It would keep all his necessary bits covered and away from Matilda's eyes.

Hearing the lock turn, with nothing either of them could do, Blythe and Michail separated their clothes. She reminded herself it was better John de Warenne locked them in a chamber together than either or both being in the dungeon. They were quick to dress, Michail helping her with the laces. Once they were ready and Michail placed his boots on with his knives still in the hidden sheaths, and the dirk from beneath his pillow was tucked into his waistband, they were ready to go.

He rapped his knuckles on the door, signaling to the guards they were ready to join the meal belowstairs. They made their way with guards surrounding them until they reached the keep's Great Hall. As they entered, then strode past people on the way to the dais, silence fell among those who watched them. By the time they reached the high table, they'd created a wave of quiet. But once they climbed the stairs, everyone who saw them pass by was abuzz with gossip.

The couple took in their surroundings. Michail, in particular, paid attention to the number of guards, the number of entrances and exits, and where the passageways led from the Great Hall. He noticed the weapons on the wall and the weapons the de Warenne guards carried. Blythe noticed who sat at the dais. She could easily guess the level of nobility of those they dined alongside. Blythe recognized the couple to Matilda's right must have been of equal stature as they. The others seemed like lesser nobility, barons at best. Their clothes were clean and well-tailored, but they were hardly as ornate as the other two English couples'.

Blythe and Michail took their seats at the farther

end from de Warenne and Matilda. It suited them fine not to be too close to their hosts. It allowed them to continue to observe those around them. Michail nudged Blythe when he spied his men and hers. They sat at tables well below the salt, but none looked any worse than when they arrived. It made both Blythe and Michail wonder where de Warenne gave the men accommodations. Certainly, no one locked them in the dungeon. It was obvious since they appeared no filthier or battered, and they were present for the evening meal. Were they truly prisoners, they never would have left the doomed crypt.

Blythe and Michail watched as servants brought out trenchers. They waited as women placed food from the communal platters and bowls before the others. It reassured them they weren't being poisoned if they gave them the same food as those sitting around them. But they both knew to eat sparingly. They could only hypothesize they were safe. They couldn't guarantee it. After a priest blessed the food, they listened attentively to discussions about the tournament, which piqued their interest.

Michail briefly wondered if Ric and Isabella had traveled south. He wondered if, at that very moment, his brother- and sister-by-marriage were in attendance. But he realized were that the case, two things would have happened. He would have found them sitting at the table, and he was certain de Warenne would have announced their relatives at once.

Or there was a third possibility. They were in the dungeon. But de Warenne would have flaunted that if it were the case.

"Lady Blythe." De Warenne interrupted both of their silent musings. "You will accompany Lady Maud tomorrow."

Blythe realized she and Michail were likely the only

people who referred to the earl's mistress by her given name, Matilda. She turned toward de Warenne, then looked at Matilda. What reason did de Warenne or Matilda have for her to accompany the Englishwoman? Seeing the question in her eyes, he continued.

"You shall be one of the Ladies in the Court of Honor amongst those watching the tournament tomorrow."

It took Blythe aback. She was unprepared for the opportunity to leave the keep and to be instructed to mingle among a crowd. It seemed like the last thing de Warenne would want if he were holding them captive. Her hand brushed Michail's knee beneath the table, and his hand rested on her thigh. Neither was sure what to make of this pronouncement. De Warenne said nothing about where Michail would be during that time.

Michail studied de Warenne as he spoke to Blythe. His manner was calm and even but hardly rude. He was merely a man used to getting his way. As Michail shifted his gaze across those sitting at the table, no one seemed to think twice about Blythe joining the ladies. At the tournament, they would sit together in a cordoned off area, provided shade and proper chairs. It seemed rather fine treatment for someone who wasn't welcome. It also signaled de Warenne didn't intend to allow Salisbury to leave with the Scottish couple the next day.

When de Warenne said no more to Michail or Blythe and turned his attention to his second-in-command, who sat to his right, the couple exchanged a silent look. It was beyond bizarre to them, but they would not argue. Both realized it was an opportunity for Blythe to explore and observe what happened around her once she left the keep. It was an opportunity to learn more about their surroundings, including who was in the crowds and who attended the tournament. They both wondered what would happen to Michail while Blythe was away.

No one else attempted to draw them into conversation, so they kept their voices hushed and spoke in Scots. The English who heard them ignored them on purpose, as though it might insult Blythe and Michail. Neither cared since it gave them time to plan.

"As long as they dinna put me in the dungeon, then all will be fine. Who kens, there might even be an opportunity for me to explore abovestairs. If I can get into one of their chambers, I might learn something to hold against them or to bribe them with."

"They'll surely lock you into that chamber. How will you get out?"

Michail lowered his voice further. "I looked at the lock as the maid announced she was there with our clothes. I believe if I'm careful, I can use the tip of one of ma *sgian dubh* to unlock the door from within."

"What aboot the guards they will be post outside?"

"I'm nae certain there'll be any once they leave the keep for the tournament. I think they'll forget I'm even here."

"Would that, that be true. But what if it isn't? Are you prepared to fight against swords when you only have dirks?"

"It wouldnae be the first, and unfortunately is likely nae to be the last. If I am the one with surprise on ma side, then I stand a chance of succeeding in ma attack. If I can unlock the door quickly and make ma way into the passageway before they realize what's happening, then I should be able to strike and move away from our chamber with nay one noticing."

"And what happens when a maid stumbles upon dead guardsmen?"

Michail shrugged. "I will deal with that obstacle when I come to it."

"That is hardly reassuring, especially when I know that I'll be so far from the keep."

"Which is to our advantage. Nay one can blame ye for being part of ma escape, and it keeps ye out of harm's way. If there's a fight, I dinna want ye near it."

"I don't want to return to the keep to discover you're dead or locked in the oubliette." Blythe hissed her last word, fearful Michail would wind up in the isolation pit. "What if there is naught to find? You will risk your neck in vain."

"Even if there is naught in either of their chambers that is of use, I'll still have the chance to learn more aboot the keep. Kenning the lay of the land is an important battle strategy."

"When we get back to our chamber, we should explore the walls. There might be a latch to hidden tunnels."

"Do you think there are?"

"It's possible. There's been a fort or keep here since William II, William the Conqueror's son. You know Cumberland was part of Scotland then, but once the English seized it, they built this castle to keep us out of what the Sassenachs claim is their land. It wouldn't surprise me if they had ways to escape. The English back then had a healthy fear of us, even if they kept trying to steal our land. They remembered the Romans never made it much past Hadrian's Wall. There was a reason why: we don't share well with outsiders. I think there probably are tunnels, or least a secret way out of the keep and past the walls."

Blythe and Michail considered what Blythe shared, both envisioning potential scenarios if they found secret passageways within the walls.

"What will you do if you find a way out while I'm at the tournament?"

"Naught. I'm nae leaving here without ye. Once I

ken where the tunnels lead, if there even are any, then I will come back, and we will plan together."

"If there's a way out, do we dare try to use it at night? Or do we make an agreement to find one another if I'm taken to the tournament again?"

"We plan for both. If neither de Warenne nor Matilda say aught aboot ye accompanying Matilda to the tournament the day after tomorrow, then we make our escape tomorrow night. If it seems like they will take ye back again as part of the Court of Honor, then mayhap I'll slip out soon after they leave and get ye away from Matilda. We can escape into the crowd."

"What aboot Cunnart and Midnight? The men?"

"I suspect they garrisoned the men in the barracks. I dinna think de Warenne or Salisbury would allow them out in the village. They ken there's too much risk the men would flee. If I can get a message to them or make ma way out of the keep and into the bailey, then I can try to get all the men and our horses out. There will be enough animals moving around during the day because of the competition that nay one will notice the extra horses."

"What if we find tunnels tonight and find a way out? Do we go now?"

"Nay. I predict Salisbury expects that of us and will have men posted around the village and the keep's walls. I wouldnae risk it this eve. It's too soon after we arrived. They'll expect us to attempt an escape. They will watch us too closely. There may be time to explore, but it wouldnae surprise me if more than one guard pokes his nose in on us tonight."

"What happens if they check on us and we're not in the chamber tonight? Isn't that just as bad?" Blythe grinned before she released an unladylike snort. She quickly glanced at the other people at the table, grateful no one was paying attention to them. "What if you find the tunnels and explore while I remain in the chamber? I can jump on the bed and make plenty of noise. Everyone will think we're coupling."

Michail grinned. "I dinna love the idea of leaving ye alone in that chamber, but yer idea has merit. We can only plan so much. It will depend on what others do around us. At least we have ideas for various opportunities. We're one step ahead of when we came down here for the meal. They havenae really restricted us since they invited us to join them. De Warenne said we were under house arrest. Mayhap when they release us from our chamber and bring us to the Great Hall, we may move freely among the people. Mayhap when the music begins, we can move into the crowd and join the dancers. I can try to talk to the men with ma back to them and make it look like ye and I are talking. We just need to get close enough for them to hear me."

"This entire situation seems too odd. Salisbury brings us here, only to dump us and storm out. He said he would take us with him when he leaves in the morn. Yet de Warenne commanded me to go to the tourney. They gave us clothes and have us sitting with them at the high table. Not only aren't our men bound and locked away, they're freely sitting and eating among the keep's people as though they're as English as the people next to them. I don't understand any of this."

"I believe de Warenne genuinely fears what he said earlier. That the entire Highlands will descend upon them, so he's ingratiating himself to us. I suspect he hopes we'll nae name him as the culprit but as our rescuer."

"Lady Blythe, you will dance with me." De Warenne's command interrupted the couple's conversation. Blythe's fingers dug into Michail's thigh, just above his knee. She didn't want to go anywhere near the man without Michail beside her. "MacLeod, you may dance with Lady Maud."

Blythe felt Michail stiffen, but there was no way for him to hide behind her while they sat side-by-side. They rose from their seats and made their way to where people now stood waiting for the musicians. Men pushed the tables and benches against the far walls, opening a space wide enough for at least fifty couples. John walked up to Blythe and lifted his bent arm. She looked down at it, forcing a mask to drop into place lest she make her disdain obvious. She glanced over her shoulder as Michail mirrored de Warenne and offered his arm to Matilda. He was not so subtle in his disinterest. He led their host's mistress into the crowd and positioned them beside de Warenne and Blythe. When the music began, they followed in de Warenne and Blythe's footsteps. It was obvious neither de Warenne nor Matilda was pleased, and it dawned on both Michail and Blythe that their host and hostess intended to separate them, likely for interrogation or seduction. They just discovered why the noble couple invited them to dine among the other nobles.

"Lady Blythe, have you attended a tournament before?" John asked, his tone supercilious. They both knew the answer already.

"I have not been to England before, my lord."

"Do you not have such entertainments on your side of the border?"

"Why would we play fight when we win battles?" Blythe's saccharine voice belied the edge to her question. De Warenne clenched his jaw, and Blythe wondered if he would cease taunting her or if he was reevaluating his stratagem. As they moved into a turn, she spied Michail and Matilda. Michail watched Blythe, but neither Matilda nor he spoke. It was clear Matilda was not enjoying their time together. Michail's icy demeanor froze Matilda's earlier ardor. Blythe caught Michail in a piercing gaze, praying he would understand her silent message that he needed to make the most of this time.

"Have there been any winners yet?" Blythe wondered.

"There have. This tournament runs for a fortnight. Our most elite knights compete this week."

"Are they crest or elimination melees?" Blythe's question surprised de Warenne, leaving him staring for a moment.

"The elimination melees took place last week. That is how we now know who the elite are among the masses. There were crest melees yesterday and today. Tomorrow we will enjoy the duels."

"Do you have a favorite?"

"Sir Richard Fitzalan." De Warenne pointed to a young man with deep brown hair, who leaned against a wall with a pint of ale in his hand. Something a man near him said made Richard laugh. Even from a distance, Blythe could see the man who'd appeared attractive only moments ago had missing and cracked teeth. It made Blythe want to ask if the man forgot to wear a helm.

"His tunic tells me he is one of your men." Blythe recognized the heraldry on the man's clothing from the banner that hung above the fireplace.

"He is my nephew, and at this time, my heir."

Blythe kept her expression studiously blank, not knowing what to say. It was well known on both sides of the border that he and his wife couldn't stand one another and that he'd petitioned more than once to divorce her so he could marry Matilda. He and his wife, Joan, got along so poorly that they weren't in the same room often enough for her to conceive a child. But he already had a passel of children with Matilda. She was certain the oldest son and oldest daughter sat with them upon the dais, which meant John's illegitimate son was neither heir nor his father's favorite. Blythe tucked that realization away, just as she had the fact that Salisbury traveled with his son and brother.

When the set ended, Blythe pulled away from de Warenne before he could trap her into another dance. Michail did the same, allowing them to partner. Neither looked at their host or hostess, instead moving farther into the crowd. Blythe quickly recounted what she learned. It surprised her to hear that Michail learned they slotted de Warenne's son and nephew to duel one another. With little forthcoming from Michail, Matilda resorted to boasting about her family.

"I wonder who's favored to win," Blythe said. She looked at the knight leaning against the wall, then at the illegitimate son who'd returned to the dais. They were of a similar build but not age. She assumed they trained together, so they would know one another's strengths and weaknesses. She found herself intrigued, not with the men, but with the competition. It was likely to end poorly.

"The nephew. De Warenne can't afford for his own son to be the victor. If aught happens to Richard, de Warenne risks his title and lands reverting to the Crown." Michail angled them so they stopped with his back to their men. Blythe peered over his shoulder, offering a small nod to the Scottish warriors. "With so many competitors, I wonder how crowded the barracks are."

Blythe watched the men. Two Dunbars shook their heads, and one mouthed "not very" while the other whispered "tents." Michail drew them out of the crush of dancers, keeping his back turned, but his voice loud enough for the men to hear.

"With so many people coming and going, I imagine

it must be difficult for de Warenne's men to guard the main and postern gates," Michail said. A MacLeod warrior's expression told Blythe that de Warenne's men were doing a poor job.

"The barracks aren't crowded because many of the competitors stay in tents pitched beyond the walls," Blythe whispered. "One of your men made it seem like they don't guard the gates sufficiently."

"I wonder if the stable hands can keep track of so many foreign horses coming and going, or which squire works for which knight."

"They don't," a Dunbar warrior whispered as he appeared to shift to avoid a passing servant.

"It seems a mon need only make his way to the bailey, then find a horse and ride away," Michail surmised. Blythe watched all their guards nod before they glanced at one another and leaned apart.

"The bailey was bursting with people when we arrived," Blythe noted. "The servants came and went carrying baskets out to the village and I suppose to the men here for the tourney. It wouldn't surprise me if they needed more hands. I bet they would accept offers of help, especially if it came from Scots forced to serve the English. But the village must be very crowded. It would become easy to get delayed or even lost." She watched as understanding dawned on the men.

"Aye. And men in breeks corralling horses to take to the list fields wouldnae seem odd," Michail surmised with a shrug. He knew Blythe's remaining guards likely had spare pairs to lend his men. It would enable the Highlanders to blend in more, especially if people saw them as mere servants, so no one expected them to speak.

"We should return to the dais before de Warenne questions why we're standing so close to our men, but we appear to ignore them. It's strange." Waves of uneasiness rolled over Blythe throughout the evening, still feeling unsettled by the odd situation.

"Aye."

Michail slid his gaze to the Scottish guards, offering them a quick nod before he and Blythe rejoined the other nobles. While they had no definitive plan in place, the couple learned valuable information. And everyone in their party understood the goal: disguise themselves to get out of the bailey and get lost among the crowd. It would be easier for the guards, and Blythe would already be away since she would attend the tournament. The only person not guaranteed an opportunity to escape the castle walls was Michail. He was determined to change that one way or another.

CHAPTER 18

*B*lythe began near the bed's headboard while Michail explored beside the fireplace, each working methodically, sweeping their hands up and down, then side to side, over the bricks. Frustration bloomed as they worked their way along the walls until they reached corners. They knew there were no hidden portals along the wall with the door, nor the one with the window.

"I've tried everywhere I can reach. What if it's behind the bed? What if they use it to disguise the doorway? I don't know that I can move something as large as that by myself. I suppose they assume there would be a mon here to do it." Blythe rolled her eyes. Nothing about the chamber said they intended it only for a male inhabitant.

Michail walked over to Blythe, looking at the wall behind the headboard. "Ye stay here, and I will go to the other side. We'll move the bed only enough for ye to slip in between. I dinna want anyone to hear the furniture scraping against the floor."

They each grasped hold of the headboard, and together they pushed the bed. It moved with shocking ease, sliding along the slick floor, making enough room for even Michail to fit. They looked at one another, stunned.

"There must be something hidden. Otherwise, why would the bed move so easily?" Blythe's brow furrowed as she looked at Michail. Standing beside one another, their hands roamed over the walls just like they had roamed over one another earlier that evening. Their fingertips brushed as they each found the latch. Exchanging a brief glance, they pressed down. A soft noise heralded the hidden portal unlocking. With a gentle push, Blythe opened the door outward.

"Wait a moment." Michail hurried to the fireplace and grabbed a log, lighting the end, then carried it back to where Blyth watched. He held it high enough into the abyss for them to see. The tunnel was shallow in front of them, but Michail shone the light to the left. The flickering torchlight didn't reach very far as they peered into cavernous darkness.

"Mayhap I should stay behind in case anybody comes to check. I can make noise and make people believe they shouldn't interrupt us."

Michail hesitated. He saw the merit to her reasoning, even if it meant leaving her alone. However, he also didn't want to miss an opportunity for them to flee if he made it to the bailey. Even though he suspected Salisbury would presume they would attempt an escape, if there was the possibility, he couldn't turn it down.

"Nay, ye come with me. We canna dawdle. We try to find the quickest way to the bailey, nae explore the entire keep." Michail looked toward the window as he tried to visualize the maze of tunnels that likely existed within the walls. From where their chamber was situated, they needed to descend a floor. He assumed the tunnel that began on his left ran along the keep's outer wall. When they arrived, he noticed only two windows on this floor, one of which was in their chamber, and the other was to the chamber behind where he stood.

Once again, holding up the lit torch, Michail entered the tunnel first. He reached back his hand and brushed Blythe's leg. She entwined her fingers with his, shuffling her feet to keep from stepping on Michail's heels. She tugged his hand as a thought came to her. "Do we need to close the door behind us? What if someone comes in?"

"Aye. The bed pushed from the wall will give away what we found, but most guardsmen and maids willna ken aboot the tunnels, or at least nae where the latch is in that chamber. Only de Warenne, and mayhap Matilda, would likely ken where to look."

They turned back the few steps they'd taken, then Blythe pulled the door closed, while Michail raised the torch to find the latch they would need when they returned. He tested it, both relieved when the door clicked open. Once Blythe sealed the portal a second time, they made their way into the void. With hands clasped and the light barely illuminating a few feet ahead of them, they wound their way through the secret passageway. They made turns they both locked away in their memory until they were certain they'd reached the ground floor. They'd heard people's muffled voices, but nothing distinguishable to tell them where they were within the warren.

While it felt like hours of inching along, they came to the end of the tunnel in five minutes. Michail handed the torch to Blythe, then drew a dirk for each hand. He pressed the lever, and they listened to the pop as the lock released. Using his elbow, his hands ready in defense, he eased the door open a crack. When no one sounded an alarm, he added a little more weight with his next nudge. A sliver of light streamed in. Instinct had them pressing their backs against the wall, breath held. Just as when the locked clicked, no one came rushing forth.

Michail handed the torch to Blythe and placed his eye to the opening. He squinted as his gaze swept over the section of the bailey closest to the postern gate. Despite it being after the evening meal, a crowded expanse bustled with people carrying baskets and barrels. The rhythmic noise from the blacksmith's forge beat a tattoo that replaced the sound of their hearts ringing in their ears. He noticed the guard at the gate watched people as they moved around the bailey but wasn't attentive by Michail's standards.

If that were ma bluidy guard nae minding the postern gate, he would find himself mucking out the garderobes. And that would only be after he swam to and from the island four times, then spent three days on duty with Ward. Ma brother would set him so straight he wouldnae even bend to take a shite.

But it gave Michail an idea. One that would only work if whomever stood guard the next day was just as inattentive as the man standing there now. He glanced at Blythe and canted his head before stepping aside for her to take his place.

She placed her eye against the opening, ensuring her nose didn't poke through. That was the last thing they needed. Her nose giving them away. It surprised her to see how many people returned to work, but she supposed the tournament just beyond the wall demanded extra labor they counted on for their plan. Twisting, Blythe caught sight of parts of the bailey Michail hadn't. De Warenne stood chatting with guards near the well. She jerked back when he turned, then reminded herself that the sliver of space between the door and its frame was so narrow that someone from the outside wouldn't be able to tell it was open. At least she prayed they wouldn't. She pinched her lips shut as he walked by them, but he never looked in their direction.

Blythe straightened and pointed back whence they came. They retraced their steps until they came to their chamber. They both placed their ear to the door, ensuring they were returning to an empty chamber. Blythe and Michail barely moved the bed back into place when they heard a key in the lock. Michail scrambled to cross the room to toss the log into the fire. He grabbed the poker and appeared to be stoking the flames when de Warenne entered.

"I came to bid you goodnight." De Warenne stared at the couple as Michail came to stand beside Blythe. They looked at him quizzically. "You've been up here some time, and yet you haven't settled in for the night."

"We were saying our prayers." Michail returned de Warenne's stare. "What else did you expect to find us doing?"

De Warenne's left eye narrowed for a second before he notched up his chin. His imperious expression made Michail grin.

"I can't say that I'm sorry to disappoint. I doubt I would react well to anyone intruding while my wife isn't presentable."

"You insist upon keeping up the pretense of that accent. Some of Salisbury's men came to the evening meal. They told my men that they heard you yammering that uncouth tongue. Plotting against Salisbury, I assume."

"Ma men and I discussed our last visit with the Sinclairs. Ye ken they are an ever-growing family. We wondered who would be next to have a bairn." Michail abandoned his accent, emphasizing each rolling syllable. "The Sinclair men arenae kenned to enjoy leaving their wives and weans, so we were speculating on how foul their tempers would be by the time they spent days crossing the length of Scotland in foul weather." Michail lowered his voice to a stage whisper. "Ma money is on Tavish being the loudest. But Alex is the subtlest, and the one I would fear most if I were ye."

"I think it'll be Ric," Blythe interjected. "He won't want to leave my sister and their children, especially not to come back to England to protect his sister-by-marriage. But, then again, he knows how to defeat the English since he knows how you fight. He killed Lord Graystone and Lord Hargate. He even did away with Arabella Fitz-Bigod. Wasn't she your mistress at court? Apparently, she was in bed with Graystone and Hargate, too. The woman threatened my sister and didn't live to tell the tale." Blythe studied de Warenne's reaction when she mentioned Ric. She caught the tiny tic of his jaw, but she couldn't tell if it was merely the mention of Ric's name or something deeper that made the English lord react.

"Ric would do well to stay on his side of the border. He won't receive a warm welcome." De Warenne's arched eyebrow didn't feel like a threat so much as a veiled warning for Ric's wellbeing. It left Blythe still wondering about de Warenne's reaction if Ric arrived on his doorstep. "If he did, he'd do well to wear his armor and not remove his helm."

De Warenne's last comment took Blythe aback, but once more, it didn't sound like a threat, but advice. She remained quiet, wondering if Michail would say anything further. When no one spoke, de Warenne turned back to the door.

"Be sure to knock next time. In the dark, I may nae wait to ask who it is before I protect ma wife's privacy."

"I'll keep that in mind." De Warenne disappeared into the passageway, and the lock clicked once more. Michail and Blythe stared at where de Warenne stood moments ago, before they turned to each other.

Michail pointed to the window embrasure, where they could talk without their lowered voices carrying.

"I have an idea, and de Warenne's suggestion aboot Ric keeping his helm on makes me think it might work."

"Are you joining the joust?"

Michail's lips pursed, while he playfully put his hands on his hips, then harrumphed. "Aye. That was ma idea. Apparently, it was yers too. I'd thought to impress ye with ma plan. I suppose ye have one of yer own."

"I do. I bet it's the same as yours though." Blythe slid her hands up Michail's chest before clasping them behind his neck. She stood on her tiptoes and pressed a tender kiss to his mouth, then settled back and rested her head against his chest. "Just promise me you'll be as careful as a warrior can."

"Ye ken I will. I wouldnae enter the joust if it werenae for getting ye away from here." Michail's steely arms encircled Blythe's smaller frame. "If the bailey is as busy tomorrow as it was when we arrived and just now, then I should be able to slip out. Now that I have breeks, I willna be so conspicuous. The issue is the armor. I'll have to pinch it from someone, and it's nae something quiet to go missing."

"And what of the crest? If you wear one, the owner will identify you as the thief. If you don't wear one, people will want to know why you came."

"I ken. And I dinna have a squire to help me dress. Ma men dinna ken aught aboot English chain mail other than where to stab to get around it. I dinna think yer men would ken much more."

"Did you watch Ric put his on?"

"Nay. He doesnae wear it anymore. Without Robbie to help him as his squire, he doesnae bother. He gave me an auld hauberk, which I have wrapped in ma spare plaid in ma saddlebag. I have a cotun in the other."

"I never imagined you wore aught but your leine and plaid in battle. Do you prefer the sleeveless cotun to a gambeson because your arms are free?"

"I prefer neither, but I wear it if there's time. It's easier to wear since it doesnae have sleeves. I also prefer that it's leather. A blade doesnae slice through it as easily as it can with linen or wool gambesons. The wool is too bluidy hot, anyway."

"Do your father and brothers wear them too?" It fascinated Blythe, since she merely assumed Highlanders forewent any defensive armor besides their targes.

"If they have time to don it, then aye. But only because ma mother kens how to make them properly. Most men find them too tight and cumbersome. Ma mother kens to keep the arm holes small, but she uses extra leather to let the cotun shift as we move while nae making us vulnerable. I dinna care for the hauberk because it doesnae shift easily and weighs ma arms down. I also canna swing as wide with it. If I wear it to joust, it isnae so bad. But I wouldnae want to wear it in an actual battle."

Michail gazed into Blythe's hazel eyes and saw the fear she attempted to hide. He didn't imagine any bride enjoyed discussing her husband riding off into battle, but it was a reality in the Highlands and the Lowlands. Whether it was fighting the English or each other, being a warrior was almost every man's calling if he weren't a priest or a peasant. His broad palm cupped her neck, his thumb sweeping over her cheek as he returned her tender kiss from just minutes ago. They eased one another's clothes off before Blythe led Michail to their bed. Their kisses were slow and heartfelt.

"I dinna want to scare ye talking aboot what I wear

or dinna wear into battle." Michail's soft voice matched the concern Blythe recognized in his eyes.

"*Mo ghràidh*, I know who I married, and I wouldn't trade who you are for aught. It's the warrior in you who makes me feel safe, who I turn to when the world is too scary. It doesn't mean I won't worry or that I enjoy hearing you describe your armor. But I also know the first thing I want your mother to teach me when we get home is how to make your cotun. I would ask Ric to teach me to be your squire if ever you wear full armor." Blythe grinned, knowing no Highlander would volunteer to don the thirty pounds of metal plating. "I know the risks. I face just as much giving birth. It's a part of our lives."

Blythe stopped when she noticed Michail's face turned ashen, and she no longer felt his breath waft against her forehead.

"Dinna say that." Michail's voice was hoarse and cracked with the last word.

"Say wha—Oh." Blythe stroked hair back from his temple. "You've never thought aboot us having bairns."

"Of course I have. Every bluidy day for three years. I didna think aboot the risk that ye might die having them." Michail's chest ached in a way he'd never felt before. It was fear, guilt, doubt, and regret tumbled together to squash his heart.

"My darling," Blythe inched closer until she rested her head against his shoulder. "I didn't mean to alarm you. I think you're regretting coupling with me. Now and three years ago because you fear what might happen if I get with child. I didn't mean to do that. I said it without thinking. Obviously, plenty of women have bairns every day and are fine. People would cease to exist if that weren't the case. Your cousin has children of her own. Your mother had three sons. Each of my sisters has children. At the rate Emelie and Dominic are going, they shall make the entire Campbell army on their own. Laurel and Brodie are no better."

"But none of them are ma wife."

"We both have risks in our lives. It doesn't mean we stop living them."

"But only one of us is endangering the other."

"Does that mean we'll never couple again? Does that mean you'll never have an heir? What if I'm already carrying?" Blythe could have kicked herself. Why couldn't she have stopped after her second question? "My point is that I don't want to miss out on building a family with you and living a full life beside you because we both fear one of us is going to die."

"I ken. I want a family with ye, and nae because I'm duty-bound to sire an heir. I want a family because ye, and nay one else, is ma wife. I mean, I've always kenned the danger was there for any woman. I just hadnae thought aboot the risk to ye."

"I promise to be careful and not take any unnecessary risks when I'm carrying our bairns. You promise me you won't take any more unnecessary risks. At all. On or off the battlefield."

"I already have. I meant what I said the other day, Bly. Ye deserve a husband beside ye and our weans deserve a father to help raise them. I see life vera differently now that I've pledged maself to ye. It's made me grow up and stop living for maself."

"I heard the maturity in your voice when you told me that before, and I see it in your eyes now. We both have too much to live for to squander any more of it." Blythe tilted her head back and kissed Michail's jaw. He snagged her mouth in a passionate kiss that seared heat from her lips to her toes. He rolled them so he hovered over Blythe. Resting on one forearm, he kneaded her breast before suckling. Her hands skimmed over his back until she could reach his buttocks. The granite beneath her fingertips reminded her of the strength she knew he possessed but had yet to see. One hand slipped between them until she wrapped it around his manhood. She stroked until Michail groaned and raised his head. She pressed his shoulder, slipping out from beneath him.

"Over." Blythe waited for Michail to roll onto his back. Her hand encircled his length once more, stroking slowly as she blew cool air over the tip. She swept her tongue over the opening before licking the length. She flicked her tongue along the ridge, making him twitch. She hadn't offered Michail such pleasure since their night together under the stars when he taught her what he liked. She sank her mouth down his manhood, allowing it to brush the back of her throat before she began to suck. With her eyes closed, she savored how Michail's body reacted to her ministrations. Using her hand and mouth, she brought him to the peak before easing her mouth off.

"What do ye want, *mo chridhe?*"

"You inside me, right now."

"Mmm." Michail nuzzled her neck. "Aught else?"

"Your mouth back on my breast." Blythe laid beside him and pressed her heels into the mattress, bringing her channel in line with the tip of his cock as he moved on top of her. She brushed the bulbous head through the dew pooling between her petals. She released him and grabbed his backside. With a small nudge, Michail thrust into her. Her moan made his bollocks ache. Gone was the tenderness of a moment ago. Passion dictated their actions as they moved together. With each surge and withdrawal, Michail brought Blythe closer to the edge before pulling back. Honoring her request, Michail latched onto her breast, his tongue flicking her nipple in between each draw he took on the turgid flesh.

"I'm going to make ye come apart," Michail whispered beside her ear. "I'm going to make ye beg for me to keep ye coming. Ye're an addiction, Bly. Every time I have ye, I need more of ye. I canna quit ye."

"I don't want you to. I want to feel you between my thighs, your cock filling me. I crave the fullness, the hunger that consumes me when we couple. That feeling that I want to climax because I can barely stand it, but I want to make this last forever."

Michail's hand caressed Blythe's thigh before wrapping his palm around it and drawing it over his hip. His chest burned, but this time it was from exertion. Blythe gasped for each breath, her heart racing. Sweat beaded over their bodies, making them grow slick. They glided together; the sound of their bodies pounding against one another filled the chamber. Blythe's nails bit into Michail's back as her core squeezed his cock. Her climax only spurred her on to want more. Michail flipped them, allowing Blythe to set their pace.

With her hair streaming down her back, and her breasts bobbing, his wife enraptured Michail. He clung to her hip with one hand while the other tangled in a fistful of hair, fighting to keep up with her frenetic pace as she rocked with his cock buried deep within. With her elbows on either side of his head, she leaned forward. The tug of her hair in Michail's grasp made her nip at his earlobe.

"Do you know how many times I made myself say extra prayers for letting my mind wander to this very act while I was in Mass? Do you know how often I thought aboot sucking your cock while I sat, bored, in the queen's solar?"

"As often as I palmed maself thinking aboot how ye taste and the sounds ye make as I pleasure ye. Do ye ken how I dreamed of falling asleep inside ye, both of us spent from making love?"

"Do you know I used to daydream aboot all the places I wanted us to couple in the keep? How I didn't care if someone caught us."

"Exhibitionist, are ye?"

"Prideful. Let all the women who stare at you at court know that you bury yourself in my quim, not theirs."

"That I do. I'd have all the Fletchers of the world hear ye scream ma name as ye come apart with ma cock buried so deep into ye that ye fear I will split ye in half."

Their confessions only inflamed their need further. Blythe leaned sideways, bringing Michail with her. Once more on her back, Blythe's hands ran over the ridges and dips of Michail's abdomen.

"I don't know why, but watching your muscles along your belly and in your shoulders bunch and flex while you're thrusting into me...it arouses me more than aught else when we're coupling."

"Watching yer breasts bounce, then swing over ma face while ye ride me makes me want to spill, just like I'm going to now." Their mouths fused together as they leaped into the bottomless sea of pleasure, waves of it pushing them deeper. They broke the surface and emerged to catch their breath once the spasms deep within their cores ceased.

"I love ye, Bly."

"I love you." Blythe reached beneath her and tugged the sheet down until they slipped under it together. Once more, Blythe nudged herself closer until her head rested on his shoulder. "What will you do tomorrow?"

Their interlude may have interrupted their conversation, but neither of them forgot there were decisions to be made. Michail stroked Blythe's hair, sometimes running his thumb back and forth along her shoulder.

"Once we break our fast, I'm certain they will bring

me back here. I'll wait until I'm sure de Warenne is at the tournament and ye're on your way. I'll bring our saddlebags with me and leave them in the tunnel for one of the men to fetch if I canna take them maself. If I can get to the stables without being stopped, then I will lead Cunnart and Midnight out. I hope walking between the two beasts will keep most people from seeing me, especially if I keep ma head down. While I'm in the bailey, I'll look for ma men. With luck, they will already be out and able to tend to all of our horses while I look for a set of armor."

"If you're free of the castle, you don't need to joust."

"I do. I will find armor, and I will challenge Salisbury. Blythe, this ends tomorrow. He will nae threaten ye and survive. And I willna let him live long enough to harass yer clan again."

"No. If you get free of here, you send word to me or give me a signal. We flee. We don't wait around, and we don't look back." Blythe's temper flared. "Besides, he plans to ride out with us in the morning. He'll likely be arguing with de Warenne or storming around ordering us brought before him. He won't be in the competition."

"He will when he hears a nameless English knight boasts he's better than him. When he hears this unknown jouster say he'll unseat him with the first pass, his pride will demand he enter."

"And if you're the one unseated? Besides, de Warenne said they already had the elimination melees. The duels are between the men who survived those."

"They will be. But jousters can still enter the duels, even if they havenae ridden in the melees. It just takes coin."

"Which we don't have."

"We do. The purse is within the hauberk. Anyone who tries to touch it will either shred their fingers if they're nae careful, or it'll make enough noise for me to ken they're taking it. Ma father sent Adan with extra coin, kenning I wasna going home but to court. Since I only went drinking one day," Michail sighed in annoyance with himself. "I still have plenty."

"Then it's just the armor you need."

"That and getting beyond the barmekin." Michail drew the covers higher over them as they shifted to both get comfier. "If I can do both, then we end this for good."

Neither said more, both lost in thought and prayer until sleep captured them and sailed them away to the land of Nod.

CHAPTER 19

Morning came with a sense of dread for Blythe and excitement for Michail. As they rose and dressed, she watched him. She could sense energy coursed through him that hadn't been there the night before. She'd never seen it in him, and she assumed it came from knowing he might take part in the tournament. She wondered if he was the same before battle.

She dreaded having to spend time with Matilda and the other ladies she'd seen the night before at the evening meal. Blythe would rather have each hair on her head plucked out, followed by each eyebrow, then each eyelash, before having to spend the day in the sun and heat around women who would natter on about things that didn't interest her. She girded her loins for the inevitable veiled barbs and outright insults.

However, Michail seemed eager to reach the tournament. Their conversation last night before and after they made love only partially reassured her. She wondered how Michail would find armor without being caught and strung up as a thief. It concerned her that he wasn't thinking realistically. Without a crest emblazoned on a surcoat or a shield, she didn't know how he would enter. Even if he were a knight with no fealty to a lord, he would still have some type of heraldry. She was about to ask that very question when a knock sounded at the door.

Michail finished pulling Blythe's laces tight and tied them in a bow. They were ready to go when the maid ushered them into the passageway. Once more, guards encircled them and escorted them belowstairs. Both Michail and Blythe spied their warriors once more sitting amongst the people in the Great Hall. Neither de Warenne nor Matilda was in sight, but others already filled the chairs on the dais. Blythe and Michail took the seats they occupied the night before. With an unrestricted view of the Great Hall and all those who dined together, the couple could see several of de Warenne's knights already dressed to join the tournament. Helms sat upon tables and metal creaked as armored bodies moved while they ate.

"Do you remember that's Richard Fitzalan?" Blythe whispered before bringing a spoonful of porridge to her mouth.

"Ye said he's de Warenne's nephew and heir. I was so interested in talking to ma men last eve I forgot to tell ye that I learned that mon's name." Michail shifted his gaze to who Blythe had guessed was de Warenne and Matilda's oldest child. "His name is William, and he is de Warenne's auldest bastard. The lass isnae his sister but his wife."

Blythe dropped her chin to keep anyone from seeing how her nose curled in disgust. She knew it wasn't unusual for a woman to marry just barely into womanhood, but William's wife could barely have been five-and-ten. As she shifted her attention to William, she realized that while he had the broad shoulders and thick build of a knight, his cheeks and jaw were smooth. With closer examination, she estimated him to be barely six-and-ten. She felt mollified, but she doubted either the bride or the groom chose to marry so young.

"The earl favors his nephew over his son to win. I think I understand now. I thought William much aulder last night, but he must be close to six or seven years Richard's junior. That hardly seems like a fair fight."

"It willna be. But William is good enough to have made it this far, or people wish to see him humiliated. For the lad's sake, I pray it's the former." Michail studied William, paying attention to things he hadn't the night before. They were of a similar height. While Michail had a thicker chest, their shoulders were the same breadth. He estimated their hands to be a similar size. He wondered if their legs would be the same length. "Do ye think he cares for his father?"

"I don't know. They don't appear warm to one another, but that's the English for you. They hatch their children."

Michail elbowed Blythe's forearm and tilted his head toward the door. De Warenne entered, his hair windblown. He straightened it as he crossed the hall and climbed the dais stairs. They watched as Matilda appeared and joined her lover at the high table. She offered a sincere smile to William and his wife, but she scowled at Blythe and Michail.

"She doesn't seem so keen this morning," Blythe noted.

"Good," Michail said around a bite of bread. He noticed William's hand curl into a fist before he flexed his fingers. The young man didn't look at his father. Michail followed his gaze and found it rooted on Richard. When Michail looked back, the loathing was clear. This wasn't a matter of a bastard son jealous of his father's chosen heir. It went deeper than that. When

Richard approached, William's arm whipped across his wife's lap as if to shield her. The young woman leaned toward William.

"What's that?" Blythe whispered. The lecherous smile Richard offered the young woman soured the porridge in Blythe's belly. Michail's hackles rose in defense of a woman he didn't know and had never heard speak.

"William, Dorothea. Pleasant morning for a ride." Richard stared at Dorothea, unblinking.

"Made better with a lance in one's hand." William's tone was offhand, but the meaning wasn't lost.

"It is certainly better when someone is holding your lance." Richard grinned, his chipped teeth on display. Everyone on the dais could see how Dorothea clung to her husband's arm which still stretched across her, the possessiveness as clear as the protection.

"You're tiresome." William sighed dramatically.

"And your wife deserves a man."

"I have one," Dorothea spoke up. "The one I want, and the only one worth choosing."

Michail took Blythe's hand beneath the table and squeezed. "I ken whose armor I'm wearing. I need only get William alone without him sounding the bluidy call to arms."

"I can make sure he doesn't. I will speak to Dorothea."

"Brave words from a woman who'll be a young widow." Richard swung his helm upward and tucked it under his left arm before spinning on his heel and sauntering away.

"Lady Dorothea?" Blythe spoke softly. The Englishwoman turned a suspicious mien toward Blythe, who leaned forward. "I fear something has come amiss with my gown. I don't know that I can make it to my chamber with no one noticing. Is there somewhere I might go? Someone who might help me?"

Dorothea opened her mouth, but Blythe tilted her head toward Michail and cocked an eyebrow as she shifted her gaze to William, who scowled at Richard's back. Dorothea nodded and rose, much to William's surprise. The young man clutched his wife's hand until Dorothea whispered something in his ear. William nodded as he looked at Blythe. Michail flashed a tight smile at William before shifting his attention to de Warenne, who had ignored the entire exchange. But Michail was certain the experienced lord and knight was aware of what happened.

The two women slipped from the dais. Dorothea led Blythe to a chamber the latter assumed was a ladies' solar. It surprised her it was on the main floor. But she cared not now that she spoke to Dorothea alone.

"I know it's not my business, but I wanted to be sure you were all right. I was aghast at what that mon said to you, and I feared it might upset you. I would be if he'd spoken such to me." Blythe didn't have to pretend the sympathy in her voice. It was genuine. "I admire your calm. I don't know that I would have been so judicious with my words."

Dorothea glared at Blythe, suspicious of the Scottish woman's kindness. Once Blythe said nothing more, Dorothea relaxed. "Richard wished to marry me for my dowry. But as you heard, I chose William instead."

"The illegitimate son instead of the heir? No wonder he's put out. I assumed you and William were an arranged marriage."

"Because we're so young," Dorothea surmised. "Neither my parents nor William's agreed to let us marry. Lord de Warenne wanted Richard to marry me, and so did my father. We made sure only William could marry me, but when I miscarried two months after we wed, both our fathers tried to get the marriage annulled. Obviously, they failed. De Warenne can't get his own marriage dissolved, so there was little hope he would succeed with ours. But ever since I lost the babe, Richard acts as though I'm a whore to be shared. I know he only half-means it. He does it to antagonize William, but my husband mostly ignores him."

"It looked like Richard frightened you."

Dorothea shook her head. "Richard forced me to dance with him last night after you and your husband retired. He made some of the most untoward comments he ever has and held me too tightly. I told William because I don't hide things from him, especially about Richard. I feared today would be the day William gutted his cousin."

Blythe glanced past Dorothea's shoulder, picking her words carefully. "Will your husband face Richard in the jousts today?"

"Yes." Dorothea shifted uncomfortably.

"Richard has more experience than your husband because of their ages." Blythe watched Dorothea nod, her fingers pressing into the backs of her hands as she clutched them in front of her. "I know someone William's size who is a match for Richard's strength and skill."

Dorothea's eyes narrowed as she once more grew suspicious, regretting she'd confided in Blythe.

"You know who I'm talking aboot. My husband hides his temper even better than your husband, but he's livid. It matters not to Michail that you're English." Blythe nearly choked on the half-truth. "He's a Highlander, and he takes seriously his duty to protect those who cannot fight for themselves. It's a matter of honor."

"You're saying your husband would joust in

William's place. And what happens to William when everyone discovers your husband lost on his behalf?"

"My husband will not lose."

"He's Scottish."

"He's a Highlander. One trained by a renowned English knight. Men from Scotland's northernmost parts are fiercely competitive and have the strength to back it up. Michail will win." Blythe prayed what she pledged was true.

"How would he even get into the list fields?"

"Let Michail worry aboot that. Which tent will William be in? Does your father-by-marriage make him share with Richard?"

"No. The Fitzalans have their own tent. William will be in the de Warenne one."

"Will his father be there?"

Dorothea stifled her snort and coughed. "He will be beside Lady Maud."

"If your father-by-marriage won't be in the tent, then William can slip away to give Michail his armor."

"You make it sound simple."

"It can be if neither you nor William give us away." Blythe stood to her insignificant height, but it kept her eye-to-eye with Dorothea. She assumed it was the lilt to her Scots accent that made it intimidating to the Englishwoman, but Dorothea's head bobbed. "We must return to our husbands. What should I expect with the other Ladies of the Honor Court?"

"They'll be bitches." Dorothea stated without affectation. "Lady Maud set her sights on your husband and is annoyed that you kept them from flirting. She wouldn't stray from the earl because she knows she has nowhere to go, not with six children in tow. She thought to make him her amusement. She will now make you such. The other ladies will follow suit."

"Any worse than others?"

"No." Dorothea didn't wait for Blythe as they left the solar. She leaned to her husband and whispered something. His eyes darted to Michail's as he listened to her. When Dorothea straightened, William looked at those gathered and still eating.

"I think that will make for a wonderful day, my darling," William said as he brought Dorothea's hand to his mouth, kissing its back. "I shall be off. My first run is in an hour and a half. I must ready my weapons and armor." He left the dais without another glance in the Scottish couple's direction. Dorothea followed Matilda when the older woman rose. Blythe assumed it meant she was to join them.

"Be careful," Blythe whispered in Scots. "Try not to get too many bumps and bruises because we may not be alone tonight for me to kiss and rub them better."

"I will find us time alone so you can reward the victor." Michail waggled his brows, his irrepressible grin making Blythe's belly flip. They cut their flirtation short when guards arrived before the dais and glared at Michail. He stood, wrapped an arm around Blythe, and kissed her soundly. He watched as Blythe followed the other ladies to the door, catching the single dip of her chin she offered their men as she passed. They glanced at him, offering him a knowing stare, before they filed out shortly after the ladies disappeared.

Michail turned his grin on the de Warenne guards before he leaped from the dais, forcing the men to make room. Once in his chamber, he reclined on the bed. He didn't doubt someone would check on him. He even suspected it might be William Montagu. The Earl of Salisbury wouldn't relent and give away his prisoners. But now that Blythe was ensconced among the ladies, it would keep Salisbury from leaving that morning.

He closed his eyes as he heard a key in the lock. The

heavier tread of a man had him opening an eye enough to spy Salisbury surveying the chamber. He watched the man cross the chamber, looking into the now empty fireplace before crossing to the window embrasure.

"You are not asleep, so you needn't play at it." Salisbury stood at the foot of the bed.

"I will be once you leave. I'm exhausted."

"Rutting your whore?" Salisbury's head slammed against the floor as Michail's weight slammed into him. Michail's fist plowed into Salisbury's face before he rose lithely to his feet. The earl spluttered as he shook his head, stars dancing before his eyes.

"You should think twice before speaking such aboot a mon's wife to his face."

Salisbury stared in shock, completely unprepared for Michail's speed and agility. He'd barely seen Michail lift his head before he found himself sprawled upon the rushes.

"You should leave before I lose my temper." Michail crossed his arms, his forearms and chest flexing, and once more returned to his courtly accent.

"You will regret that when I drag you behind my horse all the way to the West Country." Salisbury patted his cheekbone before storming over to the door. He left as quickly as he appeared. Michail settled back onto the bed for what he estimated was another forty-five minutes. When no one else disturbed him, he lit a log, gathered their meager belongings, and peered out the window. He could see the crowd in the bailey, and there were people hurrying toward the tournament fields. He inched the bed away from the wall and squeezed into the gap before opening the secret portal. Once he stepped into the tunnel, he yanked the bed back into place and snapped the door shut. He wasted no time winding his way toward the bailey. When he reached the end of the tunnel, he ground out the torch, took a deep breath, and eased open the door.

Half a dozen men with their heads bowed from the weight of the straw they carried on their shoulders provided a shield as Michail crossed the bailey with them. He still carried the saddlebags, praying no one would question why he had them instead of straw. When they passed the stables, he ducked inside.

"Michail." Stanley emerged from a stall with his horse saddled. A moment later, the other MacLeod and Dunbar guards led their mounts into the walkway. "We slipped the stableboys a few pints of whisky to let us do their job."

The mix of Highlanders and Lowlanders grinned, each remembering the first time he drank himself into a stupor. Michail rolled his eyes but hurried into Cunnart's stall, then Midnight's. Once both horses were ready, the group led the enormous animals by their bridles. The warhorses didn't differ from any of the mounts the knights rode. Hidden by the animals' height and girth, men and beasts blended into the crowd. They made their way to the far side of the tournament in silence.

Michail and the others scanned their surroundings, looking for anyone who might pay them too close attention. When they spied no one taking notice, the men eased into the woods a hundred yards from where they stopped. One of Blythe's guards took Midnight while Michail and Cunnart wound through the tents.

"Feitheamh."

Michail spun around at the Gaelic word for wait hissed with an English accent. A knight in chain mail but no plates, with his helm on, approached. Michail fought to repress his grin.

"You need more practice." Michail chuckled as Ric lifted his helm's visor.

"You sound like you've had plenty. I would take you for a Lowlander with that accent." Ric teased, but his gaze swept over their surroundings, just as Michail's did, both men acutely aware of everyone and everything.

"What the bluidy hell are you doing here?" Michail kept up the pretense of a Scots accent in case anyone stumbled upon them.

"Isa and I traveled to Kilchurn, then continued to Druchtag Motte with Emelie and Dominic. When we arrived and Blythe wasn't there, we knew something happened. Dom and I rode for the MacLellans, but we never made it that far. We ran into Hannays who volunteered information." Michail knew how those men came to offer such knowledge. He was glad for it, since they'd long suspected it was the Hannays who told Salisbury where to find them.

"Is Isa with you?"

"No. She remained with her family. Her father likely won't make it. No one told him what delayed Blythe, but I think he suspects."

"Well, brother-by-marriage." Michail waggled his brows. "You are too late to free us from the keep. But you are in time to fulfill that offer to be my squire."

"No. We leave. I found you easier than I thought. We get Lady Blythe, and we go." Ric lifted his visor once more. "Brother?"

"Aye. We handfasted just after leaving court. My wife is stuck with the Court of Honor, likely sitting just behind de Warenne and Lady Matilda." Michail twisted to look in the main tent's direction. "I intend to joust in de Warenne's son's stead against Richard Fitzalan. Then I shall beat Salisbury. One is the cost for the other."

"And when you're expected to ride before the Court?"

"I offer my wife—Lady Dorothea, that is—a rose, then turn to take my place. Richard will be so eager to humiliate William that he will not care if he misses the fanfare. He wants Lady Dorothea."

"And when you defeat Richard? When everyone wishes to congratulate you?"

"I will issue my challenge to Salisbury."

"Why the devil would de Warenne's son wish to duel the Earl of Salisbury?"

"Such nasty rumors spread through events like this. Why, William is merely defending his mother's honor." Michail's level gaze met Ric's, the resolve clear.

"You have an answer to everything."

"I have thought aboot everything, or at least, just aboot. There will be quite the coup when our host's bastard son unseats Salisbury. During that, Blythe slips away to our men. I need only William de Warenne to be ready to take my place among the crowd."

"Whose armor will you wear?"

"I was going to wear William's, but now I shall wear yours." Michail crossed his arms, smugness in his expression. "I'm accepting your offer to squire for me. If William still wears his armor, he can easily switch places me, when I make my escape."

"And whose helm shall you wear? If I take off mine, every knight here will recognize me. If you wear William's, he cannot disguise himself while you ride his horse. You do realize you have to ride his mount."

Michail's smile slipped. So he hadn't thought of everything. "Then I shall go to my original idea. I will be a knight of no fealty when I challenge Salisbury. I ride as William against Richard in your armor, but I carry William's crest. I slip from the crowd while William accepts his accolades. Then we spread my challenge for Salisbury, and I ride against him with no heraldry."

"You better make sure the right William dies, or you're liable to get de Warenne's son killed."

"We must hasten to the de Warenne tent. Where is your armor?"

"Already there." It was Ric's turn to waggle his eyebrows. "John and I were childhood friends. We grew apart as men, but neither of us likes Salisbury. We didn't as wards of the court, and we don't now. I know too many of John's secrets. His tent is the only safe place for me."

"Hiding amongst our enemies." Michail followed Ric along the outside edge of the veritable village of tents. When they reached the de Warenne tent, Ric slipped inside before signaling Michail to join him. Once Cunnart was secure to a nearby tent post, Michail slipped inside.

"Uncle Ric?" William gaped.

"Shh. Your father doesn't know I'm here, and it's best if he doesn't. You're due on the field soon, and we need to get Michail into my armor."

"Yours? I thought he was to wear mine. How do you know this?"

"Our wives are sisters. I learned Salisbury was being a menace. Again. When neither my brother- nor sister-by-marriage were at Druchtag Motte when my wife and I arrived, it took little to deduce what likely happened." Ric spoke as he peeled off his helmet and his hauberk. While he did that, Michail pulled the cotun from his saddlebag, donning that and the hauberk Ric gave him when he first taught Michail to joust. With two men to act as squires, it took little time for them to encase Michail in his garniture, a knight's full suit of armor. As they worked, they explained the rest of the plan to William. Ric helped William don his metal suit. "Where is your squire?"

"Drunk with the boys from the stables. It seems

someone's guards gave them whisky." William stared at Michail, who shrugged. "If you're thinking of being his squire, you're far too large."

Ric sighed. "Someone has to squire for Michail. He can't mount with the lance in his hand."

"I go with him and only enter the ring to hand him the lance before I come back here."

"You can't come back here," Michail interjected. "You must be ready to take my place. I'll make your horse rear and high step. I'll maneuver him out of the ring, but you must be ready to take my place immediately."

"What of the people who see us?"

"We deal with that when we must. We have no time left." Michail finished speaking as a horn signaled a call for the next set of competitors. It was William's turn. Ric led William's horse as Michail and William followed. He used the massive steed as a shield just as Michail had done with Cunnart and Midnight, hiding his uncovered head from most prying eyes. When Michail mounted, the horse didn't approve of a strange rider. It wouldn't be difficult for the uncooperative beast to convince people it took Michail out of the ring rather than the other way around.

CHAPTER 20

Ric handed Michail a rose before the Highlander spurred the horse forward. He and Richard came to a halt on their mounts before the Court of Honor. Michail offered his rose before Richard, handing it to Dorothea, who beamed at Michail then turned away from Richard's proffered flower. Michail whipped the horse around and cantered back to where he'd entered the list fields. He accepted the lance and an ecranche, a small shield to strap onto a jouster's left arm, from William, adjusting his hold on both.

"Good luck," William offered, to which Michail nodded. He glanced past the circle's opening and found Ric watching. Few people milled around, everyone interested in the imminent duel. Michail trained his focus on Richard as he urged his horse to the starting point. A horn wailed once more. Michail spurred William's horse, which neighed and tried to turn. Michail's powerful thighs squeezed the beast as he tightened the reins. The steed charged forward. Michail pressed harder against the horse's flanks, urging it into a gallop. The speed at which the horse traveled was faster than most jousters rode, but it would give Michail the force he needed.

As the distance between Richard and him shrank, he lowered his lance into position. His breath, trapped within the metal helm, made his face sweat. Every hoofbeat echoed within the helmet. The pounding gait jarred him as he fought to keep his seat, unused to the extra weight. The ground and crowd blurred past him, and he was only vaguely aware there was a world beyond his horse and their targets.

He ignored everything but his breathing and his target on Richard's body. The horse, whose name he didn't even know, sensed his urgency, and sped toward its own nemesis. Moving faster than Richard's mount, they charged past the stands, meeting Richard past the stretch's midpoint. With all the force he could muster, Michail thrust forward the lance as he twisted away from Richard. His opponent's weapon glanced off his ecranche as Richard took flight from his saddle.

Michail reined in as he watched Richard come unseated. The Englishman landed with a clatter of metal and a groan. Hearing his opponent was alive, Michail turned around and galloped back to his end of the list. With a splintered lance, he had reason to ride out of the circle having won. He maneuvered the horse so he could dismount on the animal's right while William swung into the saddle from the left, taking the ecranche from Michail's left hand. Michail followed William back into the ring, carrying the fractured lance. He watched William ride before the noble spectators and remove his helm. The heat from wearing the helm had already made sweat saturate his hair, so he looked as though he'd exerted himself. He wrapped his arm around Dorothea and kissed her soundly before bowing to his father. Michail left the list field as William remained with his family and their guests.

Fitzalan men carried Richard from the competition area.

"Well done," Ric murmured as they returned to the de Warenne tent. "We must find armor for your horse."

"Whose do we take?"

"Salisbury's son's." Ric grinned.

"Another bluidy William. Do the English ken nay other names?" With no one to hear them, Michail shed his accent.

"I'm not a William."

"Ye're nae really English." Michail matched Ric's grin. Ric's father had abandoned his English home and returned his spurs to Longshanks when he married Ric's Lowlander mother. Hallam Hartley became as much a MacLellan as any man born to the clan, and he'd died defending his family. Ric hadn't chosen to live among the English, and once he was free of his knight's tenure of service, he'd returned to Scotland and not long after, fallen in love with Isabella Dunbar.

"Thank God." Ric stepped to the tent's flap. "Salisbury's brother loathes the man. He knows he'll never be earl, but he's happy to help make his nephew one. He thinks the younger William to be a malleable whelp. He shall be surprised. But in the meantime, I kept Simon alive on more than one battlefield. He knows he owes me, and now I shall call in his debt. I spotted him during your match and told him."

"Willna Salisbury recognize his own son's armor? He likely paid for it."

"Not if Cunnart doesn't wear any insignia. He can wear the caparison with no embellishment. Cunnart needs naught draped over the croupier to cover his hindquarters' mail. The criniere, the peytral, and the flanchard around his neck and over his chest and flanks may have etchings, but they won't give away who owns them."

"How will we get them?"

"They're on the way." Ric peered out of the tent once more. "Simon is bringing them, and I suspect his nephew will come, too. They have already started spreading the rumor a knight wishes to challenge Salisbury, claiming the earl is too old and too fat to ride into battle. That he prefers to stand off to the side, then claim the glory."

"Ye're nae wrong." Michail's disgust oozed from each word.

"Not surprising. It's why they came up with it so quickly."

"Ye really trust them nae to give either of us away?"

"I left the king's service, and I avenged my parents' death and Isa's attack. I only loathed Graystone and Hargate. Now I'm not so fond of Salisbury, and I have no affinity for that bastard they call king. It doesn't mean I have no fond memories of the men I rode beside for a decade."

"They dinna think ye're a traitor?"

"They all know my horse's name." Ric laughed deeply. He'd named his steed MacLellan after his mother's people. When he received the animal as a young squire, naming his horse after the Scottish clan was an act of rebellion. It was no secret among his peers and the knights a few years older than him that he swore fealty to Longshanks to repay the king for housing, feeding, and educating him. "I don't know for certain they won't turn on me. But I believe Simon's greediness and Will's ambition are greater than their desire to turn me over."

"I pray ye're right. Once I'm in the lists with Salisbury, I need ye to get Blythe away from the stands. She needs to be with the men when I finish. We dinna dilly-dally. Once I kill Salisbury, we are away."

"Don't underestimate him and believe the rumors we've concocted. He's still a formidable man."

"I willna. I ken I likely willna defeat him with one pass. Richard was arrogant and naïve. Salisbury is only arrogant. I willna make the mistakes Richard did."

"I'll make sure Blythe is with your men, but you know she'll insist upon watching. She won't leave until she knows you're safe."

"I ken. De Warenne will probably demand she watch just to torment her, hoping she will fear what happens if Salisbury lives or if he perishes."

Their conversation ended when they heard men's voices approaching. Michail slammed the helm back onto his head, disguising himself once more. Simon and William Montagu the Younger entered the tent with three squires carrying the horse's barding. The boys placed the pieces on the ground where Ric pointed.

"Who's this?" Simon demanded.

"Your savior," Ric responded.

"Shut up, Hartley. I don't need your patronizing drivel."

"Then you don't need my friend's help. You can commit fratricide on your own. Or would you have your nephew guilty of patricide? It would keep your hands clean. You've always kept them so soft." Ric smirked. Simon and he were never close, but they'd relied on one another in battle over the years. Mutual need curbed hostility that might have otherwise bloomed. But Ric intended that Simon and in turn William remember who placed the younger man on the earl's seat. As long as he had family-by-marriage living along the border, Ric would ensure he kept at least one powerful Englishman in his debt. "Go rile up your brother while your squires prepare my friend's horse."

"How convenient you found a friend here." Simon

stared at Michail as though he might discover who hid beneath the conical helmet. Michail didn't move, appearing like a metal statue. Simon stuck out his hand toward Michail. "I would know whose debt I am entering."

Michail grasped it without hesitation, but the gauntlets he wore kept him from constricting his hand around Simon's. Infusing a raspiness his voice rarely held, hoping to disguise a poor English accent, Michail said, "I am a man your brother wronged. Now I shall right that."

"You must be more specific than that." Simon chuckled, but there was no mirth. But Michail offered no more, releasing Simon's hand instead. With nothing forthcoming, Simon turned back to Ric. "If this fails, you will die on your own. I will not come to your rescue."

"And dirty those clean hands. I never thought you would." Ric held back the tent flap. Taking their cue, Simon and William filed out. Ric nodded to the squires, who hefted the armor once more. Ric and Michail helped the boys as they prepared Cunnart for his turn in the lists. Once the steed was ready, the boys scarpered off to Salisbury's tent with orders to boast of seeing the unnamed knight challenging their lord.

It was another two hours of waiting in the overheated armor within the de Warenne tent before they made progress. Neither John nor William de Warenne came to their tent, for which Michail was exceedingly grateful. It meant he was able to keep the helm off. Ric and Michail chatted on and off, but both men were often lost in thought. Michail worried about Blythe. He'd barely noticed her once he'd given Dorothea the rose. He'd been too singularly focused on not being knocked from the horse or decapitated, that he'd not looked for her once he was through. Now he wished to see for himself that she was hale. As though conjured from his imagination, Blythe stepped into the tent.

"Bly?" Michail crossed the tent in four long strides.

"I slipped away from the other ladies wandering the market. I needed to know you're all right."

"I am. I worry aboot ye. How has it been?" When Blythe wouldn't meet his gaze, Michail lifted her chin with care, having discarded the gauntlets to ready Cunnart. "What have they said?"

"They've made passing insults aboot Scots, and Matilda said she now thinks Highlanders wear their plaids to hide their tiny cocks. They fear wearing breeks because it would give it away. I should have ignored her, but I couldn't help myself. I asked if my husband looked fearful at all last night. She looked ready to say something, but de Warenne drew her attention away. The other ladies took it as an opportunity to condemn wanton women who preferred heathens. I should have kept quiet then too."

"What did ye say?" Michail sensed he would laugh, but he knew his bride risked much by insulting the other women.

"That if their men were aught like mine, then they'd know why we're wanton. I told them it was a pity they would never know what it is to be with a mon and not an overgrown boy."

Michail pulled Blythe into his embrace, kissing her as though Ric wasn't there. Ric turned from the couple, giving them privacy. He could hardly fault them, since he'd been kissing Isabella the same way since before they wed. He smiled to himself as he remembered an entire bailey catching them kissing before they'd even announced they were courting. Now he was a father to both a son, Kirk, and a daughter, Keira.

"I must return before anyone questions where I went. Congratulations, *mo ghràidh*, I am proud of you. I wish you well." Blythe strained to whisper to Michail. "And I wish to strip you of that hideous armor so I can feel you against me. If I wanted to hold all that metal, I would bed down in the blacksmith's forge."

"I may make a squire out of ye yet, *mo chridhe*." They exchanged another passionate, albeit brief, kiss before Blythe slipped away. Michail watched as she joined the ladies, none of whom took note that she'd left.

"De Warenne!" An angry bellow sounded as Salisbury marched past the de Warenne tent. "De Warenne! I demand this black-hearted churl show himself. The one who dares claim he can best me. Where the devil is he?"

Michail donned his borrowed helmet, peeking out of the tent until William, the Earl of Salisbury, walked past. Ric and he watched him stalk away, spewing curses as he went.

"I'd say it's time." Michail untied Cunnart and walked toward the list fields' entrance. Ric followed him; his hair hanging beside his cheeks disguised his down-turned face. When they reached the end of the tilt, Michail mounted Cunnart, taking the lance from Ric, who left the field. He raised his visor so he could project his voice. "I do."

Everyone in the stands and the crowds turned to watch Michail lower his visor and nudge Cunnart forward. He executed a levée as he would if he were taking a pass. The slow lowering of his weapon only exaggerated his announcement, especially when he pointed the tip toward Salisbury.

"Bring me my horse," Salisbury demanded. Michail raised the lance and waited, Cunnart motionless beneath him. But as he waited, Michail spied Blythe, who he found sitting beside Dorothea. He focused on her, calming his breathing.

Ye have a long life to live with her. Dinna cock this up.

Pay attention. Remain focused. Dinna let aught he does rattle ye, or ye will be the one winding up dead. Ignore aught he says. Look for his weaknesses, look for the opening. Make it clean, one pass.

Michail felt the false calm settle over him just as it did before battle. His heart pounded, and sweat slid between his shoulder blades, but his mind cleared. His pulse's staccato rang in his ears as it had before, making him further loathe the helmet but giving him a beat upon which to concentrate. He reminded himself that anonymity was the only way he could defeat Salisbury. A moment's doubt flashed through his mind, making him wonder if he should let Ric duel the earl. Michail relegated the doubt to the mud beneath Cunnart's hooves. Salisbury hadn't captured Ric and threatened Isa. He'd taken Michail and Blythe, and he would defend his wife to his last breath.

He watched Salisbury mount an agitated steed before he slammed his helmet onto his head and flicked down his visor. Michail was already in position, and once Salisbury was too, the Knight Marshal rose from his place in the stands.

"William Montagu, Earl of Salisbury, accepts the challenge from—" The Knight Marshal looked toward Michail, uncertain how to announce him.

"Sir Galahad," Ric's booming voice sounded from the field's entrance. Michail grinned. While he was undoubtedly legitimate, unlike the fabled Sir Lancelot and Elaine of Corbenic's son, Michail enjoyed being hailed the most perfect knight. He supposed his three years of abstinence brought him closer to the legendary knight's renowned purity. He pulled back on Cunnart's reins, signally the horse to rear and paw the air. He would enjoy the fanfare and play the part.

"The Earl of Salisbury and Sir—Galahad," the Knight Marshal announced.

Michail patted his steed's neck. "Cunnart, I named ye risk for the one I took raising ye from a weakling to the beast ye are now. We've taken countless risks together, urging one another on. I ken yer love for speed, and ye're a competitor as much as me. We must win. There's too much of the wrong risk if we dinna. It's just like with MacLellan. Ye run a straight path, and I will do the rest, lad. I trust ye, ma friend. Make us victorious."

Michail didn't need to spur Cunnart when the horn sounded, the animal understanding the signal. Unable to lean low over his mount's withers like he normally would, Michail kept his thighs tight against Cunnart's flanks and his heels down in the stirrups. He knew he had mere seconds before the earl and he met, but he readied himself as Cunnart ate up the yards separating him from his enemy.

Lower the lance. Aye, it's balanced. He's leaning away. Aim for the shoulder joint. Push yer weight forward as ye thrust. Now!

Michail drove his lance into the weaker part of William's mail, the articulating joint at the man's shoulder. It pushed William away, but he kept his seat. Michail's lance splintered but didn't break. William managed a glancing blow against Michail's shield. Michail scored the greater points, but not enough to win. They would take another pass. Wheeling Cunnart around, Michail kept his mount to a walk, allowing them both to recover. Michail's head ached from the confined space around his pulsing temples and the heat trapped within.

Nay wonder the English lost. They couldnae think straight in these bluidy traps. They likely expired from heat before any of us cut them down.

A member of the ground crew handed Michail a fresh lance. He tested it in his hand, trusting nothing

Ric didn't hand him. He looked where he'd last seen Ric standing. His friend nodded, making Michail breathe easier. He adjusted his ecranche that slipped when William's lance nicked it. The horn blew once more, catching Michail by surprise. He'd expected some announcement to come first.

Bluidy bleeding hell. Come on, Cunnart. Come on. There we go. Dinna look at Blythe. Stop. How far do I have? He's further from the tilt. He thinks to make me reach across, bring me closer. Aim sideways. Outside of his ribs. Lower the lance. Twist left. Now. Thrust.

William's left foot came loose from his stirrup as he slipped to his right, but he kept his seat a second time. He hadn't touched Michail this time, his lance cutting through air rather than striking a target. Michail's lance shattered into severed spears. They tempted him to ram William again, so he turned away.

"Sir Galahad, the tenan, leads as the challenger with five points," the Knight Marshal announced as the men and their mounts returned to their ends. "Montagu, Earl of Salisbury, defends as the venan with one point."

Michail knew, despite issuing the challenge to Salisbury, the older man assumed he would gain the upper hand and be the tenan instead of the venan. His first pass hadn't broken his lance's tip, and he hadn't struck Michail with the second. However, Michail earned two points for breaking his lance in the first pass and three points for shattering the one during the second pass. Three points were the most a jouster could score in a single pass, so there was no scenario, short of unhorsing Michail, where William could win with only one more pass. However, Michail was unsatisfied with a mere victory. He had a last chance to unseat Salisbury and draw him into a battle on foot. He was confident the earl wouldn't accept defeat graciously and would draw his sword first.

When the horn sounded for the third time, Michail was ready. He believed Cunnart understood it was their last chance. The animal's head dropped low while his tail came up. He plowed forward as though he competed against the other horse as much as Michail competed against the other man.

"*Tu es une petite fille avec une petite chatte,*" Michail yelled just before his lance struck Salisbury in the sternum, sending him flying over his horse's hindquarters. He'd seen the shock, then venom, as Salisbury registered his words. He was convinced the man knew he hadn't called him a little girl with a little cat. No, he'd told William Montagu, the Earl of Salisbury, that he had a little cunt. As Michail predicted, William rolled to his feet, unsteady on his feet, but drew his sword.

Michail swung down from Cunnart's back as he drew his double-handed broadsword in one agile movement. Cunnart sensed the change in danger and bolted back to where they started.

"Fucking heathen. I will kill you and spit in your eye before I bugger your wife." Michail laughed as Salisbury recognized his opponent from the sword he carried. The English preferred thinner weapons, whereas the Highlanders favored claymores. The Highlanders wielded the massive swords often with one hand while the other carried a dirk, pike, or axe. Michail had none of the other weapons, but he would use the ecranche as one rather than a defense. Ducking beneath the tilt, Michail launched himself toward his nemesis.

Their swords collided with an ear-piercing, shiver-inducing scrape. The blades locked, but Michail's greater strength pushed his opponent away, forcing Salisbury into three stumbling steps. It was the time and space Michail needed to bring his shield crashing against Salisbury's helmet. He knew the cacophony of noise and the vibration would make his enemy's head ring and disorient him.

In his disorientation, Salisbury swung wildly. One blow landed against Michail's leg, sending searing pain up to his hip. He jumped back but didn't account for the added weight from the armor. He lost his footing and fell. Lying supine, he thrust his blade upward and forward, striking Salisbury in the belly. He rolled to his feet as the earl fought to catch his breath. They circled one another, both looking for an opening, both fatiguing.

Michail noticed Salisbury's armor had slipped when he thrust his lance into the earl's shoulder. It left an opening at the base of the Englishman's neck. But he would still have to pierce chain mail to reach an artery. He was growing too tired, and his leg hurt too much, to keep dancing with Salisbury. He needed to end the fight before he was the one to collapse. Leaning forward as though he were about to charge again, Michail discarded the ecranche to grip his sword with both hands.

"You are the little girl. You need both hands to play with your sword," Salisbury taunted.

"I've only ever needed one hand to play with ma sword. That still leaves one free for ma claymore." Michail exaggerated his burr as he rocked forward on his feet, telegraphing that he was about to charge toward Salisbury. The man believed the signal, running to meet Michail. But the younger fighter didn't move until the last moment. Salisbury's own momentum and Michail's unrestrained strength blended as Michail swung his sword horizontally, slicing the chain mail in the opening he found on Salisbury's neck. Blood oozed through the links, a combination of the blade and the metal abrading his skin. Stunned, Salisbury didn't expect Michail to lunge and knock him to the ground, straddling his chest. The earl fought to push Michail away, but the younger man's gauntleted fist rammed into the earl's helm. Michail crushed the visor shut before his other fist struck Salisbury's temple.

Knowing he had no choice but to offer the earl mercy, his voice filled the hushed silence. "Do ye yield?"

With his helmet too mangled for his voice to carry, Salisbury could neither accept nor decline the offer.

"I hear naught." Michail yelled to the crowd. "There will be nay mercy!"

Michail grabbed his sword from where it landed beside the men. He raised it overhead, his blade pointing down. He drove it toward Salisbury's throat, but at the last minute, held it suspended above the English knight.

"Ye harmed ma wife's kin. Ye threatened her. And I just dinna like ye. For those things and yer multitude of other sins, ye die. Say goodbye to God as this heathen says goodbye to ye." With a moment's pause, Michail drove his sword through the mail and into his enemy's throat. Blood pooled beneath the armor, and Salisbury's body shuddered as the last breath slipped from him. Michail rose and turned to the crowd. He bowed as the stunned silence turned to cheers. He swept the ecranche from the ground and hurried to the opening in the lists' fencing.

"Halt."

Michail pretended not to hear de Warenne's command, but ground marshals stepped before him, blocking his exit. With a sigh, he turned toward the Court of Honor.

"Come forward and present yourself."

Michail scanned the seated women until he found Blythe. She perched on her chair, her cheeks flushed, beaming at him. But as he came closer, her smile faltered. He was certain she knew de Warenne would order him to remove his helm, and their secret would explode. He flipped his visor open, locking eyes with his wife, before he dipped his chin. As he raised his head, he canted it to Blythe's right. Her lips pursed in a tight circle, but she eased from her seat as de Warenne, then Matilda, rose. The others seated around the noble couple also came to their feet. Michail watched Blythe slip from the raised platform. Dorothea stepped into her place, making Blythe's absence less noticeable. He ambled toward the grandstand as though he had no reason to hasten to a noble's call. Moving as slowly as he dared, Michail prayed it gave Blythe enough time to reach Ric and for them to flee to the woods, where the men still waited.

"If you were not at a joust that allows battles to the death, we would brand you a murderer." De Warenne crossed his arms, his arrogance oozing from his posture. Michail remained silent. "Remove your helmet, so I might see who takes the prize."

"Keep your coin, and I keep my helm." Michail reverted to his Scots accent. He doubted anyone thought him to be anything but a Highlander once they witnessed him wield his massive sword. But he would pray for a miracle that he might confuse people.

"A man who does not want to accept his prize of coins is a man who has accepted his prize of vengeance." Michail remained still while de Warenne surmised how Michail felt. He had no need for the coin, but he would have preferred to accept it than it be obvious that he'd fought a grudge, not a mere competition. But he would not reveal himself.

"Or he is a mon who sees those in more need than himself. Give it to the poor on my behalf."

"This knight wins not only the glory of victory." Lady Matilda held out a flower crown. "He wins the Court of Honor's sincerest admiration for his chivalry and generosity."

Bluidy bitch thinks to outsmart me when her lover couldnae. Try again.

Michail placed his fist over his heart and bowed. "Naught more would make me feel victorious than to share that with my lady. You will surely look finer in the crown than I, a grisly and filthy knight not fit for ladies' sight until I refresh myself."

The women cheered as several men rolled their eyes, but it offered Michail the chance to bow once more before he took one step back and spun on his heels. Passing through the break in the fence, he took Cunnart's reins from a groom and swung back into the saddle. He spied a man riding ahead. Wisps of blonde hair from someone in front whipped around his shoulders. Michail urged his horse to catch Ric and Blythe. They entered the trees only two feet ahead of Michail. Without a word, Michail and Ric rushed to strip the armor from Michail while his men removed Cunnart's and left it where the horse stood. He gazed in confusion at the chest that awaited the armor.

"The lads were happy to bring the chest if I didn't tell anyone they'd gotten drunk. They were too sotted to remember aught they saw." Ric placed the armor in the trunk with precision, so the lid snapped shut. He soon attached it to a pack horse Michail hadn't noticed.

Michail opened his arms to Blythe, who already awaited her husband's embrace. Their hold was tight while their kiss was passionate, but both were too brief. He helped her onto Midnight's back, then remounted Cunnart.

"We ride," Michail declared. Free of his borrowed armor, he leaned toward Cunnart's ears. "Ye are the bravest horse in all the land. Ye are the strongest there ever was. And when we reach a stable, ye shall get every apple and carrot ye wish, and ye shall have a mountain of hay to munch on till ye get yer fill. Then ye shall rest for a month of Sundays, lad. Ye have earned it."

The horse nodded his massive head and swung his hindquarters, making the entire party laugh. But it was only moments later they fled Carlisle and set their course for Druchtag Motte.

CHAPTER 21

The party rode for two hours before making camp. Everyone knew Michail couldn't push Cunnart further lest they wished the horse to drop dead. They found a place deep within the woods where they didn't dare build a fire. The flora was too densely packed to do so safely. Three men gathered all the waterskins and walked two miles to the stream they'd allowed the horse to drink from, then crossed. When she was certain a guard cared for Midnight, she slipped farther into the trees. She prayed Michail thought she merely needed a moment of privacy.

Instead, heaving, silent sobs racked her body as she wrapped her arms around her waist. The fear that engulfed her when she watched Michail enter the ring to joust against Richard had been controllable once she reminded herself to breathe. She'd been proud of Michail, wishing she could boast to those around her as they boasted about the knights representing their noble families. When she watched Michail's three passes against Salisbury, she'd once more battled the fear. But when the two men clashed on foot, she feared she would be ill. When Michail fell, she ripped a nail to the quick and shredded her cuticle before she realized she'd been picking at her nails.

She'd been conflicted when Michail demanded Salisbury yield. She knew it was the honorable action, but she wanted Michail to end the man's life without consideration. She'd accepted days ago that she would arrive at Druchtag Motte to learn her father was dead. She'd swallowed that grief until Michail had a chance for retribution. Grief flooded her and coalesced with fear, making her blood run cold.

As she stood behind the tree, the torrent of emotions poured forth. Once her fear subsided during their escape from Carlisle, rage replaced it. She knew the man responsible for holding them captive and for stealing her father from their family now rotted in hell. But she couldn't cast aside the burning need for her own retribution. She found she wasn't as satisfied watching Michail kill Salisbury as she thought. She wanted her turn. But there was no turn to be had since her enemy was dead. Her emotions swirled in a pointless circle, but they refused to subside. So her body did the only thing it could to expel them. She cried.

She knew when Michail found her, but he kept his distance, giving her the space she needed. But the moment she looked up, he came to her. Rather than terror consuming her, Michail's body and his love engulfed her. It was a place she far more preferred. He stroked her back as she clung to the leine he'd donned after scrubbing himself in the stream when the horses rested. She laid her head over his heart and closed her eyes. His heart's cadence calmed her, the last of her emotional typhoon blowing away. As she always did, she felt safe.

"Thank you." Blythe's muffled words were received with a kiss on her crown. "I needed that. I appreciate you letting me cry rather than trying to solve everything or offering platitudes neither of us would believe."

"When ye wish for me to solve a problem, ye need only ask. When ye wish for comfort, ye need only seek me. When ye wish for space, I shall give it."

"And when I wish to make love to my husband?"

"I will oblige."

"It's pointless to say it terrified me, especially when you fell. I know you're here with me and safe. But my heart isn't yet convinced. I want my husband. I want us."

"I understand. Making love to ye isnae a deed to be done. It's a promise we always mean our lives to be one."

"Quite the bard." Blythe kissed his neck and along his jaw until she reached his lips. Their mouths fused until they were breathless. Once more in a plaid, Blythe had the means to slide her hand around Michail's manhood. She stroked as he nibbled her ear. "Burn those damn breeks."

Michail's chuckle puffed warm air against her ear, making her shiver with desire. She continued to cling to his leine with one hand while the other worked his engorged flesh. She felt warm air around her calves, then her thighs. Michail's broad palm stretched wide over one half of her bottom, massaging the heated flesh. With each squeeze, his fingers dipped just beyond her entrance. Blythe rocked her hips, grinding her pubis along his length.

"We canna stay much longer."

"I don't need much longer." Blythe grazed her teeth along his stubble before nipping. Michail flipped back his plaid as he kneeled, then helped hold Blythe's skirts out of the way as she lowered her sheath onto his sword. With their heads buried against one another's shoulders, they rocked and thrust together. Their neediness drove them, a blessed reprieve coming quickly as pleasure washed over them both. With their foreheads pressed together, they released matching contented sighs. They lingered only for a few brief kisses before they settled their clothes. They each slipped to their own tree before returning to camp, hand in hand.

~

It was four days of hard riding before Blythe and Michail's journey ended. With Ric as their guide, they spent their second night of travel among the MacLellans. Ric's cousin, Laird Malcolm, welcomed them with plenty of food and comfortable beds. It was clear Ric was happy to see his cousin and his wife, Rosalind. But it was Emelyn, his mother's cousin, who Ric was most excited to see. From missives Isabella sent, Blythe knew Emelyn bore an uncanny resemblance to Ric's mother, Emelote. The women had grown up together, and when Emelyn married the old MacLellan laird, Emelote had moved with her.

Blythe and Michail were happy to watch Ric with his family, both lost in thought about their own relatives and both too exhausted to chatter. They sat holding hands, forgoing the dancing until they could politely excuse themselves. They seized the opportunity for true privacy, making a bed of pillows and Michail's plaids before the fire. With the heat from the flames flickering across them and warming their skin, they made love well into the night until neither could keep their eyes open.

Once Malcolm promised to spread word of Salisbury's death to the other Lowland border lairds, they were off. The last two days were as pleasantly boring as the first two. It was midafternoon when Blythe pointed to a mound in the distance.

"There. That's my parents' home."

"Ye ken it's still yer home as much as Ardvreck now is."

"I know. But it hasn't really felt like home in years. It's easy to think that my home is the one I will share with you. I'm certain Druchtag will feel as familiar as it always has. That doesn't change feeling like home is wherever we're going to make our life together."

"I love ye, *mo chridhe*." Michail leaned to kiss Blythe, tempted to place her on the saddle before him. They'd ridden together throughout their four days of travel, usually in the late afternoon when Blythe's endurance faded, but the men and horses could continue for a few more hours. But Michail would respect his wife and not enter her parents' home unannounced with her in his lap.

"Fear not. My mother—" Blythe swallowed. "She doesn't know everything. But she knows something happened between us. And she knows I've loved you for years."

Michail caught himself before he asked if Laird Patrick Dunbar would geld him. When Ric left to find them, Blythe's father was still alive. It was Michail who shared Ric's summation that it was probable the laird died before they returned.

As they approached, Blythe spied the banner flying from her parents' chamber. A laird was in residence, but she knew not whether it was still her father or now her cousin Alasdair. Her stomach tightened as she realized if Alasdair were laird, it was his chamber from which the banner hung. Her mother would occupy a new chamber, one Blythe doubted she would ever come to associate with her mother. Her parents weren't affectionate like she and her sisters were with their husbands, but no one doubted their devotion and the love they preferred to share in private. Agnes and Patrick were a rare arranged marriage that grew into a deep and abiding love.

As they passed beneath the portcullis, Blythe spied her cousin at the base of the steps, her heart plummeting. When she looked past him, she nearly fell from her horse as she kicked her feet free from the stirrups. She slid from her mount and stumbled over her hem. She gathered her skirts and skidded on the dirt as she ran.

"Papa!"

Blythe climbed the steps two at a time until she wrapped her arms around her seated father's neck. The older man's left arm wrapped around her, but his right remained limp in his lap. There was a jagged scar that ran through the shaved hair from his right ear to the back of his scalp. Blythe noticed none of it.

"Lass, you shall suffocate me and do what the bluidy English never could." Patrick's jest only made Blythe refuse to release him. "Lass, you have someone to introduce. He looks rather anxious."

Blythe turned her head and spotted Michail, who stood beside Alasdair. They'd met at court but didn't know each other beyond acquaintances. She kissed her father's cheek, accepting a kiss to her forehead before she straightened and held out her hand to Michail. While he climbed the steps, Blythe greeted her mother as warmly as she had her father. It was only when Michail took her hand that she lifted her head from her mother's shoulders. She laced her fingers with Michail's as she beamed as Isabella, Ric, Emelie, and Dominic.

"Mama, Papa, this is Michail MacLeod, tánaiste to the MacLeods of Assynt and my husband."

Michail frowned, something not feeling right about Blythe's introduction. He turned her to face him as he wrapped an arm around her waist, uncaring who they ignored. "Until I become laird and then only on days that I canna help it, I am yer husband before aught else. I'd rather ye introduce me as that first than ma clan's title."

Blythe's brilliant smile made Michail appreciate his sporran, which hid his unbidden arousal. When he heard two stifled deep laughs, he glanced at Dominic and Ric, who rolled their eyes. Dominic patted his sporran with a knowing grin. Perfectly timed, Isabella and Emelie elbowed their husbands. Blythe squeezed Michail's hand before turning back to her parents.

"I'm glad to be here finally." Blythe's smile faltered. "Papa, Harry and some of the other men died when Salisbury attacked."

Patrick sighed, sadness etching his weathered face. "We know. The Hannays were so kind as to dump the bodies over our border for our patrol to find." Anger coiled around each word, making clear that matters were still unresolved with their traitorous neighbors.

"Ma laird, yer men were brave while defending Lady Blythe. Ye would be proud of their loyalty and devotion."

Patrick nodded, peering around his newest son-by-marriage. "How many did you lose?"

"Most." Michail worried what Patrick would think, knowing how many MacLeods fell that day.

"Most of what?"

"Half a score. I lost six."

Patrick's somber stare matched Michail's. "I'm sorry for your loss and your clan's. But I don't doubt having so many men is why my daughter is alive. However Salisbury captured you, I know he attacked you from behind rather than face you. Those men shielded Lady Blythe."

"Aye, ma laird." Michail bowed his head, gathering

himself as he once more thought about having to tell his dead friend's wife and family what happened.

"Patrick."

Michail lifted his head to find his father-by-marriage held out his hand. When they grasped forearms, Michail chided himself for underestimating the man's strength. It was clear he'd survived tremendous wounds that would have been fatal for most men, and he still had the grip of a young warrior. Patrick's chuckle told Michail his thoughts were clear.

"Come inside." Agnes stepped forward, ending the men's silent competition. Having deduced their escape came because of Salisbury's death, she said, "Tell us how the bluidy bastard met his end. Please tell me it involved a rock."

"No rocks, Mama. But I offered him wine since we had no bread to give him." Three feminine laughs joined Blythe's as the men watched the women enter the keep ahead of them. Alasdair helped Patrick, while Dominic carried the laird's chair back to the dais. The family sat together, sharing news after Blythe and Michail recounted their tale, and Ric added how he tracked them.

"Blythe, you will find your blue gown with the silver embroidery airing out in your chamber. Your sisters and I will fix your hair once you've bathed." Agnes spoke with the efficiency of a woman used to command. "Michail, the lads will show you where you can make yourself presentable. We will meet you at the chapel steps at dusk. I am only patient aboot some things."

Blythe gawked at her mother before looking to Isabella and Emelie. Isabella looked at Emelie, who smirked at the youngest Dunbar sister. "Only one of the three of us married in a church first. Once we learned Michail accompanied you, we knew you'd handfast before you reached here. Scouts spotted you two hours ago. The feast will be ready by the time you exchange your vows in front of the kirk."

"You knew?" Blythe shot her sister a mocking stare.

"Of course. Whatever happened between you two was only made worse by being at court. Once away from there, I was certain you would resolve it. I convinced everyone else." Emelie, her belly rounded with the couple's third child canted her head to look up at her mountainous husband seated beside her. "The sooner people learn I'm right, the easier all our lives will be."

Dominic lifted Emelie onto his lap and kissed her as shamelessly as Ric and Michail kissed their wives in public. "I never doubt you."

"Humph. You just take a long time to realize you don't." Emelie giggled, then clapped her hand over her mouth when Dominic whispered in her ear.

An adolescent boy and girl approached the dais, making Blythe smile softly. The boy's blond curls were so sun-bleached as to match his mother's and two aunts' hair. The girl's chestnut hair fell in waves down her back, an exact match to her father's locks.

"Keira, Kirk, you've grown to where I nearly didn't recognize you." Blythe moved around the table and accepted her niece's and nephew's warm welcome.

"I doubt that, Auntie Blythe." Kirk's deep voice made Blythe lean away. He tugged on a lock of his hair and rolled his eyes.

"The Lord wasted it on ye," Keira teased, a Highland burr slipping from the daughter of a Lowlander and a man raised in England. "May I help with yer hair?"

Blythe dashed a glance at Isabella, who shook her head. The girl's mother winked at her daughter. "Not until you're a married woman. We would set your ears on fire."

"Mama." The twins might not look much like one another, but their aggrieved tones matched.

"Aye?" Isabella asked in all innocence.

"Never mind. Come on, Kirk." The brother and sister went in search of other teens their age.

Blythe grinned at Isabella. "You're auld. They're practically adults."

"It took Mama and Papa several years to come up with a match for me, then it took two of you," Isabella gloated, having often teased her younger sisters about the gap in age between Isabella and the two younger ladies. "Now up the stairs with you."

"You're not my mother," Blythe repeated an often-heard refrain while they all lived under one roof. "But fine."

Blythe kissed Michail before making her way abovestairs to her old chamber. The time rushed by as she bathed, and the women in her family helped her get ready. She was walking toward the kirk in what seemed like only minutes after leaving the Great Hall. Before her stood the most handsome man she'd ever seen. Long calves encased in leather boots led to a hint of muscular thighs covered by a crisp MacLeod plaid. Blythe's gaze traveled over the snow-white leine, briefly wondering how they laundered it so quickly, then realizing it was likely Dominic's. She took in the polished brooch on his shoulder and how the hilt of his sword gleamed from behind his shoulder. Michail's freshly washed hair curled around his collar, and his stubble had disappeared.

She ran a hand over the sky-blue skirts of the best kirtle she kept at her parents' home. It wasn't of courtly standards, but it was her favorite. It pleased her to wear the exquisitely embroidered gown to her wedding. She and Emelie spent nearly a moon stitching it while at court, but she'd taken it from court when she realized the cut was too modest by Stirling standards. She wanted to look her best for her groom, the man she already considered her husband.

Michail turned as the crowd shifted, giving him an obstructed glimpse of a woman in blue approaching. When people finally parted, leaving room for Blythe to walk beside Alasdair, Michail couldn't catch his breath. His bride's hair shimmered like a halo beneath the setting sun. The gown looked as though someone poured her into it, fitting better than any other garment he'd seen on a person. The skirts swished around her legs, giving a feminine silhouette as she veritably glided toward him. He found his palms growing clammy in anticipation. Just before Blythe arrived to stand before him, he unpinned the extra length of plaid from his shoulder. The priest bound their hands once they joined.

Michail would gladly drown in Blythe's blue-hazel eyes, her love drawing him as the sea's current draws a man to its depths. Crinkles appeared at the corners of his emerald-green eyes. The tiny white lines that formed contrasted to his sun-darkened skin. He experienced the same joy standing before a priest as he had when they exchanged their handfast vows before their guards.

Both spoke their vows reverently, meaning each word that passed their lips, savoring each moment of binding their lives together before God and the Dunbars. Their kiss was passionate but unhurried, neither caring about the ribald jokes that reached them. They'd waited three years to pledge their love and their lives. They'd nearly lost it all when an English earl threatened to destroy them. Now they'd received their holy blessing and were indivisible by law and by their own commitment. They would not be rushed.

"I love you, *an duine agam*." Her flawless pronunciation surprised Michail, his heart threatening to explode as it swelled with another layer of love and admiration for his bride. With a grin, Blythe explained, "Emelie and Isabella helped me."

"I love ye, *mo bhean*. In this life and the hereafter. I pledged ma life and love to ye, and I meant it from the vera depths of the mon I am. As I take ye to wife before God and yer people, I shed ma devil-may-care ways."

"But not in our chamber." Blythe pinched Michail's backside before he swept her into his arms.

"Come along, wife. We shall feast, so ye have the strength to demand yer wifely rights."

"How right." Blythe kissed his cheek as they entered the feast. They ate and made merry alongside Blythe's family and her clan of birth. They retired to the quiet of her childhood chamber, where they did things she'd only dreamed of when she once slept there. They proved marriage and duty hadn't dulled all their wildness as they explored all the ways to make love of which they could think before falling into a deep slumber, sleeping well into the next morning. They made it a routine for the next three days, sequestered in their chamber, accepting only trays and baths. They emerged blissful and ready to venture north.

Despite looking forward to reaching Ardvreck, Blythe and Michail remained at Druchtag Motte for a fortnight, giving Blythe's family time to get to know Michail and to reassure the three sisters that their father would survive. He might not fight another battle, but he was still sound of mind and loud of voice. They giggled each time they heard their father bellow their husbands' names before he went to watch his sons-by-marriage and his nephew train in the lists. It was a joyous reprieve from the dangers of traveling in Scotland.

The three couples, with their various children, traveled north. Emelie and Dominic brought their sons, Nic and Fergus, while Isabella and Ric had Keira and Kirk with them. When they reached Kilchurn, the two couples who had further to travel remained for two days while they visited with Laurel, Brodie, and their sons Broderick, Montgomery, and Donnan.

The Hartleys and MacLeods skirted Mackenzie land, Michail refusing to test the accord Ric promised that Seamus had reached with Torrian after he deposed Ulrich and claimed the lairdship. Once they traveled together as far as they could, the Hartleys and their Sinclair guards turned east, while Michail and Blythe turned west with his few remaining warriors.

After more than a fortnight of travel, Michail halted their party, allowing Blythe to have her first peek at their home. When she offered an eager—then mischievous—smile, he accepted her silent dare. They raced Cunnart and Midnight over hill and dale until they drew to the village's outskirts, slowing their mounts. They passed beneath the portcullis with rosy cheeks and windblown hair, both laughing and disagreeing over who was the victor.

Michail lifted Blythe from the saddle as his family gathered. Adan and Ward came from the lists while his parents passed through the enormous, studded metal doors to the keep. Blythe wasn't certain how Michail's parents would receive her, but Catriona's motherly smile set her at ease. It dissolved a moment later.

"Ye got the lass to say aye. And it's finally to marrying ye," Adan quipped. Michail's smile dropped as he turned a murderous glare at his younger brother. He'd confessed only to Adan what happened between Blythe and him. "I would have sworn she'd agree to murder ye before marrying ye."

Michail and Blythe relaxed, neither appreciating the poor joke at their expense. But neither feared their secret would be exposed. When they turned to greet Torrian and Catriona, the older couple's wise eyes stripped them of that confidence. But Michail's father and mother soon welcomed Blythe with embraces and sincere smiles. Ward and Adan teased Michail, but they had the sense to keep their voices too low for anyone but them to hear.

"It's over," Torrian proclaimed as they gathered a few hours later for the evening meal. Blythe and Michail had bathed and napped before returning belowstairs. Michail breathed a sigh of relief, but Blythe's brow furrowed.

"Ma father means the feud with the Mackenzies is over." Michail turned to his father. "Ric didna tell us much beyond Seamus is now laird."

"Aye. He rode back with his brother. Along with them went Liam, Callum, and Tavish. Hamish and Lachlan met them halfway. Together they had nearly ten score men. The sheer size of their force meant nay one among the Mackenzies put up a fight. Ulrich, pathetic bastard, drank himself stupid that night and fell down the garderobe. They found his mangled body the next morning lying in a pile of his own shite. He broke his neck."

"Our Lord God is a just one," Ward quipped.

"Kieran and Maude left only three days ago. They came with their weans to ensure all was well." Catriona smiled at Blythe. "I believe they married before ye arrived at court with Lady Emelie. I hope ye can meet her soon. She has the kindest and most generous heart of anyone I ken. And she throws a dirk better than anyone but her cousin Mairghread. It's quite a sight."

"I've heard Mairghread, Maude, and Blair rival most men, either with dirks or a bow." Blythe glanced at Michail and his brothers. She expected the men to scoff at her pronouncement, but they all nodded.

"Our cousin, Siùsan, is just as good. But she saves her marksmanship for hunting," Adan explained.

"And keeping her husband, Callum, alive. She's his avenging angel." Ward tugged at a lock of his hair. "It's the red. Be prepared. If yer bairns have it, ye shall be in for a struggle."

"Aye. It's a good thing I love ye, lads." Catriona rolled her eyes and shook her head. As Blythe listened to the MacLeods banter around her, including her in their jests. Michail's arm remained draped around her shoulder as she leaned against him once the meal ended. She felt a part of their family as though it had always been. She'd started thinking of Ardvreck as her home soon after Michail and she handfasted, but she'd held reservations that Michail's family wouldn't be as eager to share their home with her as she was to get there. Before the evening meal ended, Adan and Ward called her sister, and Torrian and Catriona declared her the daughter they'd needed for the past score and half years.

Torrian and Catriona talked together as the meal ended. Adan and Ward disappeared to find their own entertainment while the clan members danced. Michail kissed the silky skin behind Blythe's ear. He'd declared the day after they handfasted that he was reclaiming it as his, and that the Fletchers of the world would have to do without. She smiled as his lips nuzzled her, his touch sending shivers along her spine and tightening her belly in a way she experienced with no other man. She leaned her head and kept her voice low.

"I bet you can't last as long as me. And I dare you to reach our chamber first." Blythe was already pushing back her chair and rushing to the dais stairs. She gathered her skirts and rushed to the main staircase.

"I accept both," Michail whispered in her ear as he caught her and swung her over his shoulder. These were the only bets and dares Michail would accept, not caring whether he won or lost. They both always came out the winners.

EPILOGUE

*B*lythe scowled as she looked around the bailey. Heat rushed up her cheeks as her temper flared. "Clive!"

"Yes, Mama." A head of red wavy curls bounced toward her as her twenty-year-old son hurried toward her.

"Where the devil are Maisie and Paisley?" Blythe and Michail named one of their twin girls Margaret, but at age five, the lasses decided they wanted their names to rhyme. They'd proclaimed that Margaret was hereafter Maisie, and the lass only responded to Margaret when it was Blythe calling her when the older woman was at her angriest.

"There, Mama." Clive was as large as Michail and bore a striking resemblance to his father. He was shrewd and levelheaded, taking after both sets of grandparents. Blythe's and Michail's tendency toward wildness skipped Clive and settled with spades in the twin girls.

Blythe turned to find her fifteen-year-old twins, who inherited the Dunbars' unique platinum hair from their mother, hurrying toward her. She opened her mouth, but Paisley was faster.

"We're sorry, Mama. We ken we're late, but Da…" Paisley choked on her laughter as the girls pointed to a drenched man passing through the postern gate. "Da, bet us he could catch the rabbit with his bare hands. It's nae our fault none of us kenned the rocks were slippery. Da…"

When Paisley giggled too hard to finish, Maisie jumped in. "He slipped into the loch. We warned him ye'd be ferociously angry with him, but he didna listen, Mama. Do any men?"

"No," Blythe huffed. She looked Michail up and down as he came to stand with Blythe, Clive, Maisie, and Paisley. She frowned and sighed. "I told you, if you're going to bet the lasses that you can catch the rabbit, lay a trap for it first. But no. You don't listen. You lost the bet, you're soaking, and you're making us late. We were supposed to set off a half hour ago. You're the one who said we had a long day's ride to reach Dunbeath in time for the wedding."

"Aye, wife." Michail pulled Blythe in for a tight embrace that soaked the front of her kirtle, making it stick to her. He kissed her behind the ear. "Ye canna go around with yer gown sticking to yer breasts. It isnae proper. I suppose ye shall have to change. I can help ye with yer laces."

"While staring at my breasts," Blythe whispered before tangling her fingers in her husband's hair and pressing his head forward as they came together in a combustible kiss. Michail scooped Blythe into his arms. Their children and their travels were made to wait. It was an hour later that the family of five with a score of MacLeod guards set off for a family wedding at Dunbeath.

"I bet I reach that tree before you," Blythe called as Midnight broke free of the pack.

"And I dare ye to eat a fish's head when I beat ye."

Cunnart pulled alongside Midnight as Michail fought to win their race. As so often had been the case over the past score, their races ended in a tie.

"You like your risks."

Michail patted Cunnart's neck before plucking Blythe from her saddle and setting her before him. "And ye like yer devil."

THANK YOU FOR READING A DEVIL AT THE HIGHLAND COURT

Celeste Barclay, a nom de plume, lives near the Southern California coast with her husband and sons. Growing up in the Midwest, Celeste enjoyed spending as much time in and on the water as she could. Now she lives near the beach. She's an avid swimmer, a hopeful future surfer, and a former rower. When she's not writing, she's working or being a mom.

Subscribe to Celeste's bimonthly newsletter to receive exclusive insider perks.
Subscribe Now
www.celestebarclay.com
Join the fun and get exclusive insider giveaways, sneak peeks, and new release announcements in
Celeste Barclay's Facebook Ladies of Yore Group

THE HIGHLAND LADIES

A Spinster at the Highland Court
BOOK 1 SNEAK PEEK

Elizabeth Fraser looked around the royal chapel within Stirling Castle. The ornate candlestick holders on the altar glistened and reflected the light from the ones in the wall sconces as the priest intoned the holy prayers of the Advent season. Elizabeth kept her head bowed as though in prayer, but her green eyes swept the congregation. She watched the other ladies-in-waiting, many of whom were doing the same thing. She caught the eye of Allyson Elliott. Elizabeth raised one eyebrow as Allyson's lips twitched. Both women had been there enough times to accept they'd be kneeling for at least the next hour as the Latin service carried on. Elizabeth understood the Mass thanks to her cousin Deirdre Fraser, or rather now Deirdre Sinclair. Elizabeth's mind flashed to the recent struggle her cousin faced as she reunited with her husband Magnus after a seven-year separation. Her aunt and uncle's choice to keep Deirdre hidden from her husband simply because they didn't think the Sinclairs were an advantageous enough match, and the resulting scandal, still humiliated the other Fraser clan members at court. She admired Deirdre's husband Magnus's pledge to remain faithful despite not knowing if he'd ever see Deirdre again.

Elizabeth suddenly snapped her attention; while everyone else intoned the twelfth—or was it thirteenth—amen of the Mass, the hairs on the back of her neck stood up. She had the strongest feeling that someone was watching her. Her eyes scanned to her right, where her parents sat further down the pew. Her mother and father had their heads bowed and eyes closed. While she was convinced her mother was in devout prayer, she wondered if her father had fallen asleep during the Mass. Again. With nothing seeming out of the ordinary and no one visibly paying attention to her, her eyes swung to the left. She took in the king and queen as they kneeled together at their prie-dieu. The queen's lips moved as she recited the liturgy in silence. The king was as still as a statue. Years of leading warriors showed, both in his stature and his ability to control his body into absolute stillness. Elizabeth peered past the royal couple and found herself looking into the astute hazel eyes of Edward Bruce, Lord of Badenoch and Lochaber. His gaze gave her the sense that he peered into her thoughts, as though he were assessing her. She tried to keep her face neutral as heat surged up her neck. She prayed her face didn't redden as much as her neck must have, but at a twenty-one, she still hadn't mastered how to control her blushing. Her nape burned like it was on fire. She canted her head slightly before looking up at the crucifix hanging over the altar. She closed her eyes and tried to invoke the image of the Lord that usually centered her when her mind wandered during Mass.

Elizabeth sensed Edward's gaze remained on her. She didn't understand how she was so sure that he was looking at her. She didn't have any special gifts of perception or sight, but her intuition screamed that he was still looking.

A Spy at the Highland Court **BOOK 2**

A Wallflower at the Highland Court **BOOK 3**

A Rogue at the Highland Court **BOOK 4**

A Rake at the Highland Court **BOOK 5**

An Enemy at the Highland Court **BOOK 6**

A Saint at the Highland Court **BOOK 7**

A Beauty at the Highland Court **BOOK 8**

A Sinner at the Highland Court **BOOK 9**

A Hellion at the Highland Court **BOOK 10**

An Angel at the Highland Court **BOOK 11**

A Harlot at the Highland Court **BOOK 12**

A Friend at the Highland Court **BOOK 13**

An Outsider at the Highland Court **BOOK 14**

A Devil at the Highland Court **BOOK 15**

THE CLAN SINCLAIR

His Highland Lass **BOOK 1 SNEAK PEEK**

She entered the great hall like a strong spring storm in the northern most Highlands. Tristan Mackay felt like he had been blown hither and yon. As the storm settled, she left him with the sweet scents of heather and lavender wafting towards him as she approached. She was not a classic beauty, tall and willowy like the women at court. Her face and form were not what legends were made of. But she held a unique appeal unlike any he had seen before. He could not take his eyes off of her long chestnut hair that had strands of fire and burnt copper running through them. Unlike the waves or curls he was used to, her hair was unusually straight and fine. It looked like a waterfall cascading down her back. While she was not tall, neither was she short. She had a figure that was meant for a man to grasp and hold onto, whether from the front or from behind. She had an aura of confidence and charm, but not arrogance or conceit like many good looking women he had met. She did not seem to know her own appeal. He could tell that she was many things, but one thing she was not was his.

His Bonnie Highland Temptation **BOOK 2**

His Highland Prize **BOOK 3**

His Highland Pledge **BOOK 4**

His Highland Surprise **BOOK 5**

Their Highland Beginning **BOOK 6**

PIRATES OF THE ISLES

The Blond Devil of the Sea **BOOK 1 SNEAK PEEK**

Caragh lifted her torch into the air as she made her way down the precarious Cornish cliffside. She made out the hulking shape of a ship, but the dead of night made it impossible to see who was there. She and the fishermen of Bedruthan Steps weren't expecting any shipments that night. But her younger brother Eddie, who stood watch at the entrance to their hiding place, had spotted the ship and signaled up to the village watchman, who alerted Caragh.

As her boot slid along the dirt and sand, she cursed having to carry the torch and wished she could have sunlight to guide her. She knew these cliffs well, and it was for that reason it was better that she moved slowly than stop moving once and for all. Caragh feared the light from her torch would carry out to the boat. Despite her efforts to keep the flame small, the solitary light would be a beacon.

When Caragh came to the final twist in the path before the sand, she snuffed out her torch and started to run to the cave where the main source of the village's income lay in hiding. She heard movement along the trail above her head and knew the local fishermen would soon join her on the beach. These men, both young and old, were strong from days spent pulling in the full trawling nets and hoisting the larger catches onto their boats. However, these men weren't well-trained swordsmen, and the fear of pirate raids was ever-present. Caragh feared that was who the villagers would face that night.

The Dark Heart of the Sea **BOOK 2**
The Red Drifter of the Sea **BOOK3**
The Scarlet Blade of the Sea **BOOK 4**

VIKING GLORY

Leif **BOOK 1 SNEAK PEEK**

Leif looked around his chambers within his father's longhouse and breathed a sigh of relief. He noticed the large fur rugs spread throughout the chamber. His two favorites placed strategically before the fire and the bedside he preferred. He looked at his shield that hung on the wall near the door in a symbolic position but waiting at the ready. The chests that held his clothes and some of his finer acquisitions from voyages near and far sat beside his bed and along the far wall. And in the center was his most favorite possession. His oversized bed was one of the few that could accommodate his long and broad frame. He shook his head at his longing to climb under the pile of furs and on the stuffed mattress that beckoned him. He took in the chair placed before the fire where he longed to sit now with a cup of warm mead. It had been two months since he slept in his own bed, and he looked forward to nothing more than pulling the furs over his head and sleeping until he could no longer ignore his hunger. Alas, he would not be crawling into his bed again for several more hours. A feast awaited him to celebrate his and his crew's return from their latest expedition to explore the isle of Britannia. He bathed and wore fresh clothes, so he had no excuse for lingering other than a bone weariness that set in during the last storm at sea. He was eager to spend time at home no matter how much he loved sailing. Their last expedition had been profitable with several raids of monasteries that yielded jewels and both silver and gold, but he was ready for respite.

Leif left his chambers and knocked on the door next to his. He heard movement on the other side, but it was only moments before his sister, Freya, opened her door. She, too, looked tired but clean. A few pieces of jewelry she confiscated from the holy houses that allegedly swore to a life of poverty and deprivation adorned her trim frame.

"That armband suits you well. It compliments your muscles," Leif smirked and dodged a strike from one of those muscular arms.

Only a year younger than he, his sister was a well-known and feared shield maiden. Her lithe form was strong and agile making her a ferocious and competent opponent to any man. Freya's beauty was stunning, but Leif had taken every opportunity since they were children to tease her about her unusual strength even among the female warriors.

"At least one of us inherited our father's prowess. Such a shame it wasn't you."

Freya **BOOK 2**

Tyra & Bjorn **BOOK 3**

Strian **VIKING GLORY BOOK 4**

Lena & Ivar **VIKING GLORY BOOK 5**

www.ingramcontent.com/pod-product-compliance
Lightning Source LLC
LaVergne TN
LVHW031537060526
838200LV00056B/4529